P9-BYH-848

Mine Eyes
Have Seen

ANN RINALDI

Scholastic Press · New York

For Ronald Philip Rinaldi III,

my fourth grandson,

may you take your father's love of history

and the family name well into the next century

Library of Congress Cataloging-in-Publication Data
Rinaldi, Ann.
Mine eyes have seen   /   by Ann Rinaldi. — 1st ed.
p.   cm.
Summary: In the summer of 1859, fifteen-year-old Annie travels to the Maryland farm where
her father, John Brown, is secretly assembling his provisional army prior to their raid on the
United States arsenal at nearby Harpers Ferry.
ISBN 0-590-54318-0 (hardcover)
1. Harpers Ferry (W. Va.) — History — John Brown's Raid, 1959 — Juvenile Fiction.   2. Brown,
John, 1800–1859 — Juvenile fiction.   [1. Harpers Ferry (W. Va.) — History — John Brown's
Raid, 1859 — Fiction.   2. Brown, John, 1800–1859 — Fiction.3. Abolitionists — Fiction.
4. Fathers and daughters — Fiction.]   I. Title.
PZ7.R459Mi   1997   [Fic] — dc21   97-10680

Printed in the U.S.A.
First edition, February 1998
The text type is Centaur.
Design by Kristina Iulo

Acknowledgments

On a trip to western Maryland in November 1996 in pursuit of research for another novel, I met some interesting people who introduced me to the area. Two of them were instrumental in bringing me to do the story of Annie Brown: John Frye, curator of the Western Maryland Room at the Washington County Free Library in Hagerstown, Maryland, and Mary K. Baykan, director of that same library. In the course of a tour of the area, they took me to the Kennedy Farm.

Like most people I had never heard of the place. But when I saw that log cabin sitting on that rise in the foothills of western Maryland and read the marker to John Brown's Provisional Army, which had just been dedicated the previous week, then found out about fifteen-year-old Annie Brown being a part of this dramatic moment in our history, I knew I had a story.

So I am indebted to both John Frye and Mary Baykan for leading me to it, to Mr. Frye for referring me to the proper reading material, for answering my questions in the ensuing months, and for leading me to Jean Libby in California, instructor of African American History at City College of San Francisco and author of *Black Voices from Harpers Ferry* (about Osborne Anderson and the John Brown raid) as well as "John Brown's Maryland Farmhouse" in *Americana Magazine* and "John Brown's Family and Their California Refuge" in

The Californians. Ms. Libby also supplied me handwritten sheets from the Boyer Collection at the Boston Athenæum.

Thanks also go to the Columbia University Rare Book and Manuscript Library where I did research on Annie Brown, and to the good people at the National Historical Park in Harpers Ferry, West Virginia, who gave me a pamphlet entitled "The Wives and Children of John Brown" and directed me to bookstores in the area where I might run down out-of-print books on the subject.

As always there are no words to express thanks to the authors of the many published books on John Brown who supplied such wonderful works that bring the facts to life so dramatically. And, once again, thanks go to my son Ron. It's been a long time since I wrote my first historical novel. But it and those that followed would never have been written without his inspiration. As far as the direction my writing career has taken, Ron has had more influence than anyone.

Thanks are also due to my editor Anne Dunn, who immediately saw the merits of this story. And to Scholastic for its faith in me.

Prologue

My pa considered himself Moses. He said caution was another word for cowardice. When Pa wasn't fancying himself as Moses, he was fancying himself as Benjamin Franklin. He had a fearful lot of sayings. "Diligence is the mother of good luck," he would tell us. Or, "One today is worth two tomorrows." Sometimes he would say, "A small leak will sink a great ship." And, "A ploughman on his legs is higher than a gentleman on his knees." My brothers told me that when they misbehaved when small, Pa would rap them on the head with the handle of his pocketknife. He had a saying for that, too. "Ringing the bell," he called it, because my brothers said it made their ears ring as if someone had sounded a bell in their heads. Somehow I don't think Moses or Benjamin Franklin ever did that to their children.

COME DOWNSTAIRS AND PLAY CHECKERS WITH US, Annie."

"I hate checkers."

"Sarah said you played the game all the time at the Kennedy farm with the men. She's gone to the post office. I thought we'd play some checkers when she comes back."

Sarah's always saying things, that's the trouble. What does she know about what I did at the Kennedy farm? She wouldn't have lasted two days there, sitting those endless hours on the porch, lying in bed at night and listening to Oliver and Martha stirring some soft into their bed, wondering when Hazlett and Leeman would take it in their heads to run off into the woods or even go down to Harpers Ferry in the middle of the day and bring the wrath of Virginia, Maryland, and maybe Pennsylvania down on us.

Sarah. It makes me laugh. How would she have managed old Mrs. Huffmaster? What would she have said to Pa when he was out of his head and called her his Kitty?

Sarah is my sister, and she's three years younger than I am. I love her. But she knows nothing at all.

I stood looking out the window at the locust, maple, and oak trees on the rise in back of the house. Such a pleasant place. They called it Orchard House. "You're lucky to be invited, you and Sarah," Mama had said. "The Alcotts are good people. Make the most of it. It was your pa's wish that you have a good education."

It was Pa's wish that my education prepare me for the harsh realities of life. I didn't need to come here, to Mr. Sanborn's school, to do that. Pa did that for me. All by himself.

My eyes fell on the clean lines of the barn out back. Two stories. "Pa would have liked that barn," I told Louisa May.

"Would he?" She came up behind me. She's a lady writer, like Harriet Beecher Stowe. Only she doesn't write about slavery. Her mother says her stories are lively, wholesome, and American. But they have nothing to do with real life, far as I can see. She says she knows it and wants to do better. Sarah and I had been invited to stay with the Alcotts so we could go to Mr. Sanborn's school. Mr. Sanborn was a friend of Pa's.

Louisa May's black bombazine dress rustled. She wears black all the time. If not for the lace collars you'd think she was in mourning. "My sisters and I produced plays out in that barn not too many years ago," she said wistfully.

"We had a barn like it out in Ohio. On our farm. The one they called Westlands."

"Did you play in it?"

"It was before I was born. My brother Jason told me about it. He and my brothers John and Owen holed up in it all night with Pa when the creditors came to take the farm."

I thought of the posse Jason had told me about and smiled. How would she take it, this woman who lives in this old three-story clapboard house on this fairy-tale street, who talks downright biblical about being an abolitionist, like they all do here in Concord? But talk is all it is. Pretty talk.

"The sheriff sent a posse to arrest my pa and brothers at Westlands," I told her. "Pa said, 'Shoot him if he puts his head in the door.'"

I figured that was about as American as you could get. I went on. "But they were arrested, anyway. All but Jason. He ran. He's the family coward, you know."

She was properly shocked. "I'm sure your brother is no coward."

"He is. He takes pride in it. Says every family ought to have one."

She gave the conversation a new turn. "Did you enjoy the gallery we went to yesterday?" she asked.

She'd taken me and Sarah to a gallery on Washington

Street. In it was a six-pound iron slave collar. "How terrible," she'd said, staring at it. But I knew she was trying to draw me out. She was all the time doing that. Meeting me halfway on common ground, she called it. Trouble is, when she got halfway on that common ground, I wasn't there. I had no desire to be.

"No slave Pa ran up to Canada ever wore such a collar," I'd told her.

She knows nothing about slavery. None of them do here in Concord, for all their poetry readings and fancy teas she drags me and Sarah around to, showing us off like a prize Saxony sheep at an auction. "John Brown's daughters," she says, coming into a room where they are gathered and waiting for her. "Everyone, look here, I've got John Brown's daughters."

Then they all gather round us and ask questions about Kansas, like did Pa really spirit eleven slaves out of Missouri into Canada back in '58?

"There were twelve when they got to Canada," I'd say, "a baby was born along the way. They named him after Pa. And he also took two good horses and a yoke of oxen."

"How long do you remember your father talking about the Cause, child?" they'd ask me.

"Since before I was born," I'd tell them.

I'm too outspoken for them. Their faces get pale, they move away and begin talking about something else. But I won't let them off the hook that easy. They'd started it, so now they must hear. "When my pa was on his way to Kansas, he stopped at Waverly, along the Missouri River. My brother Jason's boy had died of cholera on their way West. Jason and his wife, Ellen, buried him there. In Waverly Pa dug the boy up and brought him to Kansas, so Jason and Ellen could bury him proper-like."

Gasps. Moans. They move off, horrified, the Peabodys and the Foords and the Fieldses and the Hawthornes. They turn to Sarah who loves the fuss and simpers and even manages to get tears in her eyes talking of Pa.

Sarah, who at fourteen scarce knew him. She makes up answers. Invents things, until I kick her. Then she hushes.

Louisa May put her hand on my shoulder now. "I only asked you to play checkers so you can socialize a little."

"I don't want to socialize."

"Listen to me, Annie Brown."

"No, you listen to me, Miss Alcott." I turned to face her. "I don't mean to be rude. But if Sarah told you I played checkers with the men back at the Kennedy farm, well, she doesn't know anything about what happened at the Kennedy farm. She wasn't there. Only people in the family who know are me and Owen. And he's not talking. Sarah will say anything to amuse people because she's basking like a cat in the sun for all the attention she's getting as the daughter of John Brown. I don't want that attention. You've been good to me, I know. But I don't like it here. Even if Mr. Nathaniel Hawthorne lives next door. And Emerson comes for visits and Thoreau is your bosom friend. I'm not used to these kind of people. I don't know what to say to them."

"Didn't you have friends at Kennedy farm?"

That brought me up short. "Only Mrs. Huffmaster, who told me my aura was in bad repair. And wanted to fix it."

"Did you let her fix it?"

"Yes. She could fix anything. She could fix burns by talking the fire out. Said she talked to the afflicted flesh. That she learned it from an old slave woman on a nearby plantation. Course, I never had any burns. But she helped me in other ways, so I suppose you could call her a friend."

Would this woman think me daft for saying such things? She didn't. She was smiling in a knowing way. "Then perhaps you will let me help you fix something else that is in bad repair," she said.

"What?"

"I want to say your heart, but that seems so bold. So I'll just say whatever it is in you that's afflicted. You are not happy, Annie Brown."

"Is there reason to be happy?"

"Your father wakened the whole country to slavery," she said.

"My pa was the meanest man I ever saw. And the most honorable, all at the same time."

"There, then. There is what needs fixing. Your feelings about your father. They are warring inside you."

I nodded. "I suppose you could say that. I love him and hate him all at the same time. And I don't know what all to do about it."

She took my hand and led me to a settee. I'm not the type who allows anyone to lead them around, by the nose or by the hand. But she had a way about her, this Alcott woman. Almost like Mrs. Huffmaster.

"Tell me," she said.

So I told her. "There's no help for it, Miss Alcott. Pa's gone a year and a half now and he still fills the spaces around me, bigger than he did in life. There is no space for me to move, no air to breathe. He's there, wherever I turn, taking up all the air. It's like I told Mama. We may have to go to California to get away from him."

"You're angry with him," she said.

"Angry? I downright hate him sometimes."

"I hated my father."

"You?" I stared at her. It was a trick, I was sure of it. I didn't trust her. No more than I'd ever trusted Mrs. Huffmaster for all the healing she did of my aura. Always poking around the farm, asking questions, saying nice things with her soft voice. Trying to get me to tell her what was going on. Only difference between Louisa May and Mrs. Huffmaster, far as I could see, was that Louisa May wore shoes.

"I hated my father all my life," she said, "until a year or so ago. Bronson Alcott is known as a great thinker, a talker, a teacher. But when there was no money for food he thought himself too good to take menial work. He never provided for our family. I had to do it. And am still doing it, before with teaching and hiring out and now with writing."

"My pa provided for us," I said.

"There are different ways of providing and not providing. My father never let us eat meat. And no butter, sugar, coffee, or tea, either. We got some nuts in our diet, finally. But only because my mother negotiated for those nuts."

I thought about Pa, sucking on lemons and drinking salt water to mortify his flesh. But I didn't say it.

"They want us to be womanly," she said. "Which means to be strong and comforting for them when they need us to be. At the same time they want to crush our intellect, punish our strengths, and encourage our weaknesses so we are dependent upon them."

She was talking like my mama, I thought. She had honed in on my mama's ideas like a bee on a mayflower.

"They want us to be submissive and docile. So we become that way on the outside. But in order to survive we must cultivate our real selves on the inside. They make us love them, depend upon them, then leave us paralyzed and unable to move without them!"

"My brother Watson said Pa wanted his sons to be strong as lions," I told her, "and yet afraid of him all at the same time."

"Well, then, apparently some men do it with their sons, too. I don't know about that. I have no brothers." She leaned forward. "Why do you think I write, Annie Brown?"

"You just said. To make a living."

"I could teach. Annie, my writing has saved my life on many occasions. And my sanity. Writing does that for a person. It could help you, too, if you tried it."

Me? Write? I looked at her like she had taken leave of her senses. "I can't write. Who would care what I had to say?"

"Yourself, Annie Brown. Do it for yourself. Here." She got up and crossed the room to a small desk, opened a drawer, and took out some paper. She uncapped a bottle of ink and held it up. "Talk to the afflicted part of you, Annie Brown," she said. "Talk the fire out. Write it down on paper, what you really think."

"I couldn't."

"Yes, you could. No one need see it, I promise. Not even me. Write down your thoughts. Just as they are."

Then I grinned. "Right now I think I don't want to play checkers. And I'm jealous of my sister Sarah, wallowing in all the attention."

"I've always been jealous of my sister May. She always seems the pet. She gets everything she wants."

From outside there came a sudden shouting, a surge of commotion. People seemed to be gathering in the backyard. We went to look out the window.

"Sumter, Sumter!" I saw my sister Sarah come running into the yard. "They've fired on Fort Sumter! The war has started!"

"War!" Louisa May gave a muffled cry. "They've fired on Sumter. Oh!" She gripped my hand.

Outside Sarah was jumping up and down and screaming it, like it was an occasion for joy. "Doesn't she know what war means?" I said aloud. "Doesn't she know?"

Louisa May Alcott hugged me. I let her do it. If war had started, I needed somebody to hug me.

War. For our family it started years ago when Pa and my brothers went to Kansas.

War. I thought of the men of Pa's Provisional Army at the farm. Of Dangerfield Newby, crying over his wife's letter and saying the time for writing was passed, it was time for fighting. Of Johnny Cook, saying the battle must be fought to the end. Of Kagi, the schoolteacher, trying to be a good secretary of war. Of Stewart Taylor, saying he'd be the first to die in the raid on the Ferry.

"Pa did this," I whispered to Louisa May. "It's what he started. At the Ferry."

She pulled away from me and nodded. I thought I saw tears in her eyes. I thought that she looked old all of a sudden. She was only twenty-seven. Had just the thought of war aged her?

What, then, had my time at Kennedy farm done to me? Was she right? Did I need to talk the fire out of myself, as if I were afflicted?

Louisa May wiped her tears. She backed away to the door, scarce able to speak. "We'll talk later," she said. "I am needed downstairs." She held out her long slender hand. "Write it down, do. See if it doesn't help."

And then the door closed and she was gone. I was alone in the sun-dappled room, with the sound of shouting outside the windows as people crowded into the yard from all around. Pa, I thought, Pa, what have you done?

And I could hear his voice then, a preacher's voice, loud and certain: "The currents of life are not made of perfume."

Oh, but Pa, must they be made of blood?

I sat down at the small cherry desk and stared at the blank sheets of paper. Talk to the afflicted part of me? Talk out the fire? Oh, I can't, I thought.

And then I dipped the pen in the ink and began to write.

Chapter One

North Elba, New York,

Summer 1859

My grandpa Owen, Pa's father, once told us about how his father, name of Captain John Brown, went off to fight in the Revolutionary War. He was captain of the Train Band Nine, a Connecticut regiment. He was killed fighting for his country. Grandpa Owen told us how his mother was left with ten children to care for. Seven were girls. In the winter of '78 and '79, he said, the snows were so deep they had to go out into the fields and find the livestock and dig them out, lest they starve and die. They couldn't afford hired help, so they lost their crops and near starved themselves. "My mother was a good woman," Grandpa Owen would say. "You come from good stock. But life is hard. And you should know it now, children."

I WAS JUST SETTING OUT TO HANG SOME WASH ON THAT morning in early July when the letter came from Pa in Maryland. It was a right pretty morning. So clear and blue you could almost see the difference between the spruce, pine, and fir trees on White Face Mountain that rose to the north over Lake Placid.

That's what I was doing, gazing at the mountains, with my basket balanced on my hip. Martha was already hanging her share of the clothes. Martha was seventeen, married to my brother Oliver, expecting his child, and no longer taken with things like mountains or spruce trees.

My older sister Ruth said Oliver married Martha so she'd have a place when the trouble came. Ruth was always talking about the trouble that was coming. Ruth was thirty and married. Thank heaven she and Henry had their own place. I'd die if I had to have her around all the time, with her superior ways and her knowledge that of all the girls she was Pa's favorite.

We'd never had a real falling out, me and Ruth. But there was bad blood between us because of something that happened when I was three.

"When the trouble comes, my Henry is not going to have any part in it," Ruth went around saying when she came to visit. "He did enough for Pa in Kansas. He need do no more."

"Maybe he'll want to do more," Martha would say in that mischievous way of hers.

"Well, I don't want him to."

"She bosses him," Martha always whispered to me. "Can you picture it? And didn't you always think Henry was his own person?"

"Yes, but he adores Pa," I'd whisper back. I knew that though Henry Thompson and his ten brothers and father owned some thousand acres in Essex County, it made no never mind to Ruth. Besides, Dauphin, one of those brothers, was my friend. And he'd told me Ruth rules the roost. Though I never told that to Martha.

She waved at me now, from the hill where she was hanging the wash. Then she shaded her eyes and pointed. "Mrs. Reed is coming up the hill."

I set down my basket of wash. Sure enough, it was old Mrs. Reed, her gray-white hair streaming loose from its pins, her shawl clutched around her.

She was on a mission. Lord knows I'd seen enough people on missions around here to know that. Mrs. Reed was Negro. So many of our neighbors were. It was the reason Pa moved us here to this plain little house in the middle of nowhere. Because all around was a colony of Negroes who'd been given land to farm. Timbucto, they called it. Pa not only helped them farm; when the Fugitive Slave Act was passed in '50, which gave Northern officials the rights to return slaves to their owners, he ran around to those who were runaways and tried to spirit them up. Told them they should arm themselves and refuse to be taken alive.

The runaways refused to be spirited up. Nobody was taking them alive or dead, far as they could see. Besides which, they had all they could do farming their land. So they just as much as told Pa to leave them be.

Mrs. Reed waved. She had something in her hand.

"What is it?" Martha came to stand beside me.

"I don't know," I said.

But I knew. It was my sister Ruth's "trouble." It was Pa's "blood atonement." I had the awful feeling in my bones that the time for both had finally come.

I was right. It was there, in the letter from Pa. We ran it right to Mama in the house. She was putting breakfast on the table for us and my brothers Salmon, Jason, and Watson, who were the only boys home then. And for Belle, Watson's wife, who was a sister of Will and Dauphin Thompson, and staying with us with their newborn son. My little sisters, Sarah, thirteen, and Ellen, five, were helping.

"Come in and set," we told Mrs. Reed. We walked her to the front door. "Careful," I warned, but she tripped. Good thing I was holding her elbow. "It's that old tombstone," I reminded her. "Didn't you recollect it was there?"

"Hain't you moved it yet?"

"No. Pa wants it there. Right where it is beside the door."

It sat against the plain little house, the only ornamentation we had. If you wanted to call it ornamentation. I don't know the particulars, but my brother John says Pa carted it all over with him for years. To every house we ever lived in. It had the name of Captain John Brown on it. He was Pa's grandfather. Pa said it was what he wanted on his grave. He'd gone and put Frederick's name on it.

Our poor Frederick who sleeps in Kansas.

Mrs. Reed had nicked her ankle. I helped her into the kitchen. "Mama, look who's here."

Mama was seeing to a brown loaf in the oven at the side of the large fireplace. She turned and smiled. She was a good speciman of womanhood, my mama. That's what Pa always said. Big boned. Built for times of trouble, Pa said. Good for the distance. He described her as he would a horse. But it was her smile, her inner strength more than her build, that carried us through trouble. She gave that smile to Mrs. Reed now. "Sit, sit. Annie, get some porridge."

I ladled some mush into a bowl, skimming it off the iron caldron in the fireplace. It had been cooking since six that morning and already had a half inch of golden baked crust on top. I poured cream into the bowl and set it down in front of Mrs. Reed.

"I've a letter." Mrs. Reed handed it over.

Mama took it right up and read it. Before she was finished, Salmon, Jason, and Watson came through the door. They'd been doing morning chores.

Mama read slowly. I sat down and held little Ellen on my lap while Mama read. Belle held little Frederick.

"Your father wants me to come to Maryland," Mama said finally.

"Oh God, it's started," from Salmon.

"Yes." Mama looked across the room at the boys.

I looked, too. Belle and Watson exchanged glances. So did Jason and Salmon. Then Salmon sighed and turned to view the mountains outside. Because they were better than what he saw in the house.

Jason rested his tall, scrawny frame against the doorjamb. He folded his arms across his chest. He looked down at his boots. He didn't know what-all to do, it seemed.

Jason's wife, Ellen, was back in Ohio where they had their farm. Though he owned a third of the farm in North Elba, too. He was thirty-four. His third of our place was in grape-vines and fruit trees. He'd come for the summer, to see to them. He'd been in Kansas with Pa, he and Ellen. Jason ended up hating what he'd seen in Kansas, what Pa had done out there.

If anybody asked me what Pa had really done out there, I'd be hard put to say.

None of us knew, not even Mama. Only Owen, Oliver,

Jason, Frederick, Salmon, and John knew. Frederick was dead. John, who's in Ohio, is half crazy part of the time and in deep melancholy the other part. And the others are not saying.

Oh, we heard what Senator Toombs of Georgia said Pa did. And Wilson Shannon, the second territorial governor of Kansas. And Lieutenant James McIntosh, who beat and chained John and Jason. We even heard what Mrs. Doyle, whose sons and husband were killed, said. She said Pa and my brothers tore her husband and sons from her and killed them in cold blood. Then went on to do the same to two others. For no other reason except that they were proslavers.

I did know that both Jason and Salmon had words with Pa after the killings, which had come to be known as the Pottawatomie murders. And that Pa said he was an instrument of God's will, and God would judge him.

It looked to me now that Salmon and Jason were doing some judging of their own.

Jason plain hated violence, and had moments when he hated Pa. I think this was one of them. He and Salmon had vowed they would never fight again. The last time Pa was home he had had a set-to about it with Salmon and Jason.

What Mama sensed of all this I was not privileged to know. But she put the letter down then and gave the boys one of those smiles of hers that would have made President James Buchanan feel at ease. "He and Oliver and Owen have rented the Kennedy farm," she said. And she beamed, as if it was all she ever wanted for Pa, him renting that old Kennedy farm across the river from Harpers Ferry.

"You know what for," Jason said.

"Yes, I know," Mama answered placidly. "He wants me to come down so the place will look normal."

Jason made a scoffing sound in his throat. "When have we ever looked normal?" He went out the door, nudging Salmon, who went with him.

"Are you going, Mother Brown?" Martha asked. I could tell she wanted to go. She missed Oliver. They were so in love it was almost indecent, watching them together.

Mama looked at each of us in turn, me and Belle, Ellen and Sarah, Mrs. Reed, Martha and Watson. She looked around the kitchen as if she'd never seen it before. Then her eyes went past the boys in the doorway, out to the mountain ranges in the distance.

"No," she said, "I'm not going to go. Now let's all sit and have breakfast."

We sat. Mama handed the letter to Martha, who devoured it for news of Oliver. But nobody said any more about Maryland. And Jason and Salmon never did come in for breakfast.

The time of trouble had, indeed, come. To say nothing of Pa's blood atonement.

We'd known all of our lives that Pa was going to do armed resistance against slavery. The knowledge had grown in us, along with our sinew and bones. For as long as I could remember, Pa had been making drawings of log forts. The logs had to be laid just right to secure the roofs. And more laid outside to discourage attackers. The forts were to be in his precious mountains, of course. The southern Appalachian mountains God had put there for the slaves when they had their uprising.

And he was always studying soldiers, like Napoleon and Spartacus. And all the great European armies. Saying that slavery was like original sin. We either commit it or inherit it. And telling us about Cinque, the African chief who led the revolt on the steamer *Amistad* in 1839, killing all of the crew.

I guess I'd always known it would be at Harpers Ferry. I recollected Pa's fondness for the place. He said the site of his armed resistance had to be located inside the slave states. Plantations could be raided and slaves sent north through the mountains.

Once Sarah came home from school and told me that her teacher had talked about Harpers Ferry and how there was a big armory and arsenal there. "Why did my heart beat so fearfullike, Annie?" Sarah asked me. "Isn't that the place Pa always talks about?"

"Yes," I told her. "That's the place."

I waited until Martha went out to tend her rutabaga patch, until Watson left to finish the fence to keep the prized Devon cattle from roaming. If not for Maryland, he'd exhibit them again this year at the Essex County Fair. But he was going to Maryland. Watson had dutifully stayed home and taken care of us when the others went to Kansas. But he was twenty-three now. He wanted his chance with Pa.

Mama sent Sarah and Ellen to accompany Mrs. Reed home. And then I spoke. "Mama, why aren't you going to Maryland?"

Her back was to me. She was chopping vegetables. "I won't encourage him in this," she said. "It's madness."

The fire spit in the hearth. There was only the sound of her chopping. I heard my own heart beating, that's how quiet it was. Mama had never spoken against Pa to any of us.

"Do you think if you don't go, he won't do the attack?"

"No," she said.

"If he does it, do you think it will work?"

"There is no if," she answered. "He's going to do it. But I'll be no part of any attempt to take over the United States government."

The peculiarity of the situation was not lost on me. Mama and I in homespun there in the kitchen of our mean little cabin in the Adirondacks, two thousand feet above sea level, talking about Pa's plans to take over the United States government.

It wasn't anything we weren't used to. It wasn't anything we hadn't lived under the shadow of all these years.

I looked at Mama's broad shoulders. She was my anchor, if you needed one two thousand feet above sea level. I did. She had staying power. She held when the rest of us crumbled. Everybody said that Salmon was the sanest-minded and levelheadest one in the family, but Mama had my vote for that honor. And it came to me, clear as the outline of White Face Mountain, as I sat there and stared at the twist of bun in back of her iron-gray head.

If she wouldn't back Pa in this, it was doomed.

"Mama," I said. "You can't let him do it."

"I can't stop him. You know he's been moving all his life towards this moment."

"Why?"

"Why?" Nobody had ever asked her this. Nobody had ever asked themselves. It was enough to stop her from chopping, to make her turn around and pick up her apron, wipe her hands, and give the matter consideration. "It's got something to do with the mountains, Annie. He always says that, through history, mountains have given men the means to defeat armies, doesn't he? How many times have you heard him say it?"

I nodded. When Pa talked about the mountains, the Appalachian, the Shenandoah, he acted like God was in on his plan when He created the world.

"And it has something to do with his failures," Mama went on. "His failure as a wool merchant, and all that money he lost in Ohio in land speculation. In '38 he had three farms and ten lawsuits against him. His possessions were sold at a sheriff's sale. His farms sold to pay debts. All that can kill a man. Or turn him into something else. Your pa came around to thinking of himself as a whipped man. And so he started paying mind to the ones who were really whipped, all around him. And thinking, well, since he was one of them he might as well devote himself to making them free."

"Did you think it would be Harpers Ferry?"

"No, for a while I thought Kansas would do it for him. Give him back some of himself. But Kansas only agitated him more. He wants to set the South on fire. When I realized that, I thought, for a while, that it would be Ohio. His backers in Boston seem to think that, too."

"What does John say?" I knew she corresponded with my half brother John. They had always gotten on. John had been only five years younger than her when she married Pa. I figured that John, dragged on foot, in chains, for sixty-five miles back in Kansas when he and Jason were captured, would have words to say about the plan for Harpers Ferry. Besides, he believed in hypnotism and mediums, rappings and messages from the dead.

"He thinks Harpers Ferry is too close to Washington. And not a good place, being on a railroad. The boys have all been talking about it amongst themselves. They knew it was coming."

That was just it. It was always coming, sometime in the future. Like a train on the other side of the mountain, whose whistle you'd heard all of your life in the distance.

Now it was here. A thought came to me. "Has Pa told Ruth?"

"Yes."

Of course he had. He corresponded with Ruth and Henry all the time. Even when she was younger and not married yet, he wrote to her from wherever he was in his travels. "Be all that today, which you intend to be tomorrow," he told her once. He never told me to be all today, tomorrow, or ever. I felt a stab of the usual envy and bitterness about Ruth. "What did she say?"

"He asked for her Henry to come down to Maryland. Ruth said no."

"Why?"

"Surely, Henry did enough in Kansas. I put no blame on Ruth."

Would Pa? I gloated. Ruth, his favorite, had turned from him now in his hour of need. Like Peter turned away from Jesus in the Garden. Pa couldn't help making the comparison. He knew his Bible inside out. He wouldn't have Henry Thompson now. Or John, Jason, or Salmon, all those he'd depended on in the past. My mind was working fast. And then it stopped working.

"Are any of the other Thompson boys going?"

She smiled at me. "If you get that butter churned you can ride over and ask Dauphin if he plans to go."

"It wasn't Dauphin I was thinking of," I lied.

"Of course it was. Don't be ashamed to say. You're near sixteen. I was that age when I married your pa."

I blushed and went to pour the cream in the churn. "What will Pa do if you don't go, Mama? Who will take care of him and the others?"

She went back to her chopping. "Martha. I'll send Martha. She's dying to go. And she should go and be with Oliver."

"She feels poorly sometimes, Mama. She'll need help."

"Well, who else is there?"

"Me. I can go with Martha if you want."

"You?" That got her turned around again, all right. She stared right at me, through me. And the light in her eyes changed. She searched my soul with those eyes. She could do that.

"I know he doesn't like me, Mama."

"Don't say that." Her voice got sharp. "Your pa loves all of you!"

I clutched the handle of the butter churn 'til it hurt my hands. "I'm that 'strange Annie' to him. We don't get on. And you know why."

"Don't say it!"

I'd never heard her talk so sharp. Not even to Salmon, Watson, and Oliver the time they got some cow itch from a drugstore and put it on the seats of the outhouse used by the Perkins girls back in Ohio. Course, I was just a tyke then. But I remember the incident well.

"I'm sorry, Mama," I said.

She went back to her work. "You can go if you've a mind. But just make sure it's for the right reasons."

"What reasons are they?"

"You know. And you know what the wrong ones are, too. And you can go, if Martha says yes. But she's in charge down there. And if you go, you're to mind that. And not put yourself forward."

She poured some hot coffee into two mugs, put some mush into two bowls, and set them on a wooden tray. "The butter churning can wait. Bring this to Jason and Salmon. All the starch came out of them when I read that letter of your pa's. And they can't make it though the day without breakfast. Ask them what they think about your going. Then form your own mind."

Chapter Two

Grandpa Owen was a trustee of Oberlin College and had a cousin who was the president of Amherst. Grandpa Owen founded the Hudson, Ohio, antislavery society and helped to found Western Reserve College. He was also a stationmaster on the Underground Railroad. When Pa and my brothers were in Kansas, my grandfather sent them money. All I recollect about Grandpa Owen is that he and Pa had lively debates. They'd argue about something called predestination. Grandpa Owen was coming around to thinking that maybe we weren't all doomed, that maybe those outside the elect stood a chance of saving themselves from hell. Not Pa. He considered himself one of the elect. "I take comfort," he would say, "in thinking the Lord has known about me since time's beginning, and that He knows I am destined for glory."

I FOUND SALMON IN THE BARN, FOOLING WITH HIS .22 Pepperbox pistol that shoots five turns in a row. It had nothing to do with violence. It had to do with squirrels getting at the turnips. I set the tray of mush and coffee down on the ground. "Mama says you should eat. You need some starch in you."

He picked up the cup of coffee and sipped it. I waited for him to say something. He didn't. So I went on ahead and said my piece.

"You and Pa fought about Harpers Ferry last time he was home, didn't you?"

"Yes."

"It was a bad fight, wasn't it?"

"Bad?" he laughed. "He made me ashamed for not wanting to take part. Said he regretted my decision as he'd never regretted the act of any of his children."

Except me, I thought. But I kept my musings to myself. I felt bad for Salmon. Why should he feel ashamed? He'd served Pa well in Kansas. I watched as he recommenced polishing that Pepperbox 'til it shone. I waited some more. He'd talk soon. It was just a matter of time. I always got on with Salmon. And I was nice to Abbie Hinckley when she came round. You can't reap what you haven't sown, I always say. Abbie liked to read and I'd loaned her two books. And they weren't *The Saints Everlasting Rest* or *The Book of Martyrs*, either, but Chaucer's *Canterbury Tales* and Milton's *Paradise Lost*. Isabella Thompson had loaned them to me. We quite frequently passed books around, since there was a shortage of them in North Elba.

"How's Abbie?" I asked.

"She's tolerable."

"She ought to come visit more."

He shrugged.

"We've all had fights with Pa, Salmon."

That brought him around, all right. He grinned. "Did I ever tell you about the fight Oliver and Pa had in Kansas?"

My brothers knew they could always talk to me when Pa became too much for them. I'm not saying they didn't reverence him. They did. We all did. But Pa was a man who needed talking about, no matter who knew him. People loved him and hated him. It confused you so. It made your soul all twisted up inside like a snake.

"Tell me," I said.

"Oliver had this revolver. And he also had a friend, name of Lucius Mills. We were about to leave Kansas, and Oliver wanted to make Lucius a present of the revolver. Pa said no. And set out to take the pistol away from Oliver. They scuffled. And I was standing aside, watching, thinking that pistol would go off any minute and blow the brains out of one of them. So I took it out of Oliver's holster and told them to finish their fussing without it. Well, you know how strong Oliver is. Remember the time he wrestled thirty lumbermen to the ground in one day in that wrestling match up at the mill?"

I smiled. "Yes."

"Well, Pa was no match for him. And Pa was getting the worst of it. And Oliver had a look of blood in his eye. Finally he grabbed Pa by the arms and shoved him against the wagon. Pa ordered him to let go. Oliver wouldn't. 'Not until you agree to behave yourself,' he said."

"What happened?"

"Pa agreed to behave. It isn't that I'm scared of what's going to happen in Virginia, Annie."

"I know that."

"I've had enough of it."

"I know that, too. But I'm thinking of going, Salmon."

He stopped polishing the Pepperbox. He just looked at me with his solemn brown eyes. I could see the knowledge all coming together behind them. He blew into the barrel of the Pepperbox and set it aside. "Ma isn't going, then."

"No. She's sending Martha. I offered to go and help."

He nodded. "It'll be your last chance to make things right between you and him, Annie," he said, wiping his hands on an old rag. "Everybody knows things aren't right between you and Pa, though neither of you ever speak of it."

I felt a stab of fear. What was he saying? "You think it won't work at Harpers Ferry, then?"

"You know Pa. He'll dally, 'til he's trapped. He insists on order. Everything perfect, everything in place. Everything arranged just to suit him before he makes a move. It can't be that way. And it'll trap him. That's what I think. It'll all get out of hand."

He went back to his work. I picked up the tray and started off.

"Annie?"

"Yes?"

"I almost wish I had one more chance to make things up to him," he said.

I went to find Jason.

There was no Pepperbox for Jason. He wouldn't kill the squirrels if they got into his grape arbor. Once, in Kansas, when they were all near starving, Salmon trapped some quail, killed and roasted them. Jason wouldn't eat them. He'd rather starve than eat the birds that had suffered so in the killing. And he grew fruit and grapes instead of a money crop like corn or grains. He was always tinkering with new kinds of grapes. Cross breeding, he called it.

"I've brought you some coffee and mush, Jase. Sorry, it

may be cold. I brought some to Salmon, too, and got talking with him. We didn't want you to starve."

"You know I always carry cheese in my pockets."

"Yes, and give it away to the dog." I sat down.

He was tending his grapes. The arbor was on a hill behind the house. He took up his coffee. "You can give the mush to the hogs. I grew up on that stuff. I can do without it now."

He sipped his coffee. "What's on your mind, Annie?" Jason cut right to the chase.

"I'm thinking of going to Maryland with Martha. Mama isn't going."

He gave me a quick look, then went back to twisting some errant vines around the arbor. "Make sure you go for the right reasons, Annie."

"That's what Mama said."

"Don't go to try to make anything up to him. You can never make things up to Pa."

It was Jason who was whipped by Pa, at four, for telling about a dream he had and thinking it was real. Pa accused him of lying. Salmon and Oliver also had stories like that to tell. But when they got old enough they fought Pa back.

"And it isn't your fault, anyway, that he lost four children the year you were born," he said.

"It's more than that, Jase, and you know it."

"The other isn't your fault. Any more than it was Fred or Owen's fault that I broke my arm when they suggested we slide down that rain pipe and get out of the house to get away from the Sabbath."

He smiled, remembering. Pa had always held with long

Sabbaths. From Saturday night on through Sunday, everybody had to be inside. No talking. No moving. The boys often escaped.

"A broken arm isn't dying," I said.

"You were three years old, for heaven's sake!"

"He blames me, Jase. Always did."

"You blame yourself. And it's about time you stopped. Ruth was the careless one."

"Then why is Ruth his favorite?"

He had no answer for that. So I pushed my case. "Jase, there's something I need to know. And only you can tell me."

He sighed deeply. "Go ahead."

"If I go with Martha, do you think I'll put a hex on things?"

"I don't believe in that nonsense. If you want to talk about hexes and rappings and tappings of departed souls and hypnotism, talk to brother John."

"I'm asking you, Jase."

"No."

"Will Pa think such?"

"He's got too much else to think about."

"Do you think it will work? What he's got planned down there?"

"No."

Silence between us for a minute. "And that's the thing," he told me. "If it doesn't work, and you go, you can't take on like it was your fault. But I have to tell you, since you asked, that whether you go or not, I don't think it's going to work. And I'm as much against slavery as anybody in this family."

I nodded. "So there's no changing your mind, then."

"No," he said. "I'm staying here the summer. Then I go back to Ohio to my wife and my sheep. I've broken all the jaws I'm about to break, Annie."

Martha had no objections to my going. And she didn't philosophize about it either, which was refreshing. She was happy, plain and simple, to have me along. "He asked for you," she said.

I looked at the outline of her form in the darkened room we shared in the upstairs loft. Outside a hooty owl called. I could see the stars from my window. Then they were replaced by Martha's words. They hung like stars in front of me in the dark, lighting up the room.

"He never did."

"It's in the letter. Mother Brown didn't read it all to us. She left parts out."

"Why?"

"Oh, maybe she thought they were private."

I stared into the spinning darkness. Martha had seen the letter. "What did he say?"

"That he'd like her to come, but if she can't, he'd be glad to have Martha and Annie come on. That it won't be unpleasant. That she should bring plain clothes and a few sheets and pillow cases and no more than can be packed in a single trunk. That the bag or bags should be marked I.S. Plain. Nothing else on them to give us away."

"I.S.?"

"He's calling himself Isaac Smith down there."

I thought he could have come up with a more colorful

name for the most important moment of his life. He'd called himself Shubal Morgan in Kansas. "Why didn't Mama tell me?" I put the question forth weakly.

"Oh, I'm sure she doesn't want you to go."

"And what about you, then?"

"Oliver is there. In any case, I'd go. She knows that."

Pa had asked for me! I couldn't believe it. But then why hadn't Mama told me? Instead she'd gotten angry when I told her Pa didn't like me. It made no sense. *Would things be so bad down there that she'd risk having me think he didn't want me, rather than have me go?*

More important, why had he asked for me? Oh, I didn't care. I felt jubilant. My heart was singing. Pa had asked for me. I turned over and looked up at the stars, smiling, before I fell asleep.

"Pa asked for me to come," I told Jason the next morning. He was hitching up the team for the ride to Keene for supplies. On the way he'd drop me off at the Thompson place. "It was in the letter. Martha told me. She saw the letter. Mama just didn't read all of it to us."

Jason didn't answer. On the drive he was silent. I occupied myself with watching the tops of the mountains, all wrapped in fog. Or the scenery, which always drew the eye. My heart was singing. I'd packed already. Pa was sending Oliver to fetch me and Martha any day now, and I was on my way to see Dauphin.

At the cutoff in the road that led to the Thompson farm, Jason spoke as I got out of the wagon. "I'll be back in three hours. Wait here at the gate."

"I will."

"Tell everybody I said hey." It was an expression he'd picked up in Kansas.

"Yes."

"He uses people, Annie. He goes through them. And like everyone who uses people, he can conjure up all the charm when he wants. Look how he's charmed the people in Massachusetts to back him with money. It's hard to resist. I know."

Out of the corner of my eye I could see Dauphin coming down the path from the house with his two blond, shaggy dogs that followed him everywhere. My heart leapt, seeing him. I did not want to hear this from Jason now. "What are you saying? That Pa doesn't really want me?"

"I'm saying that he needs you, if Ma doesn't go."

"Isn't it the same thing?"

He looked sad. "I'm sorry you don't know the difference, Annie. But that's part of it. He's made you that way."

I tossed my head. Dauphin was coming closer. He mustn't hear this. "Well, I'm glad to be needed then," I said. "He's never needed me before, Jase. But if he does now, I'm going."

He shrugged. "Just don't want you fooling yourself, Annie. See things as they are. It'll be easier all around that way."

"You were glad enough to be in Kansas with him. You didn't ask if it was wanting or needing," I reminded him.

"We were in Kansas before him. We asked him to come out there, remember. And in our case it was needing," he said. Then he clucked to the horses, shook the reins, waved to Dauphin, and drove on.

I watched him go. Jason's broken, I thought. He and Salmon. Their minds aren't unhinged, like John's, but they're broken just the same. But they had their chance with Pa. And I never have. They had Kansas, no matter how it turned out. If Pa had any complaints about them when they were my age, he flogged them and got it over with. Like he did with John one time. Kept accounts. For disobeying mother, eight lashes; for telling lies, eight lashes. Then invited him into the tannery to settle the account. But John was always his favorite son, the one he depended on. What kind of accounts has Pa got on me in the old ledger book of his mind?

How many lashes do you get for causing the death of a child?

There can't be enough. He'd already decided that. So why bother settling the score? He settled, instead, for sometimes not even looking at me when he walked into the room.

Still, I was determined not to let any of this ruin my day. I turned to greet Dauphin, a smile on my face that was from both wanting and needing. And I couldn't see the fault in either one.

I'm going to Maryland, and that's that, I told myself. Had I said it out loud?

"So am I." Dauphin grabbed me and whirled me around. His dogs danced around us, barking in sheer delight.

I stopped dancing. "You? You're going?"

"We got a letter from your pa, asking us down. Me and Will are going. To hell with brother Henry. You get hitched to a woman, that's what happens to you."

I pulled away from him. "You think that?"

"Most women," he amended. "Not you. You wouldn't be like that if we were hitched. You'd let me go and fight with your pa when he asked. Wouldn't you?"

The way he said it, with such reverence, under the blue vaulted sky, with the birds singing and the sun shining down on us on that beautiful July morning, and his two blond dogs as witnesses, made it sound like a marriage vow. I knew in a minute what he was about, of course. Only Dauphin would dare to make ordinary words sound like a marriage vow on a dusty road by a gate in God's good sunlight.

Only I would pick up on what he was about and enter into the spirit of it.

"I would," I said solemnly. "And when you got finished fighting, you'd come back to me, wouldn't you?"

"I would."

"To be with me forever and ever."

"Yes."

"And at Christmas, we'll have a tree. And trim it with popcorn."

"Yes."

"And we'll never flog our children. Or make them sit still and not speak on the Sabbath."

"I promise," he said.

I looked at him and he at me. I don't know how-all I appeared to him. I did have on my second-best dress. But he, oh Lordy, he was so handsome, with his blond curls and his dimples and his gentle, trusting ways. He was full of fun and always laughing. He had to be, I suppose. He was the youngest Thompson brother. And theirs was a happy family.

When you sat at their table you were more nourished by the love and joy than by the stew and vegetables. They had dancing at their house, music, and not "Blow Ye Trumpet Blow," either. Dauphin played the fiddle, so sweetlike it wrung out your soul. His father led a country reel. They celebrated Christmas. Since I was twelve I'd sneaked over on some pretense to help Isabelle and Dauphin make popcorn to trim the tree.

My sister Ruth never took part in this ceremony. She'd sit there and do some handiwork while the others did. She never told Pa about me doing it. I suppose there's some good in everybody. But she kept my involvement hidden, like some dark secret, to be ashamed of. So that I learned to be ashamed of it, too.

"We're betrothed, official-like now," Dauphin said. Then he hugged me, and his soft lips sought mine. It wasn't the first time. It wouldn't be the last. "We'll wed when the business at the Ferry is done with," he said. "And Pa will give us a piece of land to build our house on. Just like he gave it to Ruth and Henry."

"Yes," I agreed.

"We must keep it secret, though. I don't want your pa to think I'm not a good soldier because you're down there with me."

I agreed to that, too.

"I'll be a good soldier, don't you think, Annie?"

No, I didn't think. He was too sweet, too good, too much a bumbling country boy. He had no fighting experience. It was why I loved him. He was so different from my family.

"Yes," I said, "but I have to say something, Dauphin."

"You go right ahead."

"I don't want you to think you have to do this to prove yourself a man to Pa. He doesn't expect you to be like my brothers. He won't object to our marriage."

"I still want to prove myself worthy of his daughter," he said.

"Dauphin, you're worthy now! You don't have to kill to prove it!" How could I tell him? *I wasn't worthy of Pa. How could he ever hope to be? No matter what he does, he won't be worthy once he attaches himself to me. And if I know him, he'll kill himself trying.*

"Hush." He held me close. "You know I want to go. Me and Will both. We never got over being disappointed last time we set out for Kansas to join your brothers and met them on the way back."

I held back a sob.

"I'll be with Will. We'll take care of each other. And for the rest of the summer you'll have to take care of us. It'll be fun, Annie, you'll see. We'll have a wonderful time down there."

I said yes and followed him down the path to the Thompson house.

Chapter Three

Pa was born in Connecticut in 1800. His pa moved to Ohio when he was five. He told us the wilderness was full of wild beasts and Indians. But he grew to like it. He made friends with the Indians. One Indian boy gave him a yellow marble. Pa cherished that marble. Then one day he lost it. "It took me years to heal that wound," he told us. Then he had a little bobtailed squirrel as a pet, and it died. And that near killed him, too. How must he have felt, then, every time he lost a child?

MY FIRST VIEW OF HARPERS FERRY WAS FROM the train, the Baltimore and Ohio, which chugged through the Blue Ridge Mountains. And if North Elba has the most beautiful scenery God ever created, like Pa says, then I figured God got carried away, made too much, didn't know what to do with the leftovers, and stuck them in the Blue Ridge.

Oliver had fetched us at North Elba. Will and Dauphin Thompson accompanied us as far as Troy, where Martha, Oliver, and I took a boat down the Hudson River to New York City. Then the rails to Philadelphia and on down. The Thompson brothers would stay in North Elba a while longer to see to the crops.

Martha and I each had a trunk packed to the top, with the initials I.S. on them. Isaac Smith. Martha was now a Smith. And so was I. Martha had left personal items at home to make room for yards of coarse, unbleached sheeting that

Oliver said was badly needed for mattress ticking. I filled the extra room in my trunk with half a dozen books.

We had packed food and ate on the train. To me the ride was exciting. I was going to a new place, with a new name, to meet new people. I stared at the other passengers, who all seemed to be accustomed to traveling through places like Baltimore, places I'd only heard about. I tried to fix in my mind where they were bound. And why. They all looked important. One lady at the end of our car had a wooden crate. Out of it came a cat's meow. Every so often the lady would push aside the blanket in the crate and pet the cat, and it would stop crying.

Imagine that, I told myself. A cat important enough to ride on the train. I wondered if she'd bought a ticket for it.

I could not believe the town of Harpers Ferry when I saw it. I thought at first that it was a mistake. There couldn't be a town here. No room, with all those towering bluffs. No room for anything but the raging river. But there was the town, clinging to the bluffs, roads zigzagging all the way up them. I thought, God isn't going to like this, the way men had intruded on His creation. It was unnatural. And plain as the nose on your face that God brooded on the place.

"It can employ four hundred people," Oliver was pointing out the arsenal as if we'd never heard of it before. As if Pa hadn't talked about it until we were all blue in the face. As if Sarah hadn't come home from school in a terror because her teacher had told her how George Washington had the arsenal built. "*George Washington*, Annie! When he was president! He wanted it there so it would be safe from foreign invaders! And Pa wants it!"

And that's why we were coming into it now. Because Pa was going to take it.

Oliver had to shout over the clacking of the train wheels as we went through a long, covered bridge over the Potomac. When we came into the open again, the hot air fanned our faces, cinders blew in the windows, the whistle from the locomotive shrieked. "There's Maryland Heights to the north, Loudoun Heights to the south, and Bolivar Heights to the west." He knew the place by heart. Oliver was that way. He read every book he could get his hands on.

He was Pa's youngest son. Twenty, handsome and articulate. But since he came to fetch us, I'd seen a shadow across his face. Something was wrong, and he wasn't saying.

There was bad cess to this Ferry place. I sensed it on sight. And I think Oliver sensed it, too.

"Twenty-six hundred people live here," he was telling us. "About a hundred and fifty are free blacks; about a hundred and fifty slaves. There's a grist mill, an iron mill, a cotton mill, seven dry goods stores, five shoemakers, four tailors, four taverns, and six churches. The arsenal turns out ten thousand muskets a year and stores them in the armory on Shenandoah Street."

I knew what Oliver was thinking. About the letter John wrote from Kansas. *Hundreds of thousands of the meanest and most desperate of men armed to the teeth with revolvers, Bowie knives, rifles and cannon, are under pay from slaveholders. The friends of freedom are not one fourth of them half armed. We need arms more than we need bread. And* now all these guns here, ten thousand a year made in the arsenal in this strange, beautiful, forbidding place where you heard nothing but factory whistles echoing off the cliffs and the raging waters protesting.

And there was Pa just across the river in Maryland.

And there was the shadow across Oliver's face.

"It's beautiful," Martha said of the town. And she leaned forward to take Oliver's hand. Did she know, too, what he was thinking?

"It can be deadly," he answered her. "You see right there? The Shenandoah and Potomac meet. The waters can be treacherous when it rains. Hogs roam the streets, coal smoke lies over everything, and they had a cholera epidemic in 1850 that killed over a hundred."

We rode in rocking, lurching silence, looking at the river that could be deadly, the arsenal that turned out ten thousand muskets a year, and the town that clung to the cliffs in such a precarious manner. A perfect place for Pa, I thought. Just sitting here, waiting for him.

The door of the car opened, and the clanking noises got louder. The conductor came towards us with a rolling gait, shouting that we'd soon be at the depot. The train was coming to a screeching halt.

"The town folk flock to the depot every time a train comes in," Oliver told us. "They like to stare and conjecture who everybody is and what they've come for. I'll handle everything. Don't answer any questions, and don't talk to anybody."

Oliver took us to the Wager House for supper. It was a middling hotel, but it had a nice rug on the dining room floor. I'd never seen a rug with flowers on it, and if I owned it I wouldn't put it out for men to walk across with their dusty boots. But Isaac Fouke, the proprietor, didn't seem to mind. His sister, Christine, did. She scolded Oliver. "No cheroot ashes on my rug now."

She was a spinster, Oliver told us. "She really runs the place. Gives the men what-for if they don't behave."

She gave us a table in a quiet corner. She seemed to know we wanted to be hidden from prying eyes, though the dining room was deserted. The taproom was full, and the talk was loud, the shouting frequent.

"You look tuckered out," Christine told Martha.

"A long day," Martha allowed.

Christine's eyes went over Martha. "And the travel. It isn't easy on those cars. We have some good soup. And I'd suggest a small glass of brandy."

"Yes, bring us two brandies," Oliver agreed. "Have you seen Mr. Isaac Smith about?"

"Left for his place just before the train arrived. Complaining that he hasn't found any good cattle to buy yet. Said he'd be back to fetch you all before dark. What will it be, then, the soup? Or the Brunswick stew?"

Oliver said Brunswick stew.

Christine patted his shoulder. "You're a good boy. You don't spill ashes on my rug, like that no-count Cook."

"Has he been in tonight?" Oliver asked.

"No. We're not rowdy enough for him. Spends his evenings at the Galt House, telling hurdy-gurdy stories."

The Brunswick stew was good. I think the meat in it was rabbit. It was a dish new to me, but Oliver said they made it in Virginia all the time. "Remember you're in the real South now," he joked. "For breakfast here they serve grits."

"What are grits?" I asked.

"Same as Ma's mush. Only with a fancier name."

"Do they really keep slaves here?" I asked.

"Mostly house servants," Oliver said, "though some labor in the fields. Cook says George Washington's great-grandnephew, who lives in a big old house four miles from here, has five."

"How does Cook know?" Martha asked.

Oliver paused before spooning some stew into his mouth. "There isn't much he doesn't know. He's been here a year now, mixing with the people. Taught school, knocked on every door selling Bibles, even married his landlady's daughter. Gotten into every quarters and talked to the slaves. Made friends with Mayor Beckham and Hayward Shepherd, the free black porter at the station. Even went to target practice at Beall Air, to see how many guns Washington had in the house. Pa couldn't do without his reports. Now he has a job tending a lock on the canal."

"I thought you said he talked too much," Martha said.

I felt jealous, left out. It was obvious that Oliver had told Martha things I was ignorant of. I would have to listen and learn, if I wanted to keep up. If there was anything Pa hated, it was somebody who didn't keep up.

"He does," Oliver said, "but he makes up for it in providing information."

"Who's at the farm now?" I asked. I wanted to sound intelligent.

"Just me, Pa, Owen, and Jeremiah Anderson. The others won't be along for a coupla weeks. But it isn't fit to live in. You girls are going to stay with the Nichols tonight. They're good people who live a few miles from the farm. Just remember, Pa's down here to buy cattle, like Christine and everybody else think."

"The Nichols are Dunkers," Oliver told us.

"I thought only Germans were Dunkers," Martha said.

Again I was outside the conversation. What were Dunkers? They sounded like the bread Mama fried in fat that Salmon dunked in his coffee.

"Most are German," Oliver told her. "But they've joined the sect. There are a powerful lot of Dunkers around here. They have a small church. Pa has preached in it. They're abolitionists."

Pa never did come back. Oliver hired a horse and wagon and drove us to the Nichols's. I don't remember much about the Nichols house that first night except lights in the distance as we rode with Oliver through the sweet July darkness. There were june bugs and frogs croaking, katydids singing, and always somewhere in the distance the sound of rushing water, then an open door, a welcoming couple, clean beds, and sleep. Oliver left us. He'd be back in the morning. He and Pa were scouring out the log cabin, he said, and it wasn't ready for us yet.

But in the morning, he didn't come. Nor did Pa. Mrs. Nichols was a large, quiet woman, and she and her husband couldn't do enough for us. They had no children, and she fussed over me and Martha so it made me feel strange. I was not used to being fussed over or paid mind to.

"Such a pretty child," she said of me.

Pretty? Me? I did not want to be pretty. I wanted to be useful. Where had I failed? We stayed there two days, and that first night she was stitching me a new dress out of some fabric she had laid by. I didn't want to take it. I was mortified when she asked me to try it on. But Martha nodded, rolled her eyes to the ceiling, and raised her hands in helplessness. Martha was faring no better. When Mrs. Nichols found she was expecting, she would scarcely let her move about.

We escaped from her fussing by taking Martha's un-bleached sheeting down to the stream in back and sitting under the trees and stitching it into bed ticking. "Can you imagine, she thinks I'm a child?" Martha asked. "I've been wed a year!"

The second night Mrs. Nichols knocked on the door of the little room I shared with Martha and brought in a tray of warm milk with honey in it. I almost tripped over myself taking it from her. "You shouldn't be waiting on us like this," I said. She beamed. We drank our milk, and I thought: So this is what normal mothers do for their daughters. I'd known, of course, that there were families like this. I'd met girls who had such mothers, back in school in Ohio.

Then I felt guilty. Did that mean Mama wasn't normal? I recollected Jason's scoffing remark. *When have we ever looked normal?* We weren't. And the knowledge was bred into me that we weren't supposed to be. We had a purpose in life. To sacrifice everything to Pa's cause, the freedom of the slaves. Pa would scold if he saw the milk delivered to us in the room. "Wasteful, foolish, frivolous," he'd say of such treatment.

I was glad when Oliver came to fetch us the next morning. And we could ride away from Mrs. Nichols and her special treatment, which put me in a terror of confusion. For what she thought I was, and what I knew I wasn't. Yet what I secretly longed to be.

Mrs. Nichols gave me extra fabric from the dress to take with me.

Pa was pouring over his battle maps at the dining room table when we arrived. They were pasted to heavy cambric cloth. And in the margins I saw scrawled figures.

"The girls are here, Pa," Oliver said.

Surely, he must have heard us coming, heard the creaking of the wagon as Oliver drove it up the long field in front. Or at least the scurrying noise of the chickens. Heard us trudging up the stairway that led to the second story of the log cabin.

But he did not look up when we stood there with Oliver. Though he did ask if we had a good trip.

"It was middling fair," Martha said.

"And how did you leave your mother?"

If the question was directed at me, I did not answer it. I was tongue-tied in his presence, as always. Martha answered for me. "Mother Brown is well."

He stood up then. "Maryland has nearly 84,000 free blacks and 87,000 slaves. Virginia has 58,000 free blacks and 491,000 slaves, more than any other state in the Union."

"Mother Brown sends her love," Martha said.

"We got this house at a good price," he told us. "Thirty-five dollars for the summer. That includes the small house across the road. And enough firewood to last until March."

He looks different, I thought. His beard is cropped. And he's thinner. Melting away. The fire that always burns inside him is consuming him. Doesn't anybody see it?

"Mother Brown also sends some sheeting and flour and lard for your shortcakes," Martha told him.

"I miss my shortcakes. Will you make them, Martha?"

"No, I tried, but I'm better at the cornbread. Annie's become an expert at the shortcakes."

He looked at me. "You've finally become an expert in something."

I did not know whether to be happy or to cry. "I could make some now if you want," I said.

"There's a big black stove in the kitchen off the porch. Owen bought a whole barrel of eggs. And there's potatoes, onions, and bacon. All in the storeroom downstairs."

Martha and I went to find the kitchen. And she knew whether to be happy or cry. She was near crying. "How can you let him speak to you like that?"

"It's his way."

"Well, it isn't a good way. Always, I ask Oliver, how can he *be* the way he is? The trouble is, you all make excuses for him." She started a fire in the big black stove and was slicing some bacon for frying. I began mixing the shortcake batter.

"Oliver told me that out in Kansas he had all of them under his spell. Just because he's your father, that doesn't make him God, Annie."

"I don't think of him as God."

"Then stand up to him, won't you."

"How can I do that?"

"I stood up to my pa. And Ma, too, when they didn't want me to marry Oliver." She wiped a hand across her brow. It was hot in the kitchen.

"You never told us why they didn't want you to wed Oliver," I said.

She sighed and looked around her. "Because of this," she said. "What your pa's doing here. What he's got planned. Oh, I know all about it, Annie. Oliver told me. My folks were bitter against your father because of his abolitionist views. And we aren't slavers."

"But you came here anyway."

"To be with Oliver. But I don't like it, Annie, I can tell you. I have bad feelings about all this. I lay awake nights worrying. What's going to happen to them?"

"What does Oliver say?"

She looked at me. And I saw her as old, though she was just seventeen. "'We can't let my pa die alone.' That's what he says, Annie."

I whipped the batter savagely. "I'm going to make these the best shortcakes ever," I said.

"You better make plenty." She was peering out the window. "Here comes Owen."

He came up the outside stairs and into the kitchen, carrying a sack of flour under his good arm. Owen had one withered arm, weakened from an accident in childhood. Because of this infirmity, Pa always tried to protect him. But he'd been Pa's stalwart in Kansas and had fought well. He was thirty-five and had never wed. But he was handsome, with straw-colored hair and beard.

"Hello, girls." He spoke calmly, always. And Pa always listened to him. He kissed Martha's cheek, then came over to kiss me. "Everybody at home all right?"

I said yes.

"Surprised to see you here, Annie."

"Why?"

He shrugged. "Where's Pa?"

"In the dining room with Oliver. Going over his maps," I told him.

"Old Mrs. Huffmaster's in a bad way. Got a growth on her neck, and it hurts her powerful bad. Needs to be lanced. I told her Pa would pay her a visit."

"Who's Mrs. Huffmaster?" we both asked.

Owen grinned. "You'll both find out soon enough. And wish you hadn't."

"What does Pa know about doctoring?" I turned the shortcakes over in the pan.

Owen stole a piece of cooked bacon off a plate. "When

he arrived in Kansas we were all sick as Clancy's goat after he ate the curtains. All but Wealthy and John's little boy, Jonny. We were shakin' with the ague, and Salmon had billious colic, weak as babes, livin' in makeshift tents, our crops still in the fields, our horses and cattle runnin' loose. Pa took us in hand and made us all well. That's what he knows about doctorin'."

"If I hear one more Kansas story I'll get billious colic right now," Martha said.

"Come on in here, Owen," Pa called out. "I've got the 1850 U.S. census."

Martha shoved a pile of dishes into his hands. "Make yourself useful," she said, "and tell him to get those maps and things off the table right now. We're having breakfast."

Owen took the dishes. And the orders. We're lucky to have Martha, I thought, watching her lay the bacon in strips on a plate and brush a strand of hair off her forehead. Something tells me she's got more sense than all of us put together.

Chapter Four

Pa never joined an army, no. He thought a standing army the greatest curse to a country, because it drained off the best of the young men and left farming and the industrial arts to inferior men. But he went to war at age twelve. He drove a herd of cattle more than a hundred miles west from Ohio, around Lake Erie, and then northwest into Michigan to the army of General Hull at Detroit. It was during the War of 1812. He did it alone. On this trip he stayed overnight with a man who made a great fuss over him. This man also owned a boy slave about Pa's age, and Pa and the boy struck up a friendship. Then Pa became distressed when the man beat the boy. I guess right about there Pa came on to hating slavery.

MY SHORTCAKES FOR THAT FIRST BREAKFAST were the best ever, if I have to say so myself. And I did take pride in them. It all has to do with the right amount of lard used in them. It has been my experience that shortcakes can be ruinous with too much or too little lard. And the pan must be just the right temperature, too.

Everybody said they were good. Except Pa, of course. I didn't expect him to say anything. Then Martha went and pressed him for an opinion. "Aren't these the best shortcakes you've ever had?"

"Nothing wrong with them far as I can see," Pa said.

It caused Martha all kinds of vexation. She just didn't

understand Pa. That was his way. There was no sense in taking on about it. All it would do was bring her to grief.

After breakfast, and before he and Oliver left to attend to Mrs. Huffmaster, Pa called me and Martha aside and cautioned us, in his most solemn manner, how to handle strangers.

"The outside world must, in no way, discover that John Brown has taken up residence in the neighborhood," he intoned in his best preacher voice. "How you divide up the household chores does not concern me. But Martha, you are in charge of the kitchen. Annie, you are to help. When the men come, I expect that some of them will live in the house across the road. They will be arriving in twos and threes any time now, through August. They are all good men, but I must ask you to refrain from speaking of my plan to them. I expect them to do their own washing. Annie, your main responsibility is constant watchfulness."

This brought me up short. I just stared at him.

He was in fine fettle now, warming to the subject. "Constant watchfulness. That is the byword you must live by here, Annie Brown. When you are not sweeping or fetching or helping dish up the victuals, I expect you to sit out there on the porch and be a lookout."

Well, that near undid me. "A lookout?"

"Yes. I expect you to have the eye of an eagle. Read or sew out there, I care not which. Just look busy. Day and evening. You must never set aside your watchfulness. And if any stranger approaches find out first who they are before entering into conversation. And warn me or whatever men are in the house immediately. No one must ever discover how many men live here. No one must become suspicious. I am depending on you for this, Annie Brown. Do you think you can be depended upon?"

The way he put it to me was like a minister asking if you were ready to come forth and accept Christ Jesus. Had God revealed himself to me in a burning bush in the backyard, I could not have been more filled with dread. And fear. "Yessir," I said.

"I hold you to this, Annie Brown," he said. Then he left.

Afterward Martha and I were cleaning up the dishes in the kitchen. We worked in silence, and her face was all tight and not pretty as it usually was.

"Don't let Pa vex you," I said.

"His saying there wasn't anything wrong with those short-cakes was an insult."

"From Pa it was a compliment."

"Can't he ever pay you one that doesn't come in the back door? He acts like you're no more than a piece of firewood. And if Oliver acted like that, I'd never cook for him again."

"Pa ate the shortcakes, didn't he? Now if he didn't eat them, that would be an insult."

She just looked at me, real sadlike. "And to think that your ma is friends with Lucretia Mott."

I didn't know what Mama's friendship with Lucretia had to do with my old shortcakes. Yes, she was a suffragette, but I knew personally that she couldn't cook to save her soul. But before I had the chance to make sense of the matter, a man came up the outside stairs and stood there at the kitchen door.

"Where is everybody?"

Annie and I glanced at each other. The man looked to be near thirty and was dressed like a peddler or a farmer. Yet he had an almost elegant bearing about him, as if he had seen better times.

"You must be Annie and Martha," he said.

"And who are you, sir?" Martha asked.

He took off his floppy hat. "Jeremiah Goldsmith Anderson." He gave a little bow. "Grandson of Virginia slaveholders, twice arrested by proslavers in Kansas, and alumnus of Fort Scott prison in that benighted territory. Veteran of the slave raids into Missouri with John Brown."

"Anderson," Martha breathed, "of course. My husband has told me of your exploits. You were in Fort Scott prison for ten weeks."

"At your service, ma'am."

Martha opened the door. He came in. "I'm just back from a run to Chambersburg. Got some cases of guns in the wagon. If it's all right, I'll be bringing them into the house."

"Cases of guns?" Martha looked shocked. "In the house?"

"Revolvers and Sharps repeating rifles. They're in the house now," he told her. "What do you think is in those wooden boxes setting right there in the dining room?"

Martha and I both stared to where he pointed. "We sat on those boxes before," I said. "Pa said they were furniture."

Anderson grinned at me. "Well then, I've got three more

cases of furniture in the wagon. Compliments of your brother John in Ohio, who's forwarding arms on to Chambersburg. Well, what say you, ladies? Want to tell me where to put it?"

Anderson's revelation to us, that we'd been sitting on Sharps rifles and more were to come, only brought us face-to-face with the real purpose of our mission at the farm. "After all," Martha said dully, "we aren't here to make short-cakes. We might as well resign ourselves to it."

Her calm amazed me. Before she'd confessed to having bad feelings about this venture. Yet now she seemed to be taking things in stride.

Like the fleas and the sleeping arrangements. I don't know which bothered me more.

We discovered both in short order. No sooner had Anderson set the boxes of rifles down than Martha and I looked around to decide where we were going to sleep.

"Your pa and the men are upstairs in the garret," Anderson told us. "And that's where the men have to stay all day, so they aren't detected."

He took us upstairs. The stairway was in the dining room. The garret was close and hot and in the kind of disorder you'd expect to find when men live together. There were crude pallets on the floor, stuffed with hay, magazines strewn about, a game of checkers, clothing, shaving strops and mugs, a pile of military tactics manuals, a Bible, a copy of the *Baltimore News American*, a deck of cards.

"I guess we'll take the small room downstairs," Martha said.

We went to inspect it. There was one window that overlooked the backyard. The room was swept clean and held two beds. "You can have the one by the window," Martha volunteered, "Oliver and I will take one over there."

I stared at her. "Sleep in the room with you and Oliver?"

"And why not?"

When she put it to me that way, with her clear, blue-eyed innocence, I could not say why not. But I thought it. Because you and Oliver haven't been together since June sixteenth, when he left North Elba with Pa, I thought. Because I know you can't wait to be alone together. Because it isn't decent.

The absurdity of the whole thing came over me. Pa was forming a Provisional Army of the United States here in this very house. To take over the government. Sleeping in the same room with my brother and his wife paled beside that.

"We don't mind if you don't," Martha said. Then she smiled. "Sew a curtain around your bed if it's privacy you're after."

"Out of what? All the sheeting must go for bed ticking."

"Mrs. Nichols gave you extra fabric, didn't she? Ouch!" And she slapped her ankle. "Something bit me."

I'd had to scratch, too, a moment ago, but I thought I'd picked up a case of poison ivy on the ground at Mrs. Nichols's house.

Martha picked up her skirt. "Fleas! The place is loaded with them!" She ran outside on the porch, whipping her skirts around her. "Annie, find Jeremiah and ask him if there's any lye soap to scrub with! I've got to scour that room!"

She emptied all the old bed ticking of the foul-smelling straw and set Jeremiah Anderson, grandson of slaveholders, to boiling it in the big washing pots in the backyard. Then she made him fetch new straw from an adjacent field and set me to sewing more bed ticking with the sheeting she'd brought down from North Elba.

I felt guilty sitting there in the morning sun, overlooking the peaceful hill that led down from the farm to the road, stitching a not-too-fine seam, while Martha, two months into having a child, scrubbed out our room on her hands and knees.

"I'll scrub, you sew," I called in the window to her.

"Your pa said you're to sit and watch. So do as you're told!"

When Pa and Oliver returned about noon, our room was scrubbed clean, the old bed ticking was placed on bushes in the backyard to dry, there was a pot of soup on for lunch, and I'd stitched a whole new ticking to be stuffed with clean straw.

Martha's hands were red from lye soap. But she seemed no worse for her morning's scrubbing. "What's that?" She stood with one hand over her eyes to shield the sun, laughing, as Pa and Oliver came through the fields.

"Isn't he the ugliest creature you ever saw?" Oliver asked.

A little dog, all long ears and snout, was tagging after them. And he was the ugliest creature I'd ever seen. And also the most endearing.

"Name's Cuffee," Pa said. "Mrs. Huffmaster gave him to us for lancing her boil. Come on down here and make him feel to home."

"More fleas," Martha growled. And she went into the kitchen to see to the soup. I went down to see Cuffee. I missed our dog at home, and it was good to kneel down and have Cuffee kiss me. He got right up on his short hind legs to do so. And gave little whimpering sounds of greeting. My heart went out to him. He was underfed. But more than that, he was underloved. Anybody could see that. At least I could.

"You don't have to worry," I told him, "I know what it's like. I'll give you all the love you need."

"He doesn't come in the house!" Martha called out from the kitchen. She was banging around pots and pans, getting the noonday vittles. I found Cuffee a rope, tied him in a cool place under a tree, fetched him some water, and went in to help Martha.

Pa was saying grace. "From winter, plague, and pestilence, good Lord, deliver us!" he finished.

Across the table I looked at Martha and she at me. "Especially the pestilence," she said. "This house is full of fleas."

"'Thou shalt not be afraid for the pestilence that walketh in darkness,'" Pa quoted.

"They walk in daylight," Martha said. "All over the place. And I've been bitten. I'm not afraid, I'm angry."

"She's been scrubbing all morning," I added. "The fleas are as big as dogs."

"Don't lie, Annie," Pa said, "I hate lies."

"Well, at least small dogs," I amended.

"Annie," Jeremiah Anderson put in, "let me give you a piece of advice. Always tell the truth, the whole truth, and nothing but the truth. But if you do have to tell a lie, tell a whopper."

Everybody laughed. Not Pa. It made me so mad, I just burst right out with what I was thinking. "Aren't we living a lie here not telling our real name?" I asked.

Pa looked down. He said nothing. And then everyone else went silent, too. I got up and ran from the room. I went right into the room Martha and I and Oliver were to share and got down on the floor looking for a flea. It didn't take long. I soon sighted one. Then I ran for Martha's sewing box, got a pin and stuck it right through the flea, and brought it into the dining room.

"Here." I showed Pa. "Here is a flea. Look how big it is."

He raised his eyes to mine. And for a moment he didn't speak. "If you are ever obliged to kill anything, Annie," he said quietly, "kill it quickly, causing it as little pain as possible. And don't ever kill to revenge anything. At any time. Not even a flea."

How like Pa, I thought, to put such a light on it that I felt in the wrong, when I knew I was right.

I was sitting out on the porch later, stitching the extra fabric from Mrs. Nichols into a bed curtain, when Owen came out of the house and just stood there. He had some mending in his hands. Owen liked to sew. Even back home he'd mended his own clothing. He especially liked to darn socks.

To mark shirts or trousers as his, he put an O.X. on them. It meant "Old Xcentricity," he once told us.

"Mind if I sit a while?" he asked.

I shrugged. He sat down on the wooden planks of the porch and commenced to sew.

"Don't ever make Pa look wrong, Annie," he said. "He won't stand for it."

I wiped a tear from my face. "I'm sorry I came. I want to go home."

"So do we all."

I sniffed and wiped a tear from my face.

"You're homesick," he said. "Ma shouldn't have let you come."

"I make my own decisions," I said.

"Then learn to live with the decisions you make."

I had no reply for that. And I couldn't be mad at Owen. He was so gentle and stalwart, always managing to do things as well, if not better, than the other boys, even with one arm rendered practically helpless. He never complained.

"You can't best Pa, Annie. I learned that when I was eight. He was shaving. His back was to me. I picked up the cat and held him over Frederick's face. Fred was two, lying in the cradle. I very carefully lowered the cat to the baby's face. Pa told me to stop it, but I wouldn't. So he told me to put the cat to my own face."

I stared at him. "Did you?"

"When Pa told us to do something, we did it," he answered.

"What happened?"

"I held the cat up in front of my own face. And got scratched for my trouble."

"Well, see what I mean, then? What kind of a father tells an eight-year-old to do such?"

"What kind of an eight-year-old holds a cat over a baby's face?"

I threaded my needle, not looking at him.

"Annie, if we succeed here, someday there will be a United States flag over this house," he said quietly. "And if we don't, it will be considered a den of pirates and thieves."

"I think it's a den of pirates and thieves now."

"All young girls think that of their families. It's normal."

"Well, this isn't a normal family."

"Exactly. We've been called on to do something special. And you and Martha are to be sent home before we do it. Which means you may be the only ones alive who can tell what it was like here this summer."

"Owen, don't say that." I shivered.

"Try to remember the good things, Annie," he said. "And not how big the fleas were."

Late that night I lay behind my calico bed curtain trying to do what Owen said, remember the good things. We'd only been here one day, but Owen had fetched water from the well and filled up two big tubs so Martha and I could bathe. Then he and Oliver carried the tubs up behind the trees and bushes in back of the house. Kissed by the afternoon sun, that water was warm enough to make that bath one of the best things I could remember in a fortnight.

Then he'd bathed Cuffee for me, using good strong lye soap. Only Owen would do that, bathe a dog. Cuffee looked a lot more presentable when it was done. And I'll wager he felt better, too.

Owen even pinned my calico around my bed for me. Now I lay, wearing my new cotton shift that smelled fresh and sweet. Mama had packed it in lavender someone had given her as a gift. I looked out my window. The stars were closer and bigger here in Maryland then they'd ever been back in North Elba. And from the distance I heard a hooty owl call to its mate.

But I couldn't sleep just the same. All I heard was Cuffee whimpering outside and, from across the room, Martha and Oliver stirring in their bed. I waited for them to settle down, but it went on and on.

"What are you two doing?" I asked finally.

"Oh," Martha said, "we're just trying to stir a little softness into our bed."

"Well, stir it and be quick about it. I can't sleep."

"It's that fool puppy," Oliver said. "We can't sleep either."

"If you'd let me bring him in with me, it'd quiet him down," I said. "He's clean. Owen bathed him."

"All right," Martha relented. "But be quick about it."

I was anything but quick. I went outside into the moon-flooded night, my face flaming. Martha and Oliver hadn't been trying to stir softness into their bed, and I should have known better. And her embarrassment was the only reason she was allowing me to bring Cuffee inside.

I stayed outside a long time with Cuffee in the moonlight. I patted him, put him in my arms, and brought him up to the porch. How long does it take to stir softness into your bed, I wondered. I wanted to give them time.

I didn't know. At fifteen, I'd been kissed by Dauphin Thompson, yes. But all I knew about that was that the world stood still and all of eternity passed across the face of the sun when it happened. After a while I went inside with Cuffee and snuggled him into my bed. Martha and Oliver were very still, likely sleeping.

Chapter Five

In 1816 Pa went East to become a minister. But he couldn't master Latin and Greek. He felt out of place, and his vision went bad. So he went back to Hudson, Ohio, to go into the tanning business. In 1820 he married Dianthe Lusk. She was neat and plain and baked good bread, and she had a way with a hymn. Pa was twenty. She was nineteen.

I AWOKE THE NEXT MORNING WITH THE SUN SLANTING in my window, the sound of chickens clucking in the yard, Cuffee licking my face, and the humiliating knowledge that I'd overslept. I pushed aside my calico curtain. Martha and Oliver's bed was empty.

I threw on my clothes and ran into the kitchen. Martha was washing the breakfast dishes. "Where is everybody?"

"Outside. Setting off to buy some livestock and return the rented horse."

"Why didn't you wake me?" I was in a panic. Never had I slept so late! "What will Pa think?"

"That the trip was too much for you, and you needed to sleep."

Pa? Was she crazy? He got up at five every morning! Shot out of bed like a bird dog after its prey. "He'll think I'm spineless and lazy." I ran out onto the porch. Below me Oliver was hitching the horse up to the wagon. I stumbled down the outside stairs. Never had I felt so ashamed. There was

Martha, expecting a child. Martha who'd scrubbed and cooked all yesterday. And I was the one to sleep late.

"Pa?"

He looked up. "You missed morning prayers."

"I didn't mean to sleep late, Pa."

"Take your place on the porch and say them there. 'Oh daughter of troops; to go to war once again.' Micah five."

"Yessir."

"If Johnny Cook comes by later, tell him to stay in the house and wait for me."

"Would you like me to make you some cornbread today?"

"Martha can do the cooking. You just set and watch. If Mrs. Huffmaster comes round, don't let her inside. She's been asking questions about the deliveries from Chambersburg. Tell her all those boxes are furniture. And we haven't unpacked them yet, because your ma is to come shortly. And is very particular and wants to unpack them herself."

I nodded.

"Tell her anything and give her anything she wants. Except information. You understand?"

I understood. I was to do what Pa considered most despicable. Oh daughter of troops. I was to lie.

"Who is this Mrs. Huffmaster that she has Pa running to lance her boil, yet he dreads her visits?" I asked Martha.

She handed me a plate of vittles and some coffee. "Oliver says she's the littlest woman you're likely to meet. Barefoot, with three children tagging at her skirts and one in her arms. Claims she communicates with the dead. And collects the first May rain to wash the eyes with. She lives about a half a mile down the road. And that garden out back is hers. She rented it from Mrs. Kennedy before we came and comes every so often to tend it."

I went out onto the porch to have my breakfast. The sun was warm, some little wrens were singing. Cuffee snuggled at my feet, and I shared some bread and cheese with him. The sky was a vault of blue overhead and crows fought in the nearby cornfield.

I wished, of a sudden, that this were my house, Dauphin's and mine. That we were wed and lived here, and that he was at the Ferry on an errand, and I was sitting here waiting for him to come home. I'd have a blueberry pie in the oven for him. And Cuffee would be our dog.

From the other side of the house came the sound of Jeremiah Anderson's hammering. It brought me back to the real world. He was building a ladder down from the garret window. Just in case, when the men arrived, they had to make a quick escape.

Inside, Martha was singing "Faded Flowers." Martha had a clear, firm voice. I felt peaceful and tried to imagine that Martha and I had just come for a little visit with Pa and the boys, who really were down here to buy cattle. And soon we'd all go back home again to North Elba. Except for Oliver and Owen, who would drive the cattle North. Just like Owen, Watson, and Salmon drove a small herd of Devon cattle from Connecticut to North Elba ten years ago now.

Then I thought I saw something in the distance and strained my eyes to see down to the road that was about three hundred yards away. Sure enough, a rider was approaching on a horse. He turned in our gate.

"Martha," I said, "we have a visitor."

She ran around to the other side of the house to tell Jeremiah Anderson, and soon the hammering stopped. I watched the rider come up our road. When he approached, I saw that he rode a fine, prancing chestnut roan with a white forelock. A Virginia horse, it looked to me. Owen said in Virginia they rode horses that nobody else had in the country.

"Can I help you, sir?"

He looked to be not quite six feet. And he had deep set blue eyes, a sun-browned face, and long, silky blond hair. He wore a canvas duster, even in the July heat. Man who wears a duster like that is hiding something, I thought. He carried a long rifle. Looked like a Virginia gun to me, too. He attracts notice, I thought, and he knows it. And when his duster fell open I saw he carried a pistol with lots of brass on it. And I thought, this is a dangerous man.

"Might you be Annie?" he asked.

"I might be. If you tell me who you are, first."

I saw a glint of appreciation in his eyes. This man likes sass, I thought. Because he is sass.

"Cook. Johnny Cook. Connecticut born, Quaker bred." He took off his hat, slipped from his horse, and tied it to a fence post all in one liquid, effortless motion. Then he gave a slight bow.

He spoke like a Yankee. Still, I had to be careful. "How do I know you're Johnny Cook?"

He grinned and winked. "Good girl. Because, as you can

see, I am impulsive, indiscreet, and loved by women everywhere. I am sure you've heard such. My reputation precedes me."

"Where do you work?" I would not be taken by flattery.

"I keep the canal lock at the North End of the federal grounds."

"You're in a fancy getup for a canal-lock tender."

"The battle must be fought to the end, and we must all play our part, or we will not triumph," he said.

"I figure you're one of Pa's men what with that kind of talk. All right, you can come up. But you'd best put your horse in the barn, out of sight."

He did so. As he was coming up the porch steps, Jeremiah Anderson burst out of the house. "Johnny, you old reprobate. How's the canal business?"

"You can now make passage to Washington for one dollar and fifty cents. Twelve hours, with meals."

"It'll never beat the railroad."

"It wasn't meant to. It's for the romantic traveler. That's what I tell people."

"What do you know of romance?"

"Ask my Mary Virginia."

"Into the house! Both of you!" Martha stood there in the door to the kitchen, wiping her hands on her apron.

Again, Cook bowed. But they both obeyed and went into the house. I heard them talking in there, as men do who haven't seen each other in a while. And when Martha called me in for my noonday soup, they were at the dining room table, eating.

57

"Don't ever let them linger where they can be seen on the porch," she whispered.

"I'm sorry."

"You must be firm with them. It's your job. Anyway, they know better. Or should. I don't know about Cook. He's so filled up with himself. Oliver said his talk is his weakness. Do you know what's he proposing in there? Listen!"

We stood just outside the door to the dining room and listened.

"I tell you, attaching the name of Washington to our cause is brilliant," Cook was saying.

"How is he related?" Anderson asked.

"A great-grandnephew of the original. Has five slaves. Lives like a lord."

"They all do down here."

"Has a pistol presented to Washington by Lafayette. And a sword that was a gift from Frederick the Great. We ought to take those slaves before our foray into the South. You know what the old man thinks of Washington!"

Anderson gave a low whistle.

Martha pulled me away, and I went onto the porch with my soup. *Cook wanted to attack George Washington's great-grandnephew and take his slaves.* The audacity of it! I wondered if Pa knew. Likely not.

Then I wondered if I should tell him. And my soup got cold, thinking on it. I was so lost in thought that I didn't even see the woman and her children step out of the cornfield next to the house until she called up to me.

"Hey, missy," the soft voice said.

I looked down to see a ragged woman in a summer shift and apron, no shoes on her feet, and hair the color of straw. At first I thought she was one of her children. Then I saw the children, three of them, pallid, skinny, not sure of whether they were supposed to be part of the light or the shadows, standing half behind her. And another in her arms.

Mrs. Huffmaster.

At first I thought: She shouldn't be about like that, after Pa just did surgery on her. Look, the bandage on her neck shows blood seeping through. Then I thought: *The men in the house. She mustn't come up. She mustn't hear them talking.* I stood up so fast, I spilled my uneaten soup into my lap. Good thing it had gone lukewarm. The bowl clattered to the floor. Recognizing her, Cuffee started to wag his tail.

She was coming up the stairs.

"Wait!" I told her. "My sister-in-law may be sleeping. She's with child, you know."

"Sleepin' in the middle of the day? I had four and I never!" But she waited while I ran into the house, right past Martha in the kitchen and into the dining room. "Mrs. Huffmaster's here. She wants to come in."

In a shot Cook and Anderson were off the crates that served as chairs and up the stairway to the garret, bowls of soup and hunks of bread in their hands. Martha and I cleared the table. Cook had been smoking a cheroot. I emptied the dish of ashes out the open window and waved off the smoke. Martha hurried coffee cups into the kitchen.

I went outside again. Mrs. Huffmaster was on the top step of the porch, her young 'uns with her. "My sister-in-law is feeling under the weather," I lied. "It's best you don't come in. Why don't you sit right here? I can get you some coffee if you like."

"Real coffee?"

"Of course."

I fixed it good and sweet. And brought out some bread and honey for the children. She sent them down the steps to play in the yard. "You watch that baby now!" she yelled down at them. "Sakes alive." She sipped her coffee. "Ain't this nice? Things do look right purty from way up here. Like bein' a sparrow in a tree, lookin' down at it all."

I'd never quite thought of it that way, but she was right. "How is your neck?" I asked.

"Comin' along just fine. All I come for is to tell you all that there's my garden out back. I planted it. I don't mind sharin' some of the vegetables. Always end up with too much, anyways. Told yer pa I'd be comin' over to weed it and he said just to tell you all first."

"Of course," I said. "Did you plan on working in it this morning?"

"Might be."

"But after you just had your neck lanced? And your dressing needs changing."

She looked at me as if my sanity was a matter of obvious doubt. "Cain't let that git in the way of my work. Ain't had time to change the dressin' yet. When I git home I aim to bathe it with the rainwater I saved from the first day of May. Best thing fer curin' wounds and tired eyes. Where's yer pa?"

"He had an errand to run. He'll be back later."

She peered at me over her coffee mug. "He's a right good man, Mr. Smith."

"Mr. Smith?"

"Yer pa."

"Oh, yes, he is."

"Where'd he learn his doctorin'?"

"Oh, here and there."

"I do my own doctorin'. Planted lots o' herbs in that garden out back that I use fer it. The summer savory is good to expel phlegm. I notice yer pa has a gathering in his head. Put some in his tea. And the berries on my current bushes make good sauce. Put that in tea, too, and drink it two hours before sunset. You'll sleep like a baby. Help yerself to both."

"Thank you. Maybe I could weed your garden for you today so your wound doesn't bleed anymore."

"Yer a good girl. Yer ma should be proud. When's she comin'?"

"What? Oh, she'll be here one of these days."

"Just in case yer in need of it, I kin talk fire out, too."

"Talk fire out?"

"Burns. I talk to the afflicted flesh. Heal it. Learned it from an old slave woman on a nearby plantation."

I nodded solemnly, fully convinced that she was crazy.

"That's not all I talk to. You got somebody on the other side, honey?"

"The other side?"

"Somebody who passed on? I kin see yer aura is ragged. You troubled 'bout somebody who passed on?"

I felt a chill. And for a moment the world all around me

seemed to recede, and the space between me and Mrs. Huff-master seemed sealed off from it. Bird song, the screeches of her children below, Martha banging things about in the kitchen, all seemed part of another world. "My aura?" I asked.

"Everybody got one. Like a light around the head. Every-body got a different color aura. Yours is a nice pale yella, but it's all ragged. Means only one thing."

I balled my hands into fists, to keep from touching the space above my head. "What?"

"Yer troubled. Young girl like you, I figure it cain't be any-thin' 'ceptin' yer troubled by somebody who passed on. Do you need their forgiveness? I kin talk to them if you want."

I felt my heart hammering. A cold sweat broke out on my arms and neck. "Mrs. Huffmaster, I think you should go home now," I said.

She stood up. "S'all right, honey. I understand. Jus' re-member what I said. I'd make contact fer you in a minute if you want. Wouldn't take anythin' in return either. No sir. Yer pa did me a good turn." Then she winked at me. "Doan git much chance to do it and I like to keep in practice."

I thought of Pa's orders. *Tell her anything and give her anything she wants. Except information.* "Maybe next time," I said.

"Yer right, honey. Guess I should be leavin'. Lookit them kids. Cassy! Johnny! Jodine! Don't pull that baby so." She set down the cup and gave me a smile so full of love that for a moment I felt dizzy. "Be around agin now. An' doan you for-get 'bout them currant bushes."

Then she went down the steps, gathered up her brood, and disappeared into the cornfield. The middling-high stalks, green and bursting with July's promise, swallowed them up, unbent by their comings and goings. It was as if I had imagined them. As if they had never been.

But I knew I hadn't imagined what Cook had said about Washington's great-grandnephew. It sat on my shoulders all day, just like unwanted knowledge always sits on us, like a wet woolen coat in the heat of July.

Pa, Oliver, and Owen came home late in the afternoon with an old wagon, a half-blind horse to pull it, a cow, and a calf in tow. Cook was still in the dining room. Waiting and scribbling. Martha said he penned poetry in his spare time.

He stayed for supper. I weeded Mrs. Huffmaster's garden and helped myself to some snap beans for supper. Martha had made light bread and we served this with mashed turnips and fish Owen had been thoughtful enough to stop and catch in the river on the way home. Cooking for five grown hungry men is no mean feat, and we had all we could do to brown that fish just right and keep everything hot at the same time the way Pa liked it.

Martha suggested we leave them alone in the dining room and eat on the porch. So I didn't argue the point. It was cooler outside. But we could hear them in there.

"He isn't telling Pa about his plan to steal Colonel Lewis Washington's slaves," I pointed out to Martha.

"No," she said. "The layout of the government buildings and the habits of the watchmen are more important."

"Don't you think Pa should know about Colonel Washington's slaves?"

"In time he will."

"When?"

She shrugged. "Then maybe he won't. Oliver said half of Cook's talk comes to nothing."

She was content to leave it lay there. But I wasn't. And after Cook had left, after Martha and Oliver had gone to the privacy of their room, after Owen and Anderson had retired to the garret, I sought out Pa. He was reading the Bible by candlelight at the dining room table.

"Pa, there's something you should know," I said.

He raised his eyes to me. He heard me out. Then he went back to his Bible reading.

I stood there, feeling as out of place as a Quaker at a Methodist social. Just like when I was in common school in North Elba and gave the wrong answer to Mrs. Nash about sums. I was never any good at sums and Mrs. Nash was inordinately fond of them.

"Are you going to let him do it, Pa? Colonel Washington's slaves?"

"It is impertinent, isn't it."

I nodded yes.

"Thank you, Annie. You should go to bed now. So you can get up on time in the morning."

I turned to leave. At the door I looked back. He was engrossed in his Bible, as if I'd never interrupted. I spoke out of turn again, I told myself. Martha hasn't said anything. I should have listened to Martha. I've made a fool of myself.

When would I ever learn? No wonder my aura was ragged.

✻   ✻   ✻

It was two days before I learned that as the result of the information I'd given Pa he'd written a letter to Cook, sternly admonishing him for his loose talk.

I found out about it from Owen. "Cook's a good man, Annie. He has three o'clock in the morning courage. Not many men have it."

I was in my usual place on the porch. It was dusk and I was watching the fireflies.

"You shouldn't have interfered."

"Owen, even Martha said Pa lives in fear of Cook giving his plans away."

"Pa never doubts Cook's bravery, honesty, or good intentions, Annie. Don't come between the men. It isn't your place."

I met his brown stare. "I thought Pa should know. So his plans aren't ruined."

He sighed. "If you just did it for that reason, Annie," he said sadly. Then he turned and walked away.

"What reason do you think I did it for?" But he wouldn't answer. He wouldn't argue with me. "It was my decision," I called after him, "and you told me to live with my decisions."

That was the trouble with Owen. He was spoiling for fights all the time, but he never would get into one. Had something to do with his withered arm. And the way Pa always protected him because of it.

I wish I could see his aura, I told myself. I bet it's ripped to pieces.

Chapter Six

When Pa first married, he and Dianthe lived on the Western Reserve in Ohio, in the middle of Indian killers, drunks, trappers, and otherwise just ne'er-do-wells. Then there were the confidence men, blackmailers, card sharps, and other assorted types to make Pa run for the Bible every chance he got. The godly were soon saying the Western Reserve was "Satan's Seat." And the men were to be more feared than the wolves in the forest. Pa set his face against all of that. He came out in "se-port of civil order and religion." My brother John was born there in 1821.

OWEN WAS RIGHT, AND I KNEW IT.

I'd gone to Pa and told tales out of school about Johnny Cook. Not to protect Pa's plan, but to put myself in good with him. There was the thing in a nutshell. I was always trying to put myself in a good light with Pa. Martha, now, she saw it different. She saw me as *taking* sass from Pa to put myself in good with him.

No matter how anybody saw it, it was my one weakness, trying to get Pa to love me. But even though Owen was right, I wasn't speaking to him. For the first time in my life, I was mad at him.

I kept to myself for a while after that, since I was the only one whose company I found fit. Oh, I helped Martha with the chores, though I didn't talk much to her, either. Mrs. Huffmaster came around one morning and didn't get further than the edge of the cornfield. I was weeding the garden, saw her coming, and handed her a bucket of tomatoes and beans I'd picked. Before she knew what was happening I had her on her way. Her neck was getting better. I said I'd tell Pa.

"Still aim to put you in touch with yer loved one on t'other side," she said.

"Next time," I told her. "I've got chores now." I wanted to ask her what my aura looked like this morning, but wouldn't let myself. "I put some summer savory in Pa's tea," I said to pacify her.

I had. Not to make up to Pa, but because if Mama was here, she'd do the same. We lie best when we lie to ourselves.

I wrote to Mama and Sarah and little Ellen, signing the letter Annie Smith and addressing it to Mrs. Smith, as Pa ordered. I played with Cuffee. I read the old copies of *Godey's Lady's Book* that I'd found under the eaves in the garret.

I didn't know what kind of a woman Mrs. Doctor Booth Kennedy was, who'd rented the farm to Pa. But I felt a strange kinship with her, pouring over the dog-eared copies of *Godey's*. I could imagine that poor woman hidden away in this backwoods country alone, with her husband dead, and Mrs. Huffmaster coming over wanting to put her in touch with him. The *Godey's* must have kept her sane, I thought. Reading about what women in New York, Philadelphia, and Washington were wearing on their heads was a sight better than having Mrs. Huffmaster talk about your aura.

The magazine addled me almost to distraction. "Mustaches, whiskers, epaulets, stars, and ribbons are badges of a Washington party," it said. "The ladies sport a chain or braid around their head with a jewel on the forehead. And all waltz like children's tops." I read about concerts in Carusi's Assembly Rooms and what Fanny Kemble, the actress, wore to tea at the White House.

Did people live like this? What kind of world was out there that I didn't know about? I thought about winters we'd spent home at North Elba, with nine feet of snow and the endless suppers of porridge and johnnycake, Ruth always patching the same dress because she never had a new one, the stories of Pa making his own coffins for the four children who died the year I was born, and all of us being told, throughout, that we needed to atone not only for our sins, but for the sins of slavery.

I hid those magazines good from Pa. And in those moments, sitting there on the porch, watching for approaching strangers, with *Godey's Lady's Book* in my lap telling me what Fanny Kemble wore to tea at the White House, I knew Pa was crazy.

I knew he was going to die as a result of this mad plan he was plotting here.

There were days I saw both these truths so clear in my mind that I started to wonder if I didn't have uncommon powers. Like Mrs. Huffmaster.

The sweet July days bled into each other, like warm honey, drowsy and calm. Then, the last week in July, they turned from honey into fire.

A very respected, upright slave man from one of the

nearby plantations hanged himself because his master had sold his wife away from him.

Word filtered out of the Ferry, the way word does in the country, like a wild strawberry vine, creeping from house to house. Everybody tasting it before it was ripe, just taking bites and never getting the true flavor. Pa wanted the true flavor. So he sent for Cook.

The man hadn't been around since Pa's letter of reproof. But he came now, full of sass as usual, certain that this news would redeem him with my father.

It did. Stories like this were meat and drink to Pa. They fed his soul. They convinced him that he was God's instrument. I was sitting on the porch sewing when Cook came. He used no flowery language this time. Just tipped his hat in exaggerated politeness and walked past me as if he was certain of his place in heaven. There is nothing more dangerous, I decided, than someone who walks in self-righteousness.

Pa was inflamed by the details Cook brought. I heard him asking how Cook got them.

"Hettie Pease," Cook said, "the freed slave. She visited some cousins on the same plantation. I'd sold her a Bible a while back and made friends. She calls me Mistuh Cook."

"We've got to get this plan into motion!" Pa bellowed. "The others must get here by the first week in August. I shall write to them tonight."

"Green wants to start on down," Owen said.

"He can't make the trip alone!" Pa was pacing back and forth in the dining room. "A Negro ex-slave."

"He wrote that our man in Chambersburg is plotting a route for him."

"Our man in Chambersburg may be in the Underground but that section of Pennsylvania is more dangerous than passing through a slave state. They hunt Negroes like they hunt rabbits. Go to Harpers Ferry, Owen, and wire Chambersburg that we're coming up ourselves to get the baggage."

Owen left to do so. I brought a fresh pot of coffee into the dining room. Pa had the contents of his carpetbag all over the dining room table. Maps of the Southern states with crosses marking large Negro populations, his layout of government buildings at the Ferry, his sketches of mountain ranges, his letters from Northern backers. And his Provisional Constitution.

My pa had his own constitution.

The one the Founding Fathers wrote wasn't good enough for him. I remember learning about that one in school, and the way everybody in the country fussed at each other because of it. And some were so afraid of it. But then the states ratified it, one by one.

I remember that word "ratified" and the way Mrs. Nash wrote it out for us. It had a nice ring to it. Like it made things certain. But all that ratifying wasn't good enough for my pa. Oh no, two years ago he met with his followers in Ontario and had his own constitutional convention.

They did some ratifying of their own. Pa's constitution made him commander-in-chief. He had a preamble, provisions, articles, everything.

I set the coffeepot down carefully on the table, a good way from the pages of the constitution. It scared me, I can tell you. Would some teacher be talking about Pa's constitution in school someday? I remember the look on Mrs. Nash's face when she spoke of the Founding Fathers. And something inside me said no.

Pa paid no mind to me. He was plotting a course for Owen to bring back Shields Green. "We should be ready to move by the first week in September," he told the others.

"The moon won't be right," Cook advised. He was a great believer in the position of the moon.

Pa looked up from his maps.

"It's better if you wait until the crops are in," Cook advised. "That's when the slaves get discontented."

"Hettie Pease again?" Pa asked.

"She keeps me informed."

"Just be careful you don't inform her of too much."

Cook was full of himself today. "After the harvest," he insisted. "By then the business with the hanging black man will be festering in their minds."

"The crops aren't in 'til the end of September around here," Pa reminded him.

"Right," Cook said. "The right moon in early October, a hanging black man festering in their souls, and no more crops in the field. The slaves will swarm to you like bees."

Pa went back to his maps. "What do you think the moon looks like over Pennsylvania these days?" he asked Cook.

"Full next week," Cook said. "Tell Owen to be careful."

*　　*　　*

Owen was to leave late that night. Martha had packed him provisions and he would wear one of the many disguises the men kept upstairs in the garret.

I lay in my bed listening as Owen came down the stairs, went through the dining room, down the front steps, and into the backyard. The house was quiet, the night outside clouding over to hide the moon. I got up and crept past Oliver and Martha's bed. I went outside. There were some bright stars overhead. Cuffee followed me as I crept down the stairs from the porch and walked across the dew wet grass.

"Owen," I called out.

He was coming down the hill behind the house, leading the half-blind horse and the small, covered wagon. "What are you doing up?" He carried a Sharps rifle, and as he approached I could see the long duster he wore, not new like Cook's, but old and ragged. A floppy hat was pulled down over his ears. Then I heard the geese under the canvas of the wagon.

"What are you supposed to be?" I asked him

"A peddler."

"Geese?"

"A couple. And a jug of peach brandy, some old pots and pans I picked up at the Ferry, a blanket or two, an old horse harness. I'll pick up more things in the North for the trip home."

"Is this Shields Green so important that you have to go fetch him?"

"He's a friend of Frederick Douglass."

Douglass. I shivered, although the night was warm.

Douglass was an ex-slave himself. He went around ranting and raving about slavery, preaching to whites all over the North, being received in the best places, saying how he'd welcome news of a slave insurrection in the South. He published a Negro newspaper. They loved Douglass in the North, all those abolitionist friends of Pa's, Thoreau, Emerson, Thayer, Gerrit Smith, George Stearns, William Lloyd Garrison. Douglass was their darling. He and Pa had been friends for over ten years now.

"You know how Pa feels about Douglass," Owen said. "He's convinced the man will join him. So we go and fetch Green."

"Don't you think Douglass will join Pa?"

"No. I think when the time comes, Douglass will run so fast the other way you'd swear bloodhounds were chasing him. I think he's gonna let Pa down. He always argued for peaceful means to end slavery. Him and that Garrison. And Douglass holds his place in the hearts of the whites too sacred."

"Then why do you have to put your life in danger, fetching Shields Green?"

"Because Pa can't afford to lose Douglass's backing, no how. Who said my life will be in danger?"

"Martha. She said with Green in tow, they'll think you're running slaves out of Pennsylvania."

"They'll think I'm a peddler with a half-blind horse." He laughed and patted the horse's nose. "After Kansas, Pennsylvania will be a tea party."

"Owen, I don't want you to go," I said.

He looked at me. "You mean that, don't you, little sister?"

"Yes. I know I haven't spoken to you in a week. And I'm sorry. I was so foolish. You were right about me and how I make up to Pa."

"You don't have to say that now, Annie. You don't have to make up to me, to keep me from going. You don't have to make up to me, ever. I'm not Pa."

"Owen," I said, "I don't want to lose another brother."

He hugged me. "You'll have me around a long time to tell you what to do." Then he turned to lead the horse, his Sharps rifle held in the good arm. "I'll be back in a week." And he walked off into the sweet July night. I heard the leather harness of the half-blind horse creaking long after I couldn't see him anymore.

A week later I lay in my bed dreaming of home. I was climbing the big rock that grew out of the ground a little away from the fence in the front yard. Ellen and Sarah were calling after me. "Come down, Annie, come down, Mama needs you."

But I couldn't get down. The rock, a good height off the ground to begin with, was growing higher and higher. It was growing as high as the treetops and Cuffee, who was on it with me, was growling with displeasure.

"Jump, Annie, jump!" Sarah and Ellen were screaming.

I jumped. And I woke up. Cuffee was still growling, low and serious, at the foot of my bed. Someone was in the yard. Two someones. I heard whispered voices outside my window. "Annie, are you awake? Annie, we need you!"

"Owen?" There was no mistaking his voice. I peered out.

"Annie, go and open the door so we can get in."

I crept out of bed, past a sleeping Martha and Oliver, through the kitchen, flooded with moonlight. I unbolted the door that led to the porch. Owen was holding up somebody and they were coming up the stairs. "Are you all right?" I went down to help.

"He's hurt," from Owen.

By the time they got through the door, what with Green yelling that he heard bloodhounds coming after him, Cuffee running in circles around him, barking like we'd been attacked by the local militia, and Green yelling, "Call off de dog, call off de dog," the whole household was up. Pa and the others came down holding whale oil lanterns. The place came alive with an eerie light. Owen was limping and muddy, his duster ripped. Martha went for rags to bind up his ankle. I went for ham and bread.

The man called Shields Green sank down on the floor, shivering, his eyes like round holes in his scratched and swollen face for fear of Cuffee. Then he kicked Cuffee hard with his muddy boots. The dog yelped and I picked him up.

"Get the dog out of the room," Pa ordered. "He's been hunted enough by dogs."

"Cuffee's no bloodhound. He's just doing his job."

"Get him out of the room!" Pa bellowed it at me.

"I must be crazy," I heard Green saying as I bundled Cuffee off. "I run once from slavery. Now here I be, again, in de claws of de eagle."

Then he passed out on the dining room floor. Pa and Oliver had to carry him upstairs, where he slept for two days.

✻   ✻   ✻

Cuffee didn't look like any eagle to me. Or any blood-hound. And his being kicked set me against Green right off. I soon learned about Green. He called himself Emperor. "He says he's descended from kings," Martha told me. And she ought to know. While he was recovering, she waited on him hand and foot.

He told her he'd run from his master in Charleston, South Carolina, three years ago, after his wife had died, leaving a small son, still in bondage. Somehow he'd found his way to Canada, then to Rochester, New York, where he'd met Frederick Douglass.

"Douglass took him under his wing," Martha said. "He accompanied Douglass to all his speeches, so he thinks he's ordained for special things."

One day I went up there to see her spooning soup into his mouth while he was sitting up in bed. In between spoonfuls, he was ordering her around. Fetch him this, fetch him that. It was hot, Martha was tired and I became angry. But I said nothing.

Next time I went up, Martha was sewing his shirt. "What are you doing?" I demanded.

"She's makin' me presentable," Green answered.

"My brothers sew their own shirts," I told him.

"I be a friend of Frederick Douglass."

"If Douglass himself were here, I'd say the same thing." I didn't like Green. I know it was wrong. Pa said slavery was like original sin, we were all guilty. We either committed it or inherited it. I knew I'd committed a lot of sins in my time, but I didn't inherit Shields Green, who kicked dogs, was rude, and made Martha mend his clothes. I ran from the room, crying. Owen found me outside, in tears, and asked what was wrong.

"I don't like him, Owen," I confided. "I don't trust him. He thinks because he's a friend of Frederick Douglass that makes him special. Martha's up there sewing his shirt. You do your own mending and you only have one good arm!"

"You're crying for more than that," Owen said. "Tell me."

I wiped my face with my apron. "I feel guilty not liking him. Pa's always taught us that the Negro is equal to the white man. What's wrong with me that I don't like him?"

"Maybe it's because he's a coward," Owen said. "We were chased by slave hunters. He hid in the brush and I couldn't get him out. I gave him a revolver, but he wouldn't shoot. Then we were crossing the river and he stood up in fear, tipped the wagon over, and fell in. I had to pull him out and carry him across on my back, then go fetch the horse and wagon."

"Then what good is he to Pa?"

"I don't know. They'll have to keep an eye on him."

"And all this business about being in the eagle's claw again. Why did he come?"

"Douglass sent him. One thing you have to learn, Annie. Some Negroes are good, some aren't. Some are smarter than us and some can't keep the time of day. They're people. Just like us. That's what this is all about, what Pa's doing. Because they're people, good and bad, just like us. So don't feel guilty if you two didn't get off on the right foot. Now stop crying and go to your post on the porch. We're the ones in the eagle's claw now. We're harboring a fugitive slave, this is Maryland, and whatever happens, Mrs. Huffmaster can't know he's here."

Chapter Seven

When Dianthe was having Owen, her third son, Pa got on his best horse and rode off, hard, to fetch a doctor. On the way he came across two men stealing some apples in an orchard. Pa pulled up the horse, ran after the men and caught them and made them bring the apples back to the owner. He thought it was more important to stop the men from committing a crime than to bring back the doctor to attend Dianthe. Owen was born anyway, of course. But I don't think he ever forgave Pa for that.

'M GOING TO A DUNKER MEETING; WHO WANTS TO accompany me?" Pa asked the next morning at breakfast.

Nobody answered. Shields Green was just coming down the stairs, affecting a limp. Martha looked down at her porridge. Jeremiah Anderson was not particularly interested in religion, but managed to look respectful when Pa stood and read from the Bible every morning before breakfast.

Now Pa looked at Owen and Oliver. "Must I give up on your unredeemed souls?"

Neither took offense. "Afraid so, Pa," Owen said.

"You think of the Bible as fiction," he accused.

"When I think of it at all," Oliver admitted.

"I'm preaching this morning," Pa persisted.

Nobody seemed very taken with the idea. Pa always preached back home, when the local minister was not available. When ministers were available, he argued with them about doctrine. Predestination was the favorite argument. Pa held fast to the notion and many ministers didn't. But the reason he left one church was because the minister didn't allow a slave to break bread with him. In North Elba he preached on Sunday afternoon, the time reserved for Negro services. But we belonged to no congregation, there or anywhere. It never occurred to us to belong. Pa was the only elder we'd ever known.

Now he looked at me. "Annie, go get your white cap and come with me."

"I don't have a white cap, Pa."

"Then get a piece of muslin and put it on your head."

I looked at the others for sympathy, but none was forthcoming, so I went into my room and rummaged around and came up with a square of white cotton. "Why do I have to wear this on my head?" I asked him as I climbed into the wagon.

"Because it's what their women wear."

"Why do I have to go to a Dunker church?"

"So it appears as if we're a normal family."

Thank heaven Mrs. Nichols was there and recognized me. She ran and fetched a proper white cap, put it on my head, and was leading me to a pew when a sour-faced woman came over and asked me about the condition of my soul.

I told her it was middling.

"The Lord is always with us," old Sour Face said, "even though our soul is only middling."

"Her soul is in good standing with the Lord," Mrs. Nichols said. "I vouch for her." And with that she led me to sit in her pew. I thought for a minute there that the two women were going to come to blows over my soul. And I didn't think it worth coming to blows over.

Pa preached that day better than I ever heard him, I have to give him that. Standing up there in his old black frock coat with the tails, he told the congregation that "nothing but an incomprehensible stupidity on our part can keep us from breaking out at once in strains of the most exalted praise when we reflect that God is ever reasonable."

But he didn't break out in any strains of anything to me, on the way to the church or on the way back. He didn't speak to me at all, as a matter of fact. And I waited. Oh, how I waited! I thought, Now that we're alone he'll talk to me. But he didn't. So I put it down to his habit of keeping silence on the Sabbath. We lie best when we lie to ourselves.

When we got home we had bad news.

"Mrs. Huffmaster was here." Martha stood at the top of the steps. "She came right up the stairs and into the house, before I even knew she was on the property. She saw Shields Green in the dining room. And she wants to know if you're running slaves North." I have to give Martha credit for nerve. I'd sooner have a tooth extracted than break such news to Pa.

"What did you tell her?" he demanded.

"That you're not running slaves North." And Martha went back to her baking. "I told you that woman was trouble," she said. "She's not coming round here just to weed the garden."

"Annie, go pay her a visit. Martha, do you have anything fresh baked from the oven?"

"Just some light bread."

"Send a loaf over with Annie."

Martha took up a loaf of her light bread that smelled so good it made my whole being ache with wanting. Martha wrapped it in a piece of cloth and handed it to me.

"What'll I tell her?" I asked Pa.

"That Shields Green is a free Negro visiting relatives in the quarters over to a plantation in Hillsboro. It's about eight miles from the Ferry. That he came here wanting to talk about the slave who hanged himself. Because the slaves on that plantation are all cast down from the hanging. And that I prayed with him."

"She knows all the free Negroes around here, Pa. And most of the bound ones. An old woman slave taught her to talk out fire."

"Talk out fire?"

Too late I realized what I'd said. "Talk to the flesh when people have burns."

Silence. I waited, holding my breath, for him to say something now about this thing that lay between us. But there was no bringing him around. "That's crazy," was all he said.

"She's crazy, Pa. Says she can contact people who are dead."

"Well still, she doesn't know every free Negro visiting here abouts. So you stick to that story then, listen to her. You've heard your brother John talk about being a medium often enough to be able to talk to her. Listen to her ravings if you have to. Agree with her. Do anything and say anything you can to put her off about Shields Green."

I left with the golden-brown light bread in my arms to talk to Mrs. Huffmaster. To lie to her on the Sabbath. To do what Pa had whipped Jason within an inch of his life for doing when Jason was only four years old.

"And take that cap off your head," Pa called after me.

I took it off, stuffed it in my pocket, and pushed some cornstalks aside in the field. Oh daughter of troops, I told myself, you are going to have to let her contact your dead sister in order to get her mind off Shields Green. You know that, don't you?

First thing I noticed was the shelf of herbs in the small kitchen. She was heating water for tea on the big old black stove. Right off she put the baby in the cradle and chased the children outside. "Sakes alive! Ain't this nice? A real visit! I ain't had a visit since old Israel Granger came round and told me he found the cure for cancer."

"What is it?" I asked.

"Put a frog under a cast-iron pot under the full moon. Walk around the pot four times. Then take the frog out and hold against the place of affliction. Repeat twice a day for a week."

"Must the frog be alive or dead?"

"Dead. And a male frog. Sit, do. My mister is out. Course, he's always out. See yer eyein' my herbs."

"Yes. What are they?"

"Bloodroot and sassafras. That jar up there holds a salve, made from bee balm and mutton tallow. There's boneset, snake root, ginseng root. And more. I grow 'em all myself.

Sit, do." She poured some hot water into a broken cup. "Jim-sonweed best for rheumatism," she said, "chestnut leaf tea for asthma. Fence grass boiled, to keep fever away. Branch elder twigs and dogwood berries for chills."

"Where did you learn all this?" I asked, pretending interest.

"From the local slave women." She nibbled at Martha's light bread. "That colored man over to yer place. He a run-away? Is yer pa helpin' him north?"

"No, of course not. My pa wouldn't do such. It's against the law! He's a free Negro visiting relatives on one of the plantations over to Hillsboro. You know how they always have to go back to the quarters once they're free and show how wonderful it is on the outside?"

She nodded yes. She was listening carefully. This woman is not as dimwitted as they make her out to be, I told myself. I must be careful.

"Well, he came over to tell Pa how cast down he and the bound Negroes are because of that slave who hanged him-self. When we got home from church, Pa prayed with him. He does that, you know. Prays with people who are afflicted. My pa was set to be a minister, except that his eyes went bad when he was back East studying."

"Rainwater caught in a bucket the first day of May cures that," she said.

I nodded. "Well, that Negro went right back to give those slaves comfort. Who knows what would have happened if Pa hadn't been there to pray with him? Those slaves might be planning an uprising this very minute!" I surprised myself with my abilities to lie. I had no idea I had such talent in that direction.

She nodded vigorously. The topknot of straw-colored hair on her head shook. "Law," she said. "Yes. 'Ceptin' for one thing. I know all the free Nigras round and about here. And I doan recognize him no how."

"He's just visiting," I repeated steadfastly.

She digested that with the light bread.

Now's the time to make my move, I told myself. So I did. "Mrs. Huffmaster, what I really came to see you about is my aura," I told her.

She perked right up. She peered at me. "It's still ragged," she said.

"I was wondering if you could help me."

She nodded. "You'll need to drink strawberry leaf tea to cleanse the body. The spirit now, that's something else. It has to be healed."

"How do I do that?"

She got up and went to the door to check on the children. Then she came back and leaned over the sleeping baby for a minute. She caressed its head. Coming back to the table, she sat down, satisfied that her house was in order, and reached across the table to take my two hands in hers. "Now you jus' tell me, child. Who you got on the other side that you need forgivin' from?"

"My sister Amelia," I said.

I hadn't said her name aloud in thirteen years. Nobody had. Oh Amelia, now I'm really going to need your forgiveness, I thought. First I caused you to die, and now I'm walking all over your grave, just so this crazy woman can forget she ever saw Shields Green in that kitchen.

"Amelia." The name, repeated, brought back so much. A golden-haired baby, I remembered so well, though I'd been only three when she died. I remember my delight in being allowed to hold her sometimes, the way I'd taught her to shake her head and say no at only eight months, the way she used to creep around the floor before she learned to walk and grab on everybody's legs.

Amelia. My personal responsibility. Because I was the smallest, the closest to her in that house full of large, busy people. She reached her little arms out to me. I had made myself responsible for her.

"And then what happened?" she asked.

I realized then that I'd been speaking the words out to her. This tiny woman in this shabby house so far away from home. I'd been telling her about Amelia.

"One day, a warm fall day, my sister Ruth was doing some washing. We lived in Ohio then. Pa was away. He was always away. There was a tub of scalding water on the ground. Amelia was running around outside. So was I. Ruth told me to watch her, and turned away to bring a bundle of clothes over to the line. I remember seeing a red bird and wanting to chase after it. I turned to chase the bird and in the next minute Amelia was in the big pot of scalding water."

Silence in the kitchen. From outside came the cries of her own children at play. Or was it Amelia's cries, come down through the years to haunt me. I was crying without knowing it. Tears coursing down my face. "She screamed so. Like there was a fire in her."

"If I'd a been there, I'd a talked it out," she said.

"She screamed for hours afterward. Then she died. Pa never did come home, even when Mama wrote to him. He wrote instead. Mama read the letter. Do you know what he said?"

"What?"

"'Divine Providence places a heavy burden on us,' that's what he said. And 'don't cast an unreasonable blame on my dear Ruth.' I know Mama told him my part in it. I know Ruth told Mama. But he said nothing about me."

I wanted to say more, then something stopped me. No, I couldn't tell her that in the same letter Pa had talked about the Negro slaves sold away from their families and separated forever. And how our plight should make us feel more for the slaves who would never meet again this side of the grave. Because that would bring us back to Shields Green again. And I was here to keep her from thinking about Shields Green.

Or was I? What was I doing here? I'd never confided any of this to anyone. Not even Dauphin Thompson!

"My pa's never forgiven me for Amelia," I whispered. "I know it."

"Never mind 'bout your pa," she said. "You hafta forgive yerself!"

Forgive myself? Never had I heard such folderol! Next thing I knew she'd be telling me to put a frog under a pot and walk around it three times under a full moon.

"You be yer own best friend," she said. "You gots to

forgive yerself. And be at peace. An' you gots to let Amelia go, so's she kin be at peace. Onliest way to do that is fer you to know that Amelia doan blame you fer what happened. And no, it ain't got nuthin' to do with frogs or full moons."

I stared at her. Could she read minds, too? My brother John believed some people could. Mental telepathy, he called it. Pa called it crazy.

"How can I know Amelia doesn't blame me?" I asked.

"It's easy. An' I kin do it right now."

"How?"

"I'll just close my eyes an' contact her."

I shivered. "Into this room?"

"You won't see her. Only I kin do that. An' we'll see what she has to say. You want I should do it?"

I tried to remember what John had said about séances. Because I knew that's what she was talking about. John had been to many. He believed in all this stuff. He'd studied phrenology in New York City. It was a science, he said. You could tell all about a person by examining his skull. It drove Pa to distraction when John talked that way. John talked about some people being able to see into the future, too. And he believed in hypnotism.

Well, it hadn't hurt John, had it? I asked myself. Of course it hadn't helped him too much, either, half crazy as he was from Kansas. But who knows? Maybe without all of it he'd be full crazy from Kansas.

"All right," I said.

Again, she got up and went to the doorstep to check on the children. Then the baby. Seated at the table once more, she spoke softly. "I may look like I'm asleep," she told me, "but I won't be. Then I may open my eyes. But doan talk to me. And doan be frightened." And with that she closed her eyes and took some very deep breaths.

I could hear her breathing. It was labored at first, then got calmer and calmer, and I felt the rhythm of it, felt bathed in it, so that a veil of peacefulness seemed to settle over the shabby room.

Then, she opened her eyes. But she was not looking at me. She was looking past me, to the wall, the shelves, the jars of herbs. But not seeing them, either

"I see this baby," she said. "This Amelia. She's wearin' this little blue dress. Fer some reason it's a right special dress."

Yes, I thought, of course. It's the outfit Ruth made for her out of Ma's old wedding dress. Amelia's eyes were blue and Ruth had begged for Ma's old dress. To make something for herself and for the baby.

"She's runnin' across the yard. Lookin' up at some steps. They look to be right high."

It couldn't be, I told myself. How does she know about those steps that went up to the hayloft of our barn back in Akron? Pa wouldn't have told her. He'd told nobody around here anything about our past.

"She's tryin' to climb them ol' steps. An' yer goin' after her."

Yes. It had always been my job to keep Amelia from those steps leading to that hayloft. She'll be killed if she climbs up there, that's what Mama always said.

"She's at the bottom of them ol' steps. Laughin' at you. Holdin' out her arms."

Amelia had always teased me by climbing onto the first two steps. Then laughing at me and holding out her arms. I closed my eyes, seeing her laughing, the sun dancing off her baby curls, part of them.

"She's sayin' somethin' now. Wait." Mrs. Huffmaster shussed me, though I wasn't speaking. "She sayin' it weren't your fault that she died. She sayin' you be jus' a little girl yerself. An' too small to be responsible. She sayin' she happy where she is, but it be better if'n you let her go. You let her go and she say she wait fer you there. Like she used to wait fer you to come git her on them ol' steps."

I don't know what happened next. I felt a great rushing of feeling. Like something hard inside me broke open and I was being drained of a flood of fear and hurt. Next thing I knew I was sobbing into my arms that were folded under my face on the table. And Mrs. Huffmaster was standing over me, patting my shoulder.

"You best git on home now," she said, "looks like it's fixin' to rain out there. Here," and she thrust something into my hands.

It was a jar of tea.

"Strawberry leaf, to cleanse the body," she said.

I nodded my thanks and stumbled out the door. The sunshine was gone. Dark clouds filled the sky. The wind whipped around, gathering leaves and small twigs upward in a spiral motion. I heard thunder in the distance. Mrs. Huffmaster called her children inside. "Hurry home!" she told me.

I hurried, clutching my jar of tea. Usually such wind and rain, such thunder in the distance would frighten me. But I was not frightened now. I knew the reason for the rain and the wind that seemed to be lifting everything in spiral motions to the heavens.

I was letting Amelia go. She had to travel somehow, didn't she?

"Oh, Amelia!" I stood, wind-whipped, my face soaked by the rain starting to fall. I looked up at the tossing branches overhead. I felt a lightness inside me, as if my own soul were rising, lifting, upward, too. "Amelia, you can go all the way to the top of those steps now. And wait for me there!"

I felt her presence, standing there. *I knew she was with me.* And I knew, too, that she forgave me and that it didn't matter if Pa did not. *Amelia!* I screamed her name. The wind tore it out of my throat and carried it upward.

Then I ran home, clutching my tea. But I never drank it. If I cleansed myself any more, I thought, there would be nothing left inside me.

Mrs. Huffmaster never mentioned Shields Green again.

Chapter Eight

Pa's uncle Frederick was a judge back in Medina County, Ohio. Pa had, by now, set himself up in righteousness. His uncle Frederick was giving Pa warrants for horse thieves and the like. Pa would go out and arrest them. One young criminal Pa brought back all the way from upstate New York, talking to him all the way about God's love. Then Pa persuaded his uncle not to send the boy to jail, but to apprentice him to the man whose horse he had stolen. The young criminal died years later, a man of respectability, always thinking highly of John Brown.

IT WAS TWO NIGHTS LATER. TUESDAY, THE LAST WEEK in July. Oliver had just returned from Chambersburg, where he'd gone to see if any "baggage" had arrived. When one of my brothers went to Chambersburg after "baggage" it was for Negroes come to join Pa. He was expecting a whole bunch of them from Canada. Since the trip bringing Shields Green here, Owen didn't make the run to Chambersburg anymore, lest he be recognized.

So Oliver had left yesterday morning. And baggage had arrived. It stood there in the light of the whale oil lamp in the dining room. Over six feet, his close-cropped hair part gray, wearing shirt and breeches.

"Hello, Dangerfield," Pa said.

"Good to see you, Captain."

"I'm writing up General Order Number One. Have you eaten?"

"Nosir. I been hidin' in that wagon all the way."

"Martha!" Pa yelled, "get Dangerfield Newby and your husband some vittles! What word about the Canadian Negroes who are supposed to join us, Newby?"

The man named Dangerfield Newby lowered his head. "They ain't comin', Captain."

"Not coming?"

"That's what I was told to tell you. Only one, Osborne Anderson. He's comin'. Nobody else."

Pa slapped the table with his hand. "Well, they escaped once from bondage. Why should they put themselves in danger again now? Why indeed?" But you could see he was hurt. And disappointed. He'd been counting on those colored recruits from Canada.

Then he saw me, standing behind Newby. "What are you doing there, Annie?"

"I'm bringing the supper, Pa. Martha's tired. I said I'd do it." I pushed past Newby and Oliver and set the plates down on the table.

"I told you to stay outside and watch. Why aren't you on the porch?" Pa asked.

He was lashing out at me for the colored recruits who had failed him. "I'm eating supper, Pa."

"Well, eat on the porch," he said.

My face flamed and I started out of the room, almost bumping into Newby, who was coming towards the table. He stopped short. I looked up at him. He bowed. Right in front of Pa. I stood looking at him, the heat of shame on my face. "Thank you for the vittles, Miss," he said.

I saw the pity in his eyes. For me. For the way Pa had spoken to me. Oh, the shame of it! That Pa should speak to me like that in front of a stranger.

The man smiled, showing gleaming white teeth. "Dangerfield Newby," he said. "Happy to make your acquaintance."

He did not look Negro. There was something else in him, I couldn't say what. But still, the way things were he could be three quarters white and he'd have to be fetched as baggage. So he knew enough about being treated badly to recognize it on sight.

I liked him right off, for that. And for treating me as if I was somebody. I flashed him a smile and left the room, my face flaming.

For two days since my visit to Mrs. Huffmaster, I'd felt good about myself. For some strange reason I'd allowed myself to be fooled into thinking that what had happened to me at her house involved Pa, too. I knew now that Amelia forgave me. I expected things to be different with Pa. Well, they weren't, were they?

I took my plate from the kitchen table and went out onto the porch to finish my supper. Things would never be different with Pa. Well, they would be different with me, I resolved. No more would I go out of my way to please him. I'd do my job as his watchdog, yes. I'd do my duty. But no more.

Maybe that's why, the next day when Hettie Pease came around asking for Johnny Cook, I never told him about it. I never told anybody.

*   *   *

She came early in the morning, when I was in the garden. It had rained during the night and if you looked straight down to the road from our log cabin you could see the mist sitting over the field and blurring the lines of the fences. If an army was coming I couldn't have seen them for looking. So I decided to go out back and pick some tomatoes. Martha had a way of baking them that made you not mind if there wasn't any meat for supper.

I was kneeling on the soft, warm earth when she called out. "Miss? Miss?"

More a hiss than a whisper. Then a nervous rustling in the trees beyond the garden. Since the ground was high here the mist was thin. I stood up. "Who's there?"

More hissing. "Come on over heah, Miss, won't you?"

"No. You come out."

"Cain't. Doan wanna be seen. Please?"

I made my way to the end of the garden where somebody had once erected an old grape arbor. There were no grapes but plenty of tangled vines. Likely they need trimming, I told myself. Jason would know what to do with them. I pushed my way through the vines and into a small clump of trees where I saw a figure huddled. "Who are you? What do you want?"

"Name's Hettie Pease."

What did I know about her? Why couldn't I think? She was thin as a sapling, and looked like she'd bend with the wind, too. She was wearing a dress made out of some dark fabric. It had no sleeves and seemed to hang on her thin frame.

And then it came to me. "She calls me Mistuh Cook," Johnny had said with pride.

"Please, Miss, you gots ta' help me. I'se lookin' fer Johnny Cook."

"He isn't here. Why would you think he was?"

"Tol' me hisself he knows Mr. Smith. This here's where Mr. Smith live, ain't it?"

I never could get accustomed to anybody calling Pa Mr. Smith. "Yes, but Cook isn't here. Are you in trouble?"

"They's lookin' fer me."

"Who?"

"All them official mens in town."

"Why?"

"'Cause I tol' my cousins that Mistuh Cook, who sold me the Bible, gonna turn this town on its ear one-na these days, sure nuf' an' they tol' their massa. And Hayward Shepherd, the freedman who carries baggage and sweeps the ticket office at the station, tol' me that them official mens in town wanna question me."

I tried to make sense of it. I knew all the names by now, Beall Air and Hayward Shepherd, but only one thing came through to me, like sun through the mist. "Johnny Cook told you he's gonna turn this town on its ear?"

"Yes, Miss. An' now I need him to say he tol' me such. Fer true. Lest they think I be lyin'. Please, Miss. I gots ta find Mistuh Cook! Nobody gonna believe a Nigra gal what's been freed. Do you know where he be?"

"No." It wasn't a lie. It was the truth. I thought fast, standing there. Lord forgive me. Hettie Pease looked so scared you'd have thought Beelzebub himself were after her.

"No, I don't know where he is. But anyway he never comes here. And anything he told you about knowing Mr. Smith isn't true. Johnny Cook lies. You mustn't believe a word he says. And you must never repeat it."

"Oh Miss!" She rolled her eyes to the heavens. She wrung her hands. "I neveh shud of told what he said to me."

"No, you shouldn't have," I said severely.

"Now if they catches me, they's gonna question me. An' 'cause I be's from Virginia, I ain't gots no right hangin' round after I wuz freed."

"No right?" I asked.

"No, Miss. You gots ta have a sponsor if'n you stays. I gots nobody. So I'se not supposed to be round an' about. But I gots relatives hereabouts an' it ain't easy leavin'."

It isn't easy keeping your mouth shut either, is it, I thought. But I didn't say it. I was busy thinking other things.

I could tell Pa. I could go in the house right this minute and wake him and he'd help her. I know he would.

But Hettie Pease wasn't a slave. She was free. If she didn't know what to do with her freedom once she got it, that wasn't Pa's job, was it?

But I knew he would help.

Then I remembered how mad I was at Pa for the other night and what he'd done to me in front of Dangerfield Newby. And how I'd sworn off telling Pa anything. Hadn't I? Hadn't I promised myself I would do my job? My duty, but no more? That I wouldn't go out of my way anymore to try to please him?

Besides, if Pa knew what Cook had told Hettie Pease, that would be the end of Cook, for sure. And Owen had told me not to come between the men.

"Go hide," I told Hettie Pease. "Away from here. And don't come back. Ever! And if they catch you and you tell them Johnny Cook knows my pa, I'll come to town myself and say you lied."

Her fear was something terrible to see. It was alive, palpitating. I could feel it swirling around her feet. Her eyes went wide. Her hands shook. "I'se goin'," she said. And then she ran, quickly and lightly as a deer through the woods. In two minutes she was out of my sight.

Two days later we heard they had caught her. She was in jail at the Ferry.

Next thing we heard was that she was being sold. At auction at Charlestown, Virginia.

Cook came around and told Pa. "They sold that Hettie Pease. Sold her South, just because she didn't leave Virginia after she was freed."

Cook had tears in his eyes. And I wondered how much he blamed himself for what had happened. "It's an outrage," he told Pa. "They hauled her into jail for questioning, they didn't believe a word she said. Sold her back into slavery."

"Can they do that?" I asked Martha.

"Yes," she said. "Why do you think your pa is here? Why do you think Oliver and the others are planning to risk their lives to end slavery?"

I had to go out on the porch and sit down by myself and stare at the stars, which seemed so much closer to earth here in Maryland than at home. Sold back into slavery. All because I was mad at Pa, and didn't tell him. I tried to console myself, saying I did well getting rid of her. She would have led the "official mens" at the Ferry to Pa. Ruined his plan. Maybe he would have been arrested. But I did not believe it for a minute. I was so addled I could not eat or sleep. And the worst part of it was I couldn't tell anybody. Not even Martha.

At the end of the week Dauphin and his brother Will and my brother Watson arrived. I had purple circles under my eyes by the end of the week. Dauphin thought it was from missing him. And I lied and told him it was.

Chapter Nine

Pa supported John Quincy Adams, the Northern Whig, when he ran for president in 1824. When Henry Clay was nominated in 1830, 1831, and 1834, Pa didn't support him. Not only because Clay was for slavery, but because he'd fought a duel. Pa'd always considered himself a peaceful sort. Wouldn't even hunt or fish. And he considered the Declaration of Independence right up there with the Sermon on the Mount.

I WAS SO HAPPY TO SEE DAUPHIN AND THE OTHERS, I could scarce contain my happiness. And as soon as they came, I could see the mood change in the little log cabin, go from dour to near festive.

Owen, Oliver, and Jeremiah all had their spirits cast down. As if they were under some cloud of worry. About what, I often wondered. Of course, Shields Green and Dangerfield Newby were anxious to get on with things. But Pa made them stay, days, upstairs in the garret, where they played cards and checkers, and, I assume, regularly checked each other's sanity for volunteering to come into a slave state. They only came downstairs for meals. Those were Pa's rules.

Now, with the coming of the others, things changed. They came from the outside world, where none of us except Oliver and Owen had been for weeks.

They came from home. With bundles from Mama.

Grapes from Jason's arbor, jars of jam, more cloth for bed ticking, a whole side of bacon, potatoes, onions, vegetables, bags of raisins and hard candy, new shawls Mama had knitted for Martha and me out of wool from our own sheep. Copies of newspapers. Mail for Pa. And news.

Pa insisted we all eat together at the dining room table that night. Even me, since the meal was after dark. I tied Cuffee on the porch. He'd let us know if anyone was approaching. And Martha and I worked all afternoon on the meal. Stuffed chicken, baked potatoes. Roasted corn that the "boys," as Pa called them, had brought along.

"I hope you didn't steal it," Pa said.

"Of course not," Watson assured him. "We bought it from a farmer at the depot."

I don't think Pa believed him. Neither did I. But somehow that made the corn taste twice as good.

Watson had news. He was bursting with it, I could tell. But Pa made him wait until we were all at table, then made him give the family news first.

He did. His baby boy, Frederick, was already turning over in his cradle. Mama was well, Sarah teaching little Ellen to spin. "Jason and Salmon are keeping the place going, Pa," Watson said cautiously. "Just like I did when you were all in Kansas."

"I don't want to hear about Jason and Salmon," Pa said. "The cock has crowed three times for them."

Martha and I got up to clear the table and get the coffee and blueberry pie. "Do you think he'll ever forgive them for not coming?" she asked me in the kitchen in a whisper.

"No," I said. He hadn't forgiven me for Amelia, had he? But I didn't say that.

"With all this quoting the Bible? Did you hear that business about the cock crowing? He compares himself to Christ before His crucifixion. And Peter betraying Him before the cock crowed three times."

"He sees only what he wants to see in the Bible," I told her. "It's why Oliver and Owen don't pay mind to it anymore."

She stood there with the blueberry pie in her hands. "Suppose he fails here? Suppose he does worse than fail? Suppose he dies without forgiving them?"

I reached to the stove for the coffeepot, burned my hand and put it to my mouth, grateful for the burn. *Suppose he dies.* Yes, what about that, Annie Brown? Dies not forgiving you? I had no answer for Martha. I had none for myself.

When we went back into the dining room, Watson was talking about a safer subject. Money. I knew Pa had money problems. He had funds from a secret committee in Boston, and I knew, too, that those funds were running out. Daily he went over his books, figuring and looking none too happy about it. Still, money talk was safer than talking about Jason or Salmon, for whom the cock had already crowed three times.

"Sam Howe from our Kansas Committee sent fifty dollars. Your friend, Sanborn, one hundred fifty-five dollars. How's the money you got from Boston holding out, Pa?"

"I'm going through it fast for freight costs, supplies and expenses for your brother John. He's traveling across New York, Massachusetts, and Canada to raise more recruits, weapons, and funds."

"Maybe that's throwing good money after bad," Watson suggested quietly.

"What do you mean?" Pa asked.

Nobody could give Pa bad news like Watson. He didn't shilly-shally. And he spoke quietly, in a reasoning tone. "Looks like the recruits we had aren't going to show."

"Who? Come on Watson, get it over with. Tell me."

So Watson told him. Luke Parsons, Richard Hinton, Charles Moffett, and George Gill seem to be backing out.

Pa's face went white. Parsons, Hinton, and Moffett had been guerrillas in Kansas. Gill had been an eager recruit in Iowa. "Gill? I can't believe it! Just two weeks ago he wrote saying 'At the right hour, by all you deem sacred, remember me.'"

"Talk's cheaper than action, Pa," Oliver said.

"What about the Negroes from New York and Massachusetts?" Pa asked.

"Not coming either," Watson said.

"I'm doing this for them!" Pa growled. "Where are they?"

Silence for a moment. We could feel the despair settling over him. He heard that cock crowing again. If it didn't stop soon, we would all suffer. Then Dangerfield Newby spoke. "You gotta realize, Captain, you're asking them to come into a slave state. To make a foray deep into the South to rescue more slaves."

I looked up quickly. Owen caught my eye, shook his head, and studied his piece of blueberry pie as if he'd never seen such a specimen before. Oliver and Watson seemed uncomfortable.

It was then that I knew that not all of the men knew Pa's

plan. Some of them thought this was another slave rescuing expedition, like Pa had done in Missouri. Hit and run. They were all ready to have at it.

When was Pa going to tell them? Was he doing more lying to these men? How could he expect Negroes to join him if he didn't tell them what he was really about?

"When are the others coming?" Martha asked lightly. "You boys should tell me. I'll need to prepare food and sew more bed ticking."

"Any day now," Watson said. "And we've had word from Douglass."

Watson had saved the best for last. Pa's eyes went all dark and bright at the same time at the mention of Douglass.

"He'll be getting in touch with you shortly," Watson said. "He wants to set up a meeting."

Thank heaven for Frederick Douglass, I thought. And thank heaven for Watson, who knew enough to save that piece of news for last. It put Pa in a good enough mood so that when Dauphin and I slipped away from the table, he scarce paid mind.

We ran, hand in hand, round the back of the house. I led him through the garden and the arbor to the spot where I'd met Hettie Pease.

Our kiss had the joy of reunion and the pain of time running out. His hands were all over me, my hair, my face, my back, my shoulders. It took all the willfulness I had to pull us apart. I finally seized a fistful of his yellow curls and pulled his head from mine. "We have to talk," I said.

"I like what we're doing better."

"Dauphin, be serious."

"I don't like serious. There's too much serious in that house. My God, how can you stand it? Did you hear that business about the cock crowing three times?"

"It's Pa's way, Dauphin, and it's what we've got to talk about."

He gave a little groan and sat down on the ground. "My pa's got eighteen children and he doesn't take on like that when one of us displeases him." We could see the yellow whale-oil lamp gleaming inside the house. Hear the cicadas and frogs. The moon was in its first quarter and hung over the distant mountains. "God, this is beautiful country," he said. "I'd like to chuck this whole business and marry you and settle down right here. In that house. Just us, Annie."

I sat down next to him. "I know. I sit on that porch and pretend it's our house and you're going to come riding home any minute. I want it so bad, I hurt from the wanting. And it's nothing hundreds of other people don't have."

He waited. "But what?" he said. "I know there's a but in there somewhere."

"There is. Pa. I know how quick you are, Dauphin. Quick to fight, quick to defend those you love. But you've never been around Pa that much. He gets all mooded up. He yells a lot. And he yells a lot at me. He doesn't mean it. And I can't have you all over him when he does it."

His eyes were riveted on me. He nodded.

"And I don't want anything to come between you and him, anyways. Or between you and the other men. Especially not me. I don't want to ruin things here for you."

I'd done a lot of thinking on the matter, wondering how I could prepare Dauphin for the way Pa gave me the rough side of his tongue sometimes. And I'd finally gotten a fix on how I was going to put it to him. I would appeal to the bond I knew he had with the others for their cause.

He sighed. "I know your pa's a tough old man. Watson warned me. So did my brother Will. I understand, Annie. This is an army. That's what we are, aren't we? A Provisional Army? And your pa's the captain. We all decided that. I've got that much fixed in my head. So you don't have to worry 'bout me that way."

I smiled. "I'm always having words with Martha about it. She can't abide the way Pa talks to me sometimes. It's his way. I just thought I'd tell you."

"You don't go against your commanding officer," he said firmly.

When he put it that way I wasn't so sure I liked the idea of him understanding the matter. An army meant war. And war meant killing.

We went back into the house and Dauphin was true to his word. When Pa said that he and Shields Green and Danger-field Newby should bunk in the small house across the road, he didn't argue. Just gathered his things, gave me a soulful look, and moved to obey. I loved him all the more for it. I stood a long time on the porch, watching their feeble lantern light as they went down the hill, across the road, then disappeared behind the trees.

☆   ☆   ☆

Oliver had told me about a place about a dozen miles north of us called Devil's Backbone. It was an Indian name given to the ridge that sat between two bodies of water.

Beaver Creek ran west on one side of the small ridge. On the other side, running parallel, was Antietam Creek. Its waters ran east.

"You can imagine how spooked the Indians were when they saw it," Oliver said. "So they named the ridge Devil's Backbone, because they figured only the Devil himself could be in charge of such a place."

And of course, being Oliver, the reader in the family, he went on to explain that the Indians were either the Catawbas, up from North Carolina, or the Delawares, down from the Susquehanna.

I didn't care what Indians they were. "Did you see these two streams?" I asked.

"Yes. When I went to fetch Dangerfield Newby."

"Do you think I could go and see this Devil's Backbone some day?"

"Of course, Annie," Oliver said. "I'll take you."

But I knew I'd never get there. Because Pa didn't let any of us out of the cabin. He only let Oliver or Watson go to town once a week, to get the mail or the *Baltimore News American.*

At the end of the first week in August more of Pa's Provisional Army arrived. Six of them, two by two, like the animals came to Noah's ark.

First came the Coppoc brothers, Edwin and Barclay. Barclay the Younger, as he called himself, was not yet twenty. He reminded me of Dauphin, in that they were both yellow-haired and trusting. His brother, Edwin, was twenty-four. They were Quaker bred, from Iowa, but had settled in Kansas.

"Is that where you met my pa?" I asked.

"Anybody worth knowing he met in Kansas," Barclay the Younger said.

They lost their own father when Edwin was six. And you could see how they looked up to mine.

Next came Charles Plummer Tidd and Albert Hazlett. Hazlett was twenty-two, a good-sized and fine-looking fellow who seemed to be brimming over with good feeling for everyone. He too had met Pa in Kansas. He brought Martha a bouquet of wildflowers he'd picked on the walk from the depot at the Ferry.

They brought tears to Martha's eyes. "What kind of a place is this Kansas," she murmured, "that it grows such good men?"

"Kansas didn't grow them," I told her. "They were born elsewhere."

"But Kansas made them what they are," she said simply. Martha's logic sometimes escaped me. In some ways things were simple for her, black and white. Other times she got downright philosophical.

Tidd had met Pa in Tabor, Iowa, but served with him in Kansas. He'd been on the run into Missouri to free the slaves. He was originally from Maine. He was not much on education, but he made up for it in good common sense. He was also quiet and kind. And he had a fine singing voice.

Then there were Stewart Taylor and Aaron Dwight Stevens.

Taylor was twenty-three, a mystic who before this had earned his living as a wagon maker. Before he met Pa. He was from Canada, where apparently they also grew good men. He loved history and was heartily afraid that whatever Pa was planning, he wouldn't have a good part in it. He believed in signs of all kinds, everything from the crows that perched on the rooftop (they boded ill will) to the weather (hot and dry, God was smiling on us). He believed in dreams and just about every "ism" there was. He asked Martha to put a cross on the bread before she put it in the oven. I must ask him, I thought, if he collects the first rainwater of May.

Stevens, at twenty-six, had already served in the Mexican War, fought against the Navahos and Apaches out West, was court-martialed for protesting the punishment of a fellow soldier and condemned to be shot, was marched across the plains with a ball and chain on him, had his sentence commuted by the president, served in prison for a year, escaped, and hid among the Delaware Indians. He'd served in Missouri with Pa. He was six feet two, stout and strong.

Where had Pa found them? Martha and I just kept looking at each other. Their devotion to Pa was unmistakable. He held sway over them. They hung on his every word. They pouted and sulked if he paid more mind to one than the other. And Pa encouragaged such behavior. He also encouraged debates amongst them, about religion, history. The discussions at the supper table were worthy of the most elegant drawing room in Washington.

But I liked what happened after supper best. Tidd would sing. So would Martha. Dauphin played his fiddle. I'd pop some corn and bring it in. Times like these Pa would sit out on the porch.

"They want you inside with them, Pa," I'd venture out and tell him.

"No, no. I fear my presence will spoil their enjoyment. They don't feel so free with me around. You go on in with them. I'll keep watch."

Times like these I'd love him. I'd want to go and put my arms around his thin shoulders. But of course, I did not. "Who you watching for, Pa?" I asked.

"Leeman. He's a good man, but impulsive. In '56 when my men were holed up in Springdale, Iowa, with friendly Quakers, I cautioned them against fighting or molesting anyone, except for helping escaping slaves. After I left, Owen had a difficult time controlling Leeman. Of course, he was only seventeen at the time. I'll feel a sight better when he gets here."

Leeman arrived the next night. He was just twenty and very handsome. In the first five minutes, I learned that at age fourteen he started working in a shoe factory in Maine. At seventeen, he'd gone to Kansas, just for the adventure of it.

The house was crowded now. But things were not always good. Sometimes I thought I couldn't bear it. Sometimes I thought, like the Indians did about the Devil's Backbone, that only the Devil himself could be in charge of such a place.

Chapter Ten

My mama had been sixteen when Pa proposed, back in Pennsylvania.
When she said yes, he sent her to Miss Sabrina Wright's school. She needed
more learning, he had decided. But her head was so turned by the idea of
Pa, she couldn't learn. So he married her on the second floor of the tannery
he owned. In between having thirteen children, losing seven in childhood,
and raising five from Pa's first marriage, Ma educated herself. She read
The Book of Martyrs. *And* The Saints Everlasting Rest. *Oh,*
she was given to long silences. Being married to Pa, who wouldn't? But she
had her own ideas and held them close.

PA SET THE RULES RIGHT DOWN FOR THE MEN. NO
going outside during the day.

When they found that out, I thought they would mutiny
right off, good as they seemed.

Here they were, fifteen men spoiling for a fight against
slavery, most of them veterans of guerrilla warfare in Kansas,
accustomed to riding the open plains, living under God's
good sky, and fending for themselves.

Here they were, hungry and sassy, in as fine a fettle as
you'd ever expect men to be.

Here they were, confined to a small log cabin in the
wilderness of Maryland. And where in Kansas they'd fought
Border Ruffians, here they were expected to run upstairs on a

moment's notice whenever little Mrs. Huffmaster took it in her head to visit. Of course, Mrs. Huffmaster could be as much trouble as a Border Ruffian any day.

She took it in her head to visit three times the first week they all arrived.

Twice, they had to do the drill they'd practiced for such occasions. Scoop up the tablecloth with everything in it and carry it right upstairs. Martha and I got to wash tablecloths a lot that first week.

I swear, Mrs. Huffmaster knew something was amiss. Her third visit that week she overstayed her welcome, if she had any left. She'd come without her children, leaving them home in the care of the oldest, who was eight. So as to kill off any suspicions she may have had, Martha invited her in and offered her coffee and pie.

Mrs. Huffmaster talked and talked. Then she talked some more. It came on to suppertime. Martha was making venison stew.

"That there's an awful big pot of stew," Mrs. Huffmaster said.

"Well, I like to cook up a lot. Saves me the trouble tomorrow," Martha said.

Pa and Owen, Jeremiah and Oliver took their places at the dining room table. They were all the men Mrs. Huffmaster was supposed to know we had. Martha handed me bowls of stew to bring inside, slabs of bread and cheese.

Still Mrs. Huffmaster stayed.

It was coming on to dusk. I knew the men would be famished. And how long would they hold still up in that garret, all but hog-tied, lest she hear footsteps above? So I did the only thing I could do. "Pa wants more stew," I told Martha.

"Sakes alive," Mrs. Huffmaster said. "That Mr. Smith is so skinny! Would you ever think he ate so much?"

I carried the pot into the dining room. Thank heaven the men's bowls and spoons were already on the table. "You could carry this pot up the outside ladder and hand it in the upstairs window," I whispered to Oliver. "I'm afraid if they don't eat soon, they'll come down anyways."

"Good girl," Oliver whispered back. Pa just nodded in approval and said nothing. So Oliver and I did just that. I held the ladder while he carried that old pot of venison stew up to the window and handed it through. I gave him the bowls and spoons.

Martha had to finally give Mrs. Huffmaster a whole berry pie to get her to leave. So we had no dessert that night. Since my visit to her house when she'd contacted my sister Amelia, I felt a lot more kindly toward her. But not so kindly that I could forgive her for walking off with our blueberry pie.

I think she came on to knowing we were hiding something at our place. Every visit after that, Martha and I ended up giving her something to make her leave. One time it was a bowlful of freshly churned butter. Another time it was a small sack of coffee beans. The worst, though, was when Martha gave her the new shawl Mama had made.

That day Mrs. Huffmaster came through the yard, right up the porch steps without so much as a by-your-leave and said, "Your menfolks has a right smart lot of shirts."

The men had done their washing that morning. Martha

and I spread the shirts on the fence and bushes. I felt a thrill of fear. Mrs. Huffmaster was staring at me just like Mrs. Nash when I couldn't answer a question about sums.

I knew what the question was, of course. "If you have only four men in the house and it's been one week since the last wash day, how many shirts should be laid out to dry?"

You had to be the village idiot not to know the answer was four shirts. Or at best six. And not nineteen or twenty. I felt just like the village idiot. I could think of no answer.

"It was such a nice day we thought the sun would bleach them all out," I said.

She knew I was lying. And she was disappointed in me. I'll bet my aura is so ragged now it will never be able to be fixed, I thought. I invited her into the kitchen. Martha put up coffee. I loved coffee.

"You ain't drinkin' yer strawberry leaf tea," Mrs. Huffmaster accused.

"No," I said.

She just grunted. "Some people could drink a bucket a day and wouldn't wash 'em clean, inside or out."

She was disappointed in me because I'd lied to her about the men's shirts.

I was disappointed in myself.

Martha had her shawl hanging there on the kitchen wall. And Mrs. Huffmaster took a fancy to it right off. Martha thought our house was so plain that she hung things. Dried herbs, an old basket or two, her favorite copper pot that she'd brought down from North Elba, and now the new shawl. She had Oliver tack it on the whitewashed wall for her. When Mrs. Huffmaster walked out with it, I wanted to cry.

"She knows," Martha said to me.

"What?"

"She knows we're hiding something. It's a game with her now. She just walks in, bold as a brass-bound monkey, makes some remark to scare the wits out of us, then won't leave until we give her something. It's blackmail. And she enjoying every minute of it. But how can she know? We're so careful!"

I wanted to tell Martha she was a psychic. But I didn't. Martha didn't hold with such.

"If she finds out anything for sure," Martha said, "there will be an investigation. And Pa and the men could be arrested." She was frightened. I'd never seen Martha frightened.

"I still don't think you should have given her your shawl."

"We have to give her anything she wants. And keep playing her game. If we do, I think it'll make her happy."

So then, Mrs. Huffmaster, for all her healing of people and reading auras, was no better than a common thief, holding us up for things, threatening us. Why was I so disappointed? Look at Pa. He cherished the Word in the Bible. He hated lying. And he had us all here living a lie, inventing a new one every hour.

It helped me some, fixing on that. But not much.

Of course, the men got antsy. How long could you play cards and checkers? How long could you swap Kansas stories? How long could you study military tactics? How long could you listen to stories about what somebody's great-grandfather did in the Revolution?

So they cleaned their rifles. They made holsters. They drilled. Stevens was the drillmaster. He'd had the most time in the army.

Martha and I left them alone up there in the garret. Shields Green, Dangerfield Newby and Dauphin spent the days in that garret, too. Every morning they came from across the road for breakfast. Before first light, so nobody would see them.

My whole being came alive when Dauphin came in early mornings. I'd be ready with his coffee. In the half-light of the kitchen, and me fussing with the fire in the stove and Martha stumbling around making breakfast, we'd stand as close as we could, smiling at each other, hands touching. Then Pa would summon everybody into the dining room for prayers.

After breakfast, of course, Dauphin had to go upstairs with the others. He didn't want to go. He'd linger. "Move along," Pa had to tell him. One or two of the other men would snicker, so I'd turn and go back into the kitchen. Dauphin wanted so much to be one of them, to be a good soldier. He was the baby in a family of eighteen. Somehow, I knew he could never be a soldier. Somehow that made me glad.

At the end of the second week in August, Leeman and Hazlett sneaked out the window, climbed down the ladder, and went to the cornfield next door, the cornfield Mrs. Huffmaster always came through. The cornfield her husband owned. He farmed, though he seemed to spend more time in taverns at the Ferry. Sometimes I saw one Negro field hand on their place, hoeing or weeding.

Leeman and Hazlett stole a whole mess of corn and brought it into the kitchen for roasting.

None of us knew they were outside the house. Martha and I were downstairs in the storeroom, taking inventory of our vittles. Pa and Oliver had gone to the Ferry to post some mail. Owen and Jeremiah Anderson were chopping wood in a distant field. Martha and I got suspicious when we heard a scuffle going on upstairs.

What happened was this: Leeman and Hazlett had left the corn to roast in the oven, then gone back outside. One of the other men had stolen downstairs, taken the roasted corn from the oven, and brought it upstairs, where the men had a midday feast before Leeman and Hazlett came back in.

Now the men were throwing the empty cobs down the stairway at Leeman and Hazlett. There were yells of "Here's your corn!" To Leeman and Hazlett it must have sounded like, "If they mean to have war, let it start here."

Those old corncobs were being thrown up and down the stairway and such yelling and screeching you never heard.

"Stop it, all of you!" Martha scolded. "Stop the noise at once."

"Aw, c'mon, Martha," Ed Coppoc said, "can't we have a little fun?"

"Fun? I'll give you fun! You just come down here, all of you, and clean up this mess you've made in the dining room! Or you'll be sorry this day you ever drew breath!"

They were shamefaced then. They came down and had to

sweep and wipe the splatter off the whitewashed walls. It was all cleaned up by the time Pa got home. But while they were doing it Owen came in and asked where they got the corn.

"That field next door," Hazlett said.

"That's Mrs. Huffmaster's field," Owen said.

That was all he said. But the next morning, he didn't come to breakfast. He'd gotten up early and left. Everybody speculated, but nobody knew where he'd gone. Just before noon he came back, hot and dirty, with a sack of corn over his shoulder. He set it down on the kitchen floor.

"Cook this for the boys," he said to Martha. "So they won't be tempted to take any more from Mrs. Huffmaster."

"Why there's at least four dozen ears here, Owen! Where did you get it?"

"Antietam," he said. "Bought it from a farmer. Got it cheaper 'cause I picked it myself."

"You walked all the way to Antietam and back? Look how hot and tired you are. Annie, get him some lemonade." I knew what Martha was thinking.

With that withered arm? You picked corn and hauled it back to keep us honest?

I fetched the lemonade. Owen drank it in two gulps. "I hate to think we can't be trusted to live next to a field of corn without stealing it," he told us. "We'll be gone from here soon. And everything we do here will be remembered, for good or for bad. I'd like to be remembered, after I'm gone, for honesty."

Martha stared at him. "What do you mean, after you're gone, Owen?"

"You know what I mean, Martha."

A pall settled over us. I sat on the kitchen floor shucking the corn. Martha started rolling pie dough. Then, as if things weren't bad enough, Stewart Taylor wandered into the kitchen.

"Sorry about yesterday, Martha. I was thinking, do you have any pencil and paper? I'm a stenographer. I know that newfangled shorthand. I could teach the men."

Martha fetched pencils and paper.

Taylor stood there holding them. I got the feeling he'd come for more than supplies. "You don't have to worry about being gone, Owen," he said.

Owen raised weary eyes to him. "How's that, Stewart?"

"You'll live a long life. I'm going to die on this expedition. I'll be the first one to die."

I stopped shucking corn. Martha stopped rolling out her pie dough.

Taylor laughed softly. "It's no matter. It's my duty to do what we're doing. Even though I'm going to my end. Thanks for the paper and pencils, Martha. I'm sure I'll be able to keep the men busy for a while." Then he was gone.

We stared at each other. "He believes he's going to die," Martha said.

"No," Owen corrected her, "he knows it."

"But he doesn't even know what Pa is planning yet, does he?"

"He soon will," Owen told us. "Pa's going to tell them all tonight. And I'm not a spiritualist. But I can tell you now, there's going to be fireworks when they find out."

I thought Owen was a spiritualist. In his own way. And he was right again, too, about there being fireworks.

Chapter Eleven

*In Franklin, Ohio, back in 1836, Pa got up in church one Sunday and in-
terrupted the sermon of the Reverend Avery. It was the Congregational
Church. Pa told the good reverend how afflicted he was to see that the colored in the congregation had to be seated in back. The reverend was hard put
to know what to say. But he made no move to put things right. So Pa took
his family to the rear of the church and led the Negroes up to his pew. Next
day some deacons came to Pa's house to pray with Pa, 'til he could see the
light. Pa said he saw only darkness in their presence and soon they left.
Every time Pa took his family to church after that he sat in back with them.
And put the Negroes up front, in his pew.*

HERE WAS PA'S PLAN.

Attack Harpers Ferry. Capture the government arsenal, armory, and rifle works. Hold the town until sympathetic
whites and Negroes came to join them. Word would spread.
Fast. Across the plains, even down to the tidewater country.
Negroes would rise up and head to the Ferry in a mighty
stampede. Slaveholders would be too confused to fight back.

After Pa and his men took all the guns from the arsenal,
they would move south and liberate even more slaves. He
would confiscate provisions. He might even take hostages. If
any slaves wanted to be free without fighting, he would send

them up North through the Allegheny Mountains, into Canada.

"If I can conquer Virginia," Pa said, "the rest of the Southern states will nearly conquer themselves, there being such a large number of slaves in them."

But he expected support, too, from slaves in Tennessee, Alabama, Mississippi, and the Carolinas. Georgia was good, too, he said. Slave rebellions there would spread like fire.

It would work, his plan. He'd have thousands of slaves with him. They would head to the hills, just as the Negroes had done in Jamaica and Guiana. He couldn't fail. He just couldn't. He'd have the slaves with him, thousands.

The slaves, maybe. But not his own men.

Martha and I stood at the foot of the stairs that led to the garret, listening. For a while after Pa spoke there was silence. Then Owen spoke.

"Pa, there's no way out of the Ferry. Once down there we'll have the mountains at our back. You've got two rivers converging there. We'll be trapped. Cut to pieces." Owen spoke calmly, like he always did.

"By whom?" Pa challenged.

"Local militia," Owen said, "possibly federal troops."

"From what we saw of them in Kansas they were dunderheads," Pa said. "Don't you remember that?"

"You'll be cutting yourself off from your base of supplies, which is here at the farmhouse," Tidd reminded him.

"This is our base of supplies only until we attack the

town," from Pa. "Once we attack, the arsenal and town will be our base of supplies."

"You're dividing your forces," from Oliver.

"You men will be officers. All the slaves who join us will be your troops. Each one of you will be at a strategic place with your troops. When the time comes you'll cut right through the militia. You learned how to spill blood in Kansas. You men are trained. The local militia isn't."

"You have no plans, beyond occupying the arsenal and the town," Tidd accused.

"The slaves will rise. Our faces will be southward. That will be enough," Pa said.

Then an explosion. "For God's sake, Pa! We aren't a bunch of Dunkers you're preaching to. We were in Kansas, that's just it! You can't be sure of the slaves!" It was Owen. "This isn't the Indies, where you have absentee ownership of slaves." Owen had lowered his voice. "The owners are present on the plantations. There's a certain loyalty the slaves have for them."

"What are you saying, Owen?"

"It won't work. I'm saying it won't work. We'll be trapped and cut to pieces in that town."

"You dare say that to me? In front of my men?"

"I have to say it, Pa. It's what I think," Owen answered.

"The trouble with you, Father, is that you want your sons to be brave as tigers but still afraid of you," Watson said.

"What if it doesn't work, Captain?" asked Stewart Taylor.

"You afraid, Stewart?"

"Nosir. I already know I'm going to die. Willing to. But I'd like to die for something that works."

"So would I." Dauphin spoke up now.

"You little buttercup, with your yellow hair," Leeman yelled at him. "You and Barclay are no more than two good girls. You'll never make soldiers."

A movement. An overthrown chair. A scraping of feet on the floor. "Who's a girl!" from Dauphin. "C'mon over here, Leeman, and I'll show you who's a girl!"

"What'd you come for, anyway, Buttercup?" Leeman sneered.

"I came because my brother couldn't," I heard Dauphin say. "He's a married man. I came in his place."

So, I thought. Ruth gets to keep her husband. And I may never get to have mine.

"There's plenty of married men here," Leeman flung back. "Oliver's married and his wife is having a baby. Watson's wife just had one. What about Newby? His wife is a slave in Virginia, the state we're going to invade!"

"Doan worry 'bout me none," Newby said in his soft voice. "I'm here 'cause I wanna be."

"We all are," Will Thompson put in. His voice was firm and clear. "We all came because we believe in fighting slavery. But I'll tell you here and now, Leeman, my brother is no buttercup. And first chance he gets he'll be willing to demonstrate that to you."

More scuffling. I think Will must have grabbed Dauphin to constrain him.

"Quiet!" Pa bellowed it.

They got quiet. Pa could make a dog leave the room with a look. "All right, now," he said, "it's clear we're going to have to have more deliberations. And we might as well all be in on it. Somebody send for Kagi and Cook."

Somebody came clambering down the stairs. Martha and I ran for the kitchen.

Everybody was walking on eggs. At supper that night the usual camaraderie was missing. Nobody looked anybody in the eyes. Martha and I had made their favorite meal, good Virginia ham diced up into small pieces and fried with potatoes and green onions. There was cold cider. Pa said a prayer from the Bible.

"'And ye shall proclaim liberty throughout all the land unto all the inhabitants thereof: It shall be a jubilee unto you; and ye shall return every man unto his possessions, and ye shall return every man unto his family.'"

When he sat down to eat, he looked around the table at everyone. "I knew Reverend Elijah Parish Lovejoy, the anti-slavery editor in Illinois," he said. "His presses were often smashed, his home invaded, and his wife persecuted in St. Louis. He fled to Alton, Illinois. He was shot and killed, guarding his press with a musket in 1837."

Nobody said anything.

"I know Harriet Tubman. She penetrated the South. One little black woman. Rescued hundreds. Conducted them to freedom through miles of swamp and forest land."

Still nobody spoke.

"America is bleeding," Pa said. "America has got a serpent in its belly. We have to go in and get it out."

"I'd feel a hell of a lot better going after the serpent in America's belly if those pikes you ordered from Charles Blair would come on down from Chambersburg," Oliver said.

That broke the mood. Everyone laughed. After that it was all right. Pa called the men "my young Turks" and assured them the pikes would soon be here. So would Kagi and Cook. And then they'd all have at this matter again.

After supper they were allowed to stay downstairs, with darkness coming on. And use the outhouse, finally. After supper they emptied the chamber pots they'd used all day. And washed them out. They brought out their books and magazines.

I'd sneak into the dining room and watch them, on some pretense. I'd bring in coffee.

There would be Shields Green, leaning over Taylor and telling him for about the fifth time how he was descended from a king in Africa. There would be Taylor, believing it. Asking to see Green's palm. Charting his destiny for him.

There would be Stevens, black hair, black beard, handsome as a Greek gladiator, studying a military manual. Newby reading the latest letter from his wife. Hazlett and Leeman in a corner smoking. Leeman taking a flask out of his pocket and offering it around, to have it accepted by only a few of the others.

There was Watson writing another letter to Belle. Tidd

and Anderson debating whether the money contributed to Pa had come from orthodox church members or liberal Christians, with Tidd saying he'd bet on the liberal Christians.

There would be Oliver, reading Tom Paine's *The Age of Reason*. Owen mending some clothing. Will Thompson doing a perfect mimicry of Pa, who was, of course, out on the porch. There would be the Coppoc brothers, playing checkers. Dauphin softly playing his fiddle.

Within the warm circle of light from the whale oil lamp they read, brooded, played, argued softly, smoked, conjectured, and sustained each other.

How I envied them and what they had here. You could feel it in the room, a warmth of companionship, all arguments aside. A bonding of spirit. I wished I had that with someone. I feared I never would, not even with Dauphin. I had terrible moments when I felt he had more affection for these comrades in arms than he had for me.

Then I'd set the coffeepot down and creep out, taking one last look at them maybe, seeing them in my memory already. Seeing them as gone. And knowing this was only a tableau, like you'd see on some old painting in some old forgotten room.

Chapter Twelve

Pa held Harriet Tubman in great esteem. He called her "the general." But Pa himself led many a slave to freedom. Without even mentioning the ones he ran out of Missouri, there were the slaves back in Hudson, Ohio. He called it his "midnight work." He helped slaves get from one point to another on the Underground Railroad, by wagon, horseback, or even by foot. Many of his neighbors were doing the same thing, of course, but they didn't talk it up amongst themselves. Nobody wanted to know much about their neighbor who might be a conductor on the railroad. This being so that if they were arrested, they wouldn't give away the activities of a neighbor. Pa told us that sometimes he'd take five or six slaves at a time on their way to freedom.

THE NEXT EVENING KAGI CAME. AND THEY ALL WENT upstairs to have at it again.

I thought I'd seen just about every variation of man in Pa's Provisional Army. But when I met John Henry Kagi, I knew I hadn't.

He was different. First off he was as fine a specimen of man as you'd ever want to see. Tall, and with some air about him I couldn't put a name to at first. And then I knew. Owen called it "aristocratic melancholy." He said all the men he'd met in the South had it. Owen got words like that out of books. He read almost as much as Oliver did.

"What do they have to be melancholy about?" I asked him.

"Well, from what I've seen of the South, the men think such a pose helps them capture the fancy of the ladies. But Kagi's melancholy is for a different reason."

"What?"

"Talk to him five minutes and you'll find out."

The second thing about Kagi was, he was Pa's secretary of war. I'd never met a secretary of war before. But when he leaped down from the seat of the wagon, brushed off his trousers, looked up, took the measure of the whole place in one glance, me included, and smiled, I knew a secretary of war when I saw one.

Watson had fetched him down from Chambersburg. Watson now led the horse and wagon up behind the house. Kagi came up the stairs of the porch and took off his slouch hat.

"Hello there," he said.

I felt that electricity go through me that a young girl feels when a handsome man says hello to her. I just couldn't help it. He had a black beard, large dark eyes, and eyebrows that arched the way Mrs. Nash's did when I'd failed with an answer. Only his eyebrows stayed that way all the time. Like the whole world failed in its answers to him.

Over his shoulder was slung a brown leather satchel bursting with papers.

"I'm John Henry Kagi," he said. "Mr. Brown's man in Chambersburg."

Pa's man in Chambersburg. The position was not to be taken lightly. It was the secret rendezvous for Pa's supplies, all the guns brother John sent. The pikes Pa expected would come through there, too. "I know who you are," I said.

"Well then, I am at a distinct disadvantage. Because I do not know to whom I am speaking."

That's what I mean about him. None of Pa's men spoke like that. Not even Oliver and Owen, who were so well-read.

"Annie Brown," I told him. Oh, how I wished I had a better name! One with flourish. And three parts. Like Caroline Walton Fletcher or something. Annie Brown was so ordinary.

He nodded. "What are you reading there, Annie Brown?"

"Paradise Lost."

"Ah, a scholar."

"Nosir. I only went as far as normal school. I'd like to continue my education someday, though. I just spend so much time on this porch I figured I might as well improve my mind. There aren't many books around here and I've read this one twice before."

He nodded. His boots were dusty, his trousers shoved into them. I saw a gold watch chain just inside his jacket and a revolver in his belt.

I fixed my eyes on that revolver. "Is it true you once shot a judge, Mr. Kagi?"

He smiled. "He was a proslavery judge. He hit me over the head with his cane. I shot him, yes. He shot back. Three times. Over my heart."

"Why aren't you dead?"

"My hide-bound memorandum book took the bullets."

"Wouldn't that be a nice story if it had been a Bible."

"I think it's a nice story now."

"Pa says you have no use for religion."

"That's correct."

"Then how does he think so highly of you?"

"We have a common meeting ground. We both think slavery is a shocking social evil."

I nodded and sighed. "I suppose you have to be a man to have a common meeting ground with Pa."

The eyebrows arched even higher. "You don't?"

I'd said too much. I'd spoken my thoughts aloud. "Oh, he's just so busy all the time," I amended.

He nodded. Why did I feel he was seeing through me? I wished Watson would come back from unhitching that horse from the wagon. "This is a pleasant place," he said.

"Yes, it is."

"Still, I find it very odd for a pretty young girl to be standing guard in such a place and for such a purpose."

I blushed. "I'm Pa's watchdog. He depends on me to keep neighbors from suspecting about his plan."

He scowled. "You know about his plan?"

"I've grown up knowing, Mr. Kagi. And I know that you're here to get the men to support it."

He was looking right through me again. "I taught school in Ohio," he said thoughtfully.

"Oh, I knew you were a teacher."

"Your pa told you that, too?"

"No, it's your eyebrows. And the way they arch."

His eyes narrowed. "Who is the secretary of war now, under President Buchanan?" he asked.

"John B. Floyd."

"Who is the vice president?"

"John C. Breckinridge. A Southern Democrat. Pa says the

Southerners needed him to balance their ticket in '56. Pa also says he's a jackass."

He inclined his head. "You haven't given me any wrong answers, Annie Brown. To the contrary, if my pupils back in Ohio had half the brains you have, I'd never have left teaching, I can tell you."

I didn't know what to say then. He made me tongue-tied. Then I thought of something. "Pa said you wrote for newspapers."

"I've done some writing in my time."

"The New York Post is more than just some writing. Pa calls you his Horace Greeley. You going to write Pa up?"

"No, I am to fight with him. Like I did in Kansas. You ought to think, seriously, about continuing your education, Annie Brown."

"I don't know as I could. Normal school is all most girls my age do."

"You are not like most girls your age. I shall suggest it to your father."

Pa? I almost laughed. What did Pa care about me? All he cared about was the slaves! "Do you come from Virginia, Mr. Kagi?" I wanted to change the subject.

"Now what makes you think that?"

The way you stand, I thought. The way you hold your head. The way you think so much of yourself. But I said, "You have somewhat of an accent."

"See what I mean? You are perceptive. Yes. I was raised hereabouts. Have kin near the Ferry. Whenever I used to go home I'd run off a slave or two. Got half a dozen to freedom. I'm not welcome to home anymore. Been informed by friends that if I show my face in Harpers Ferry again they'll lynch me."

I stared at him. So that's what he had to be melancholy about. "You going to get the men to support Pa's plan? The way they feel about you hereabouts?"

He'd taken his leather satchel off his shoulder and was fishing in it for something. He drew out a book. "Because of the way they feel about me hereabouts," he said. He handed the book to me. "For you."

I took it. It was a good leather-bound copy of three of Shakespeare's plays. "You sure you want to give me this, Mr. Kagi?"

"I've never been more sure of anything, Annie Brown. Now why are you staring at me like that?"

"I've never met a real secretary of war before."

"Well? Do you think I make a good one?"

Watson was coming around the front of the house, finally. Thank heaven. "I'll wait and see," I said, "'til after you meet with Pa and the others."

They'd waited for him all afternoon. They were in the garret waiting. Cook had come up from the Ferry. Now Kagi was finally here, and I was dying to go and stand at the bottom of the stairs in the dining room and listen. Pa had said Kagi was a debater. But he'd told me sternly to stay outside and watch.

I opened the book of Mr. Shakespeare's plays and started to read. But I couldn't concentrate. Even out here I could hear the arguing going on upstairs. If they got much louder, I'd have to tell Martha to tell them to hush.

They got louder. Voices were raised almost to a shout. I heard horrible, hoarse, accusing things hurled across that garret room. What, I didn't know. I only knew the tones, the desperate anger, the outrage, the mumblings.

Were they turning against Pa? Would they back down on him now?

Then I heard Pa's voice. He was delivering some kind of a speech. It was short and vehement.

Then silence. During which the frogs did a whole chorus of what sounded like "Nearer My God to Thee."

I could have told John Henry Kagi more if he'd asked me.

The Democrats were divided over slavery, for instance. The Republicans were getting stronger. Buchanan didn't have the mettle to be president. Pa said he'd never run for re-election.

Why was Kagi so surprised that I knew things? You couldn't be Pa's daughter and not know things. I'd cut my teeth on Dred Scott, the slave who'd sued for his freedom when his master moved him from Missouri, a slave state, into Wisconsin Territory, in the 1830s. I knew that Ralph Waldo Emerson had said, "Cotton thread holds the Union together," that Stephen Douglas came out for the Missouri Compromise only because he wanted Southern backing in his drive to be president.

The men started to come downstairs. They trailed the argument with them, like an old coat nobody wanted. They were throwing it back and forth. And it was getting more tattered by the minute.

"Supper!" Owen yelled.

I saw whale oil lamplight spill out onto the porch from the dining room windows, heard Martha scurrying back and forth setting the table. I should go in and help. Did Pa want me still out here, watching? He'd be all mooded up now and I didn't want to walk into him. It would be like walking into a brick wall.

The door opened. Cook came out. He went right on past me, down the stairs, and around to the back to get his horse. Then Tidd came out. He paused to light a cheroot. He had those newfangled matches. They illuminated his face. He was scowling.

He didn't look at all like the man who could sing "Home Again" in such a way as to bring tears to your eyes. He flung the match away and walked past me.

"Aren't you staying to supper, Mr. Tidd?"

He turned, looked at me as if he had no idea who I was. Then I saw his eyes focus, remembering. "No," he said. And he began to walk down the stairs. "Is there an extra horse around here?"

He was leaving! I ran down the stairs after him. "Where are you going, Mr. Tidd?"

"I said is there an extra horse around here?"

"There might be."

"Then I might be leaving."

"You're not allowed to leave. You're not even supposed to be outside."

That got him turned around again all right. "He thinks he's going to hold the whole goddamned town against the militia. And federal troops," he said. "And he thinks we ought to all follow him. Like lambs to the slaughter. Just because he says so! Is the man crazy?"

Oh yes, Mr. Tidd, I thought. He is pure daft. Addled in the head. Crazy. Always has been crazier than Clancy's goat. And he has always expected us to follow him.

But I made no reply.

"Ahhh," and he waved me away and started to walk up to the barn. "Cook!" he yelled, "wait up there, will you?"

"Where are you going, Mr. Tidd?" I yelled after him.

"To hell," he said.

"Well, you don't have to take the rest of us with you!"

"Do I have to answer to the daughter now as well as the father?"

We shouldn't be yelling like this. Even though it was dark and there was no one around. The very trees around here had eyes. I ran up the hill after him. "Mr. Tidd, at least tell me where you'll be so I can tell Pa."

He'd found a horse. Pa's. It was the only other horse around, one of two horses Pa had rented from Mr. Unseld, who'd told him about this house. Pa needed it for when he went to Chambersburg. I watched Tidd saddle it, mount it.

"I'm going home with Johnny Cook a while to cool off," he said. "If I don't get out of here, I'll be as crazy as the rest of them."

He started to ride by me, he and Cook. Then Tidd turned. "Annie Brown," he said, "you're a good girl. You're a sweet girl. And he doesn't treat you right. He doesn't treat any of his young 'uns right. The others, they're men, they can take care of themselves. But you? You don't need all this. Take my advice, Annie Brown. Marry your nice yellow-haired boy and get away from here. Make a life for yourself."

Then he was gone, he and Johnny Cook. Off into the night where the frogs were singing the second chorus of "Nearer My God to Thee."

How could I tell Pa Tidd was gone off the place? I was dragging my feet up the stairs when Kagi came out. I halted on the top step.

"Is Tidd gone?" he asked. I nodded. "Well, maybe it's for the better he gets away for a while. He'll be back."

"What happened, Mr. Kagi?"

"I suppose in polite language you'd call it a mutiny."

"Who?"

"Your brothers for some. Stu Taylor. The Coppocs. The Thompsons. The Negroes and all the rest seem to be with your pa."

My brothers against Pa? It didn't seem possible. "And you, Mr. Kagi?"

"I believe he can take the Ferry by surprise. I don't know about the rest of it. Taking the Ferry should be enough on its own. It would accomplish what he wants. Then we could move to the mountains to avoid capture. Cook has studied the layout of the government buildings. He knows the habits of the watchmen. He thinks it can be done, too."

I nodded. "How is Pa taking it?"

"He's resigned as commander-in-chief," he said.

"Resigned?" I could scarce get the word out. Pa had never resigned anything in his life. He did not know what the word meant.

Kagi smiled. "It's a smart move. The old man knows what he's about. We conferred. And I thought it was a good move. It'll ward off mutiny. Put it in their hands. They'll come back to him now. And when they do, the decision to attack the Ferry will be theirs, not his. Well? Do you think I'm a good secretary of war, Annie Brown?"

I did not answer him, because I did not know. Was a secretary of war supposed to look out for the army? Or send them to their destruction? And which had he done, anyway?

We went in to supper.

"Dauphin, you went against Pa?"

"Yeah." He did not look happy.

We'd stolen outside for a walk around the house after supper. Pa had taken the half-blind horse and hitched it behind the wagon to go to Chambersburg with Kagi.

"We voted," Dauphin said, "and then your pa said he'd resign. It was awful, Annie. I feel bad about it. We all do."

"You're supposed to feel bad," I told him. And then I related to him what Kagi had said. "They're counting on the fact that you'll all go back to him. And then the decision to attack will be in your hands. Only you can't tell the others, or I'll get in trouble."

"Then why tell me?"

"Because I love you. And I don't want you walking into a trap. Let's leave here, Dauphin," I said. "Tonight. Just the two of us."

"Leave? Are you crazy? Where would we go?"

"Back to North Elba."

"I couldn't go back to North Elba if I deserted, Annie. And neither could you."

"Then we'll go somewhere else."

"Where?"

"I don't know. It doesn't matter. Anywhere away from here."

"What brought this on all of a sudden, Annie?"

I shrugged. I hadn't given it much thought. It just seemed right now. "If my brothers don't agree with Pa, something's wrong, Dauphin," I said. "My brothers were in Kansas with him. They're not scared. They're right smart."

"Well, they're not deserting. And I'm not, either. I'm not running off. I'm staying and seeing this thing through."

"This isn't a real army. You can't desert from what isn't real," I pleaded.

"It's real to me. And to the others. I don't think you understand things, Annie. This is as real as it gets. We're serious here. And if we don't attack the Ferry, we'll do something else. And I want to be part of it."

"Didn't you hear me?" I grabbed his arms. "They're going to all come back to Pa. That's the way he planned it. And coming back to him means they're going to attack. And you'll all be killed. Dauphin, please!"

He pulled away from me. "Your pa won't do anything we don't think is right. He said that."

"My pa? You don't know him, Dauphin. My pa gets his own way all the time. About everything. He'll have all of you with him before this is over. You won't be able to resist my pa. He holds sway over everybody he meets."

"He won't get us killed, Annie. That isn't what he's setting out to do."

"What is he setting out to do then?"

"Put the country on notice about slavery."

"Oh, Dauphin." I felt such a large sadness inside me, I thought I would die. I stood there taking his measure. He was so handsome, so full of fun and good nature. But he was so innocent.

"Don't you think that if he and all of you get killed, that'll put the country on notice about slavery?" I asked.

He just stared me down with those blue eyes of his. "How could you say that about your own pa, Annie?"

"Because I know him. He doesn't care about anything but ending slavery. He never did."

He moved away from me. "That's crazy, Annie."

"Is it? Why do you think my sister Ruth wouldn't let your brother come down then? Because Ruth knows what I know about Pa. And she's his favorite, Dauphin. *She's his favorite, and she knows. And that's why you're here and Henry isn't.*"

I was crying then. He took me in his arms and I cried against him. "Don't you remember the night you got here? How you couldn't believe the way Pa spoke about Salmon and Jason, because they wouldn't come?" I reminded him. "You said your pa never took on like that, and you asked me how I could stand it."

"I remember," he said.

"And I told you it was Pa's way. And you had to get used to it."

"I guess I've gotten used to it," he said.

"I don't want you to, Dauphin." I was crying softly. "I don't want you to ever get used to it. It's why I love you. 'Cause you're not like my pa and my brothers. Please, don't get used to it."

He let me sob softly in his arms. He promised he wouldn't get used to Pa's way. "I'm not going to do anything foolish," he promised. "But I'm not running away tonight. With or without you, Annie. I could never go home to North Elba again if I ran now. Neither could you. Don't you want to go home with me to North Elba?"

I wanted to so bad, I'd have given an arm for it right then. An eye. Anything, except what I was going to have to give.

I dried my tears and went back into the house. We'd settled nothing.

Chapter Thirteen

Pa was a rich man at one time. In the boom back in the '30s everybody was making money, doing business on credit. Pa went into land speculation in Ohio, buying up building lots. Like everybody else, he was counting on the success of the new Pennsylvania-Ohio canal. It was to go east-west across Ohio. Pa paid $7,000 for the ninety-five-acre Haymaker farm, borrowed the money. He was going to divide it into industrial lots and get rich. Pa thought he was right smart. Then, in 1837 he lost nearly all his property and couldn't pay his debts. The canal never came into being. Land prices dropped. Stocks and cotton prices went down. Pa often had to trade leather from his tannery in Hudson for a side of beef or a barrel of pork. But he didn't worry. He said the Lord God Almighty would sustain him. And then he went bust.

PA WAS GONE TWO DAYS. IN THAT TIME OWEN WAS in charge. It made sense, I suppose. He was Pa's oldest here. In his quiet, calm way, Owen managed things. He said prayers before meals, just like Pa. He insisted everybody come to the table. He made me watch outside. He made the men continue with their drills upstairs. He wouldn't let anybody go out except Watson, who went to the Ferry for the mail.

Nobody gave Owen any grief. They'd just as soon have somebody in charge, and Owen seemed to know what he was about. They minded him.

Another thing Owen did, he called meetings. He had meetings all over the house, upstairs and down, at different times of the first day. He'd call two or three men to him and encourage them to talk about what they were feeling. And the others were huddled in small groups, having meetings of their own.

Nobody knew yet how it was going to go. Would they stand for Pa? Or against him?

I got to thinking the reason Pa stayed away was to give them time to decide.

Watson came back from town with the mail, the newspapers, some tobacco and hard candy. Almost everybody got letters and it seemed to lighten things up a bit. And then something strange happened.

I went down to the storeroom to fetch some milk and eggs for Martha. She was going to make a cake. When I opened the door, there was Dangerfield Newby sitting on a cask.

He was crying.

I stood there like six kinds of a fool, taken with the sight of a grown man crying, and wanting to run away at the same time. Then he looked up and saw me.

Newby had kept pretty much to himself since he'd come to us. He was good at fixing the small parts of guns. Owen told me he'd been a blacksmith on the plantation in Virginia, that his father had been a Scotchman who'd freed all his mulatto children. Newby was over six feet and had muscled arms, but he spoke real gentle and walked that way, too.

"I'm sorry, Dangerfield," I said. "I'll come back later."

"No, you c'mon in now, Miss Annie. I got no right to be in here."

"Of course you do." I walked on in. "It's cool in here. And nice. I don't blame you."

He nodded. "I just wanted to be privatelike when I read my letter from my wife."

"Is it bad news, Dangerfield?"

He was holding it in his hands, looking at it. "Depends. She writes me alla time like this. I was just cryin' 'cause there's really nothin' I can do for her."

"What does she want of you, Dangerfield?"

"What does she want?" he echoed softly. "Why she wants what every wife wants of her husband, Miss Annie. She wants our family to be together. She writes beggin' me to come and fetch her and the children."

"Oh." I remembered Martha telling me his wife was in bondage. "Where is she?" I asked.

"On a plantation in Brentwell, Virginia. She and the children belong to Jesse Jennings. I knew her since I was in bondage."

"Can't you buy her?" I asked. Owen had told me how some freed Negroes bought the freedom of their mates.

"No, Miss Annie. Mr. Jennings, he won't let her go. And she writes here, 'Oh, my dear husband, come this fall without fail, money or no money I want to see you so much; that is the one bright hope I have before me. Come and buy me, and the children, please. If you do not get me somebody else will.'"

From somewhere in the storeroom there was a drip, drip, dripping sound. From some barrel of food. I must tell Martha,

I thought crazily. "How many children do you have, Newby?" I asked.

"Seven. The baby just commencing to crawl. That baby, she's mine, Miss Annie, but her little body belongs to Mr. Jennings. They all do, all my children. And I can't do what my wife wants. And it's killin' me."

I felt his wrenching heartache. His powerlessness, he who had shoulders and muscles so strong he could lift the crates of guns off the wagon with ease when they arrived from Chambersburg. I thought about Watson and how he wrote to Belle all the time, and said, "give the baby a kiss for me." I thought how crazy Oliver was over the idea of Martha's baby. I remembered how John and Wealthy had mourned their little Austin, lost to cholera on the way to Kansas.

It's wrong, something cried out in me. It's wrong.

"Maybe my pa can help," I said. That was it. Pa would know what to do. "Why don't you show him the letter when he gets back. Maybe he can write to this Mr. Jennings for you."

He said two things to me then that I shall always remember. "Time's past for writing, Miss Annie," he said. And then: "Your pa is helping. That's why we're all here. That's what this is all about."

I stared at him. He was so certain. Something had come together in him, fused into some powerful force. The Scotchman and the Negro, I thought. They have met.

It was his provisional constitution. Not written on paper. But there in his eyes. And it was in that moment that I knew I'd been wrong. That Dauphin had been right.

"Trouble is," Dangerfield was saying, "trouble is, if we do

this here raid and fail, Mr. Jennings'll sell her away for sure when he finds out about it. He'll sell her South. And that's bad."

South. I thought about Hettie Pease. She'd been sold South. Everybody knew there was nothing worse for a slave. And I was responsible for Hettie Pease.

"But if we don't do this here raid, she's lost to me anyways. So I'm gonna vote to do it, Miss Annie. I gotta do it. For my wife and babies." He stood up.

He'd made his decision. I could make mine now, too.

I could help Dangerfield Newby. There were men upstairs who were still conferring, still uncertain. I was sure that if they knew about this letter it'd end their confusion. They'd vote to support Pa. Because it was here, right here in their midst, what the fuss was all about.

As Dauphin said, "This is as real as it gets."

So I made my decision now, too. Not only for Dangerfield Newby's wife and baby, but for Hettie Pease. "C'mon upstairs with me," I said. I took hold of his shirtsleeve. "You show that letter to the men upstairs. You tell them about your wife and children."

The second day Owen set himself up at the table in the dining room like Pa did, with a lot of paper around him.

One of those papers was the letter from Dangerfield Newby's wife.

Owen summoned the men to him, one at a time, to confer. Martha and I kept the coffee coming and with it some fresh gingerbread. The men loved gingerbread.

All day the conferring went on. At supper the second day Pa still hadn't returned. Neither had Tidd. I know Owen was waiting for Tidd. His vote was important. He could be a holdout.

"Let me know the instant he comes, won't you, Annie?" Owen asked.

I was taking the last of the supper dishes off the table. We were alone in the room. "Suppose he doesn't come back?" I asked.

"He'll come."

I saw Owen had a paper in front of him with all the men's names on it. And check marks next to each one. How had they voted? I did not expect him to tell me. He just sat there with a fresh cup of steaming coffee in front of him on the table, holding his bad arm with his good one. Did it ever hurt him? I wondered. He never said.

"Can I ask you something, Owen?"

"Ask away."

"Did the letter from Newby's wife help?"

He looked real melancholy then. And it was as aristocratic a melancholy as any Virginia gentleman's. "It helped," he said. "You did good, Annie. Real good. I don't know what we'd do around here without you. You've got more sense than a lot of these men."

I left the room with tears in my eyes and a warm feeling in my heart. Yet I felt sad, too. Pa would never say such to me. Owen had to do it. And busy and worried as he was at the moment, with all that responsibility on him, he'd not been too busy to know he had to do it.

Tidd rode up the hill about twenty minutes later.

"Owen wants to see you," I told him when he came up the steps.

"Don't you ever get tired of sitting out here?"

"It's better than sitting in the house and listening to all of you fussing."

"Don't you ever want to ride into town? It's a fine town. It has shops, churches, everything."

"I want a lot of things. But I don't go running off in a snit just because I don't get them."

He smiled at me. "I have a temper, Annie. I know enough to remove myself from things when it flares. When you wear a gun, it's the best thing to do."

"You could take the gun off."

He shook his head and laughed. "Women," he said.

"Women have tempers, too, Mr. Tidd. Only we don't carry guns to back them up. Or have the luxury of running off, 'cause we're afraid we'll use them."

"But they have sharp tongues. And they're as good as guns, aren't they?"

He smiled, so I smiled, too. He was righter than he knew about women. Hadn't I told Newby to show the men the letter? "You'd best get inside," I said, "Owen's waiting for you."

In the end they all stood with Pa, of course.

They waited in the dining room for him, drinking pot after pot of coffee. Dauphin played his fiddle. Tidd sang. The others played cards and wrote letters.

Dangerfield was writing to his wife. I didn't ask, when I poured his coffee, what he was writing. But he gave me a blissful smile when he thanked me for the coffee.

Then I went back on the porch to keep watch, Cuffee at my feet. Overhead the night was full of stars. The cicadas were singing. I was worn out, pure and simple. The night air was like silk. The wind whispered in the treetops. I must have dozed off, between the sound of the wind and the comfort of the murmured voices from inside.

Pa woke me. He was standing over me. "You should go to bed, Annie."

"I was waiting for you. Everybody is."

"They haven't killed each other yet?" He was making a feeble joke. I thought how he would never know how the men had anguished over the right and wrong of their decisions, had walked over hot coals in their minds for him. "No, Pa," I said, "Owen's kept everybody in line."

"Well, I've got good news. My man in Chambersburg just got word. Fred Douglass wants to meet with me. In two days. Isn't that wonderful? Douglass himself. Who better represents the plight of the slave?"

Dangerfield Newby's wife and seven children, I thought. But you don't see it. Because he's right here in front of you. Just like you don't see me.

"Yes, Pa, it's wonderful," I said.

"When the men hear this, they'll be with me for sure," he said. And he started inside.

"Don't tell them, Pa. Please."

He stopped to look at me. He waited for me to elaborate. He would never ask my opinion on anything, but I'd started this, so now he was waiting to hear me out.

"Let them tell you what they've decided first, Pa," I said. "Without it having anything to do with Douglass."

He paused at the door. Was he afraid they'd not stand with him? That they needed Douglass? He didn't answer me. He just took a big breath and went inside.

I got up and followed. I stood just outside the dining room door. Nobody paid mind to me. The men all stood up and stopped what they were doing when they saw him.

"Well," Pa said.

There were murmured hellos and embarrassed looks all around. I held my breath. Was he going to let them talk first? Was he just going to blurt out his news about Douglass?

Owen stepped aside from his place at the table, Pa's place. Pa sat down.

Owen spoke. "We have all agreed to sustain your decisions," he said solemnly. "I speak in behalf of everyone here. And Cook, who sent word with Kagi from the Ferry. We are wholeheartedly with you and behind you, until you have proved incompetent, and we will adhere to your decisions as long as you will."

It was over. They were going with him. It was done. And I'd had my part in it, for better or for worse. Whatever happened, I'd live with it for the rest of my life. And that is as real as it gets.

Chapter Fourteen

As far back as 1839 my pa was saying that blood atonement alone could destroy slavery. People said he was crazy then and they say it now. I don't know what I think. But I want to set things right. My pa did as much to spirit the country up against slavery as anybody. Including Frederick Douglass. Mama says it had something to do with the covenant his ancestor Peter Brown, the carpenter, signed in the cabin of the Mayflower on a cold December morning almost two hundred and fifty years ago. "We hold ourselves the Lord's free people," Peter wrote, "to walk in all His ways made known, or to be made known to us, according to our best endeavors, whatever it may cost us." As I see it, the "whatever it may cost us" part loomed large inside Pa. And never left him.

TWO DAYS LATER PA WENT TO MEET WITH FREDerick Douglass.

The meeting was set up by Pa's man in Chambersburg, Henry Watson, who was a Negro agent on the Underground Railroad.

Pa and Douglass were to rendezvous in an old deserted stone quarry near Chambersburg. My brothers all wanted to be part of it, but Pa said no.

"I'm taking only Shields Green."

"Green?" I thought Owen would break apart. "Green? He'll get you killed. Like he almost got me killed on the way here!"

"He's like a son to Douglass," Pa said.

"A son?" Owen's eyes bulged. He swung his useless arm. "I don't care if he's the Holy Ghost to Douglass, Pa! Give him a pistol and he don't know what to do with it!"

"Don't blaspheme," Pa said. "You'll hex my trip."

"Hex your trip? You're taking a runaway slave with you through Maryland and back into Pennsylvania where they hunt Negroes like rabbits, and I'm hexing your trip?" Owen walked out of the dining room. He came into the kitchen and slumped in a chair in the corner.

Green's arrogance knew no bounds. "I'm goin' wid de old man," he said. He had Martha pressing his shirt for him. He borrowed a silk cravat from one of the other men. He spent a whole day getting ready.

"Green'll get Pa killed on the way there or on the way back," I heard Owen tell Oliver. "And all for nothing. I'll wager Douglass is going to turn Pa down anyway."

Oliver was sitting in the kitchen by the stove, reading. But I think he was really brooding. He'd been brooding since they all voted to stand with Pa. "Let him do whatever he wants, Owen," he said, "he'll do it anyway."

"Pa's crazy," Owen said. "He needs somebody along who can handle a rifle. All right, I can't go, because I could be recognized. What about you or Watson? Anybody instead of that bantam rooster strutting around in there."

They left, Pa and Green, with the half-blind horse and the wagon. They were to meet with Kagi, who would take them to the quarry. "You're in charge, Owen," Pa said.

Owen wouldn't be mollified. "I'm damned if I'm going to

keep things in line any longer," he said. "Let the men do as they please. Annie?"

"I'm here, Owen."

"You're responsible. They're not to run off or go outside. You hear?"

"Don't take your vexation out on me, Owen."

"Do you hear me, Annie Brown?"

"Yes, I hear."

He left. He took Pa's horse. He needed to get away, he said. He wanted to see that place called Devil's Backbone that Oliver had told us about. "It sounds even crazier than this place," he said. I watched him go, wishing I could go with him.

Of course as soon as Owen left, the men thought they could do all sorts of things and get away with them.

They did.

First we had a fight. Then Hazlett and Leeman stole off and roamed through the woods, went to Harpers Ferry without so much as a fare-thee-well, and never came back until late that night. It was the worst day I remember in my time at the Kennedy farm. All I needed before it was through, I thought, was Mrs. Huffmaster poking around. I shouldn't have tempted the gods. We had that, too.

Hazlett and Leeman were the start of it all. Separate, they were a plague to us all. Together, they were a plague to the citizenry at large. Hazlett had a foul mouth that he took to exercising behind Pa's back. Never did I hear such language. The air was purple from it. Martha threatened, three times, to wash it out with lye soap. "Only it would be a good waste of soap," she told him.

Leeman was just wild. No wonder Owen had trouble keeping him in line in Springdale, Iowa. He liked to spit tobacco juice, miss the spittoon, and hit the clean floorboards. Martha made him mop it up when he did that. When he wasn't chewing, he was smoking foul-smelling cheroots that smelled up the house. Pa believed that some people were naturally depraved. I think Leeman was. Yet Pa liked him, because he'd fought well in Kansas. Leeman knew it. "He likes me like a son," he'd brag.

"Get down on your knees and thank God you aren't," Owen told him.

To start with, the August day boded bad things. A heavy stickiness hung over the Kennedy farm. The air was thick and humid. We needed rain. The house was so close it was near intolerable. In the distance thunder boomed. The men were all waiting for a good storm, because then they could make noise. They'd run up and down the stairs, throw things, wrestle, yell, and just be plain obnoxious.

They were waiting for it, because they had feelings in them as thick and heavy as the air outside. And they needed to let them out in that storm. They were lounging on the stairs, venturing down, wandering into the kitchen to sneak treats and bother Martha. She kept chasing them out. I kept watch on the porch.

"Anybody wants to work off steam they can mop the floor in the dining room," she told them.

Barclay Coppoc and Dauphin took her up on it, got

buckets and mops, soap and water, and were working away on the floorboards in the dining room. That's when Hazlett saw his chance. "Hey Buttercup," I heard him yell, "you finally found your true purpose, I see. Does the old man know you're so good at mopping floors?"

To give Dauphin credit, he didn't answer. Just went right on working. That's what Watson said later, anyway. He was sitting on the stairs at the time. But Hazlett couldn't leave it be. Oh no. Do pigs have wings? He kept right at Dauphin, then started on Barclay. Asking them if his mama missed him at home, and who was taking his place mopping the floors.

Dauphin and Barclay were the youngest in Pa's army. Both were twenty. Barclay's widowed mother was an abolitionist. Barclay had read me a letter from her that said, "I believe you are going with old Brown again. When you get the halters around your necks, will you think of me?"

Quakers did not fight. Oh, they fought slavery all right. But they didn't fight upstart bullies like Leeman and Hazlett. They kept their own counsel.

Not Dauphin. And it wasn't because he wasn't Quaker. It was because, being the youngest of eighteen children, he knew how to fight.

I will say that both Dauphin and Barclay took a great deal of teasing. It was when Hazlett started in on Dauphin's name that he went crazy.

"Dauphin! What kinda name is that? Your mother run outa boys' names time she got to you?" I heard the taunt, even out on the porch. I heard the scuffle start, too.

First it was a yell. Then a curse. I didn't know Dauphin could curse that well. Next it was a whooping and thumping. I heard something fall. It sounded with a great thud. I got up and ran into the house. Dauphin and Hazlett were rolling on the dining room floor, awash in sudsy water like two wild boars. Somebody had thrown the bucket. Water was all over the place.

There isn't anything more terrible than seeing grown men fighting. I'd grown up seeing my brothers doing hurdy-gurdy things at home, tussling, wrestling, roughhousing. But Pa never allowed real fighting. Not like this.

Dauphin was giving as good as he got. But he was no match for Hazlett. Then Leeman jumped on him. That was too much for Barclay, Quaker or no Quaker. Something in him told him that the underdog was the underdog, even if he wasn't Negro and a slave. He jumped into the fray, too.

Barclay tried to pull them off Dauphin. Hazlett had Dauphin's head in his hands and was pounding it on the floor. You could hear the thump, thump, thumping. Nobody's head could take that.

"Stop it!" I screamed.

Leeman was sitting on Dauphin's feet. Barclay, for all his Quaker upbringing, was attempting to gouge Leeman's eyes out. I stood there screaming. Martha was whipping at them with wet dishrags. The other men were crowding around yelling and stomping and saying encouraging things.

Oliver stopped it. He fired a pistol right out the open window. That's what it sounded like anyway. Later on I learned it was a crack of thunder. Then the rain started pouring down. A great, drenching rain. The men yelled and whooped. Will Thompson dragged Hazlett off Dauphin with the help of Watson. Edwin Coppoc dragged off Leeman.

They sat Dauphin up. He didn't look too good. He was bleeding from a cut at the corner of his eye. He looked stunned. "Dauphin!" I went to him. Will picked him up and settled him in a chair in a corner. I tried to put a wet rag on his eye.

"Leave off," he growled. And he pushed me away. It was clear he didn't want to be attended to by a girl.

I dropped the rag and ran from the room.

"Mind your manners," I heard Will say. "Or I'll start pounding your head on the floor."

I was in the kitchen crying when Will came in a few minutes later. "He didn't mean it, Annie."

"Yes he did. He always means it."

"Well, he isn't himself. He took quite a beating. Doesn't know what he's saying. None of us do. We're all going crazy trapped in this place. I swear, I never would have come if I knew it was going to be like this."

"None of us would have." Watson came in for a cup of water for Dauphin. "Belle writes that she thinks we're all crazy."

"I'm going to tell Pa we can't last much longer like this," Watson said. "The men are like caged animals. I'm worried about Dauphin, Will. All that pounding. I think he may have a concussion."

"What do you do for a concussion?" Will asked.

We all looked at each other. Pa would know, but Pa wasn't here.

"I think John had one in Kansas," Will said, "when the federal men beat up on him."

"John's still got one," Watson said. It was dark humor and showed just what a state we were all in.

"What did they do for John in Kansas?" Martha asked.

"Do?" Oliver came into the kitchen. "They dragged him in chains, sixty-five miles. Which is why he's still dragging himself around in chains. Dauphin's got to sleep," he said.

"No sleep," from Will. "I think sleep is bad for him now."

They debated the matter. Nobody knew. And then the last person in the world we needed to hear from called out to me.

"Yoo-hoo, Missy? Missy, you up there? I'm wet as a drowned cat. Got any coffee?"

We looked at each other. "Get rid of her," Oliver told me.

"No," I said. "She'll know what to do for a concussion. Get the men upstairs."

Everybody ran. I went out the door to meet Mrs. Huffmaster on the porch. From inside I heard running boots going up the stairs, shouts, laughter, groans.

"Sounds like a herd of cattle in there," Mrs. Huffmaster said. "You got company?" She trotted right down to the end of the porch to peer in the window.

I know she saw them in there, Barclay and Hazlett. Maybe Leeman, too.

"No. My brothers were just trying to clean the place a bit."

She had big blue eyes and they changed with the light. They changed, too, when you lied to her. I swear she knew when I lied. "Missy," she said, "you kin tell me. Anythin' you want. I'm yer friend."

"I've nothing to tell," I said.

The rain poured down on us. I felt bad lying to her, but what could I do? I felt so bad about so many things that one more didn't matter, did it?

"I healed you oncet, didn't I? Yer aura's all fine now. Brighter'n a new penny. I kin do it agin. It ain't nice to lie to a friend, Missy. I saw men in there, an' they ain't the ones who live here. What's goin' on? I hope you people ain't runnin' slaves outa Maryland."

"We're not running slaves, Mrs. Huffmaster. It's against the law. My pa's a law-abiding citizen."

She liked Pa. I saw her certainty vanish.

"Strange men in there," she said. "I knowed I saw strange men."

"Those are my brothers. You can't see for this rain, anyway. You know your eyes are bad. When was the last time you washed them out with May water?"

"Got none left."

"Well, see? Now why don't you come in and dry off. And have some nice hot coffee."

We went into the house. I took her wet shawl. She stopped just inside the door and peered into the dining room. "Sakes alive! A flood! What happened?"

It came to me then, a stroke of pure genius. "I was coming down the stairs with a bucket of water and I tripped and fell. Haven't had a chance to clean it up yet."

"Did'ja hurt yourself?"

Oh daughter of troops! Don't stop now. Lie your way into infinity if you must. It is for a good cause. "I fell on my head," I said. "Do you know how to treat a concussion, Mrs. Huffmaster? I think I may have a concussion."

An hour later I was propped up in my bed in my room with a cold compress on my head. Martha was getting final instructions about keeping me awake for the next twelve hours straight, and the dining room floor was mopped clean. Mrs. Huffmaster insisted on doing it. All Martha's protests couldn't stop her.

An hour! With no sound from upstairs and a houseful of men!

No sound! Did that mean Dauphin was sleeping? He could die if he slept. That's what Mrs. Huffmaster said I would do.

Would she never leave? She was taking her sweet time over her coffee telling Martha about how her oldest fell from the apple tree. "Thought she was dead. Kept her up all night. Never saw such a lump on a child's head. Cain't figure why yer sister-in-law don't have no lump."

Finally she left. I heard Martha talking to her all the way down the stairs. Then I jumped out of bed and ran into the dining room. "She's gone!" I yelled.

They started to come down.

"Where's Dauphin?"

"Fell asleep," Will said.

"You've got to wake him up! He'll die if he falls asleep! Go wake him! Now!"

Such a scramble I never did see. They woke Dauphin. Will dragged him downstairs and sat him at the table and tried to make him play cards. I ran to make hot coffee. Martha came back in, exhausted.

"It'll be suppertime soon," she said. She pushed a lock of hair off her forehead, looked around, and then stopped. "Where are Leeman and Hazlett?" she asked.

Nobody answered for a moment. Then finally Will did. "They sneaked out the upstairs window when Mrs. Huffmaster was here," he said. "They couldn't stand it for another minute."

Couldn't stand it for another minute, could they? Well, did they think the rest of us could?

Martha, cooking and cleaning all day, and her expecting?

Dangerfield Newby, crying over those letters from his wife?

Watson, who hardly even knows his and Belle's new baby boy that he named Frederick after our brother shot in Kansas?

The Coppocs, who left their widowed mother in Springfield, Ohio?

Will and Dauphin, with the harvest coming in at home and them not there to help?

Owen and Oliver, who fought already in Kansas?

Taylor, who's convinced he's going to die?

What gives them the right to just light out the window and take off? We're all wearied of it, living so close, missing people we left at home, hearing Pa talk about what his army of liberation is going to do when it gets into the heart of Virginia, and where are the pikes and why aren't they here yet. And what the mutinous slaves did in Jamaica.

I'm so crazy from sitting on that porch and watching for approaching strangers that Mrs. Huffmaster is starting to look good to me.

I'm starting to think the frogs have tired of "Nearer My God to Thee" and have now switched to "Amazing Grace." I lay there in my bed every night hearing Martha and Oliver stirring some soft into their mattress and wondering if Dauphin will live long enough so that we can wed and stir some soft into ours.

Where are Leeman and Hazlett? Will said they took to the woods. Well, I'm in the woods and I don't see anybody. I'm standing here feet and skirts soaked. I'll have foot rot soon. I'm staring through the rainy mist like some half-demented female Diogenes, looking for the truth. All I need is a lamp.

Maybe I need some bloodhounds. Wouldn't that be a hoot. I could track Leeman and Hazlett like they track the slaves in the South, with bloodhounds. What am I talking about? This is the South. There they are, the unfeeling varlets.

Leeman! Hazlett! Ho, you there! I see you. You can't hide from me. Do you think I don't see you? Do you think you're a couple of invisibles? What are you doing, picking those apples? They're not ours! Owen finds out and he'll hike all the way to Antietam again to fetch apples this time so people around here will remember us as honest. Come here, I say, or I swear, when Pa comes back I'll tell him you ran off! That's right, you heard me. All the men inside have agreed not to tell Pa. Even Dauphin and Barclay. Not about anything. The fight or you sneaking out or anything.

Why? How should I know why? Dauphin's decent and Barclay's a Quaker. Don't expect you to understand either persuasion.

You're going where? To see who? The Ferry? To see Cook? Not while

I draw breath, you're not. Look here, it's my job to keep you from running off. Pa finds out and there will be all hell to pay. Yes, I said hell. You ever seen hell, Hazlett? You think it doesn't exist? You just let Pa find out you ran off and you'll know.

Why should I let you go to the Ferry? Just tell me why?

Because if I do, you'll be back by eleven tonight?

Because every other time you sneak out and I find you, you'll come right back?

Because I'm the prettiest girl you ever saw? Don't give me that hogwash.

Because you're wearied of all the talk of what counties in the South have all the slaves? And crossing the Rubicon? How about me? I've heard it all my life.

Because you'll leave off tormenting Dauphin if I let you go?

Because you'll look out for him, real special like, when you do the raid? No, he isn't a soldier. No, he didn't rough it in Kansas. You will? You promise? Well, you better be back by eleven tonight. 'Cause I'll be waiting by that window with Oliver's pistol. And I'll shoot you both in the feet if you're one minute late. Do I know how to use it? Of course I know how to use it. And if I don't, then you're worse off, 'cause I might aim higher than the feet and shoot something else. Then I'll tell Pa about today. That's why.

Lie down with dogs and get up with fleas, I say. I'm as bad as they are now. Never mind that. It was worth it. Just for the promise that they'll leave off tormenting Dauphin. And keep an eye on him when they go on the raid. How do I know they'll keep their promise? I don't. But I can't take the chance that they won't. Any old worn out, frayed scrap of hope I have that Dauphin will come through this craziness, I have to hold onto with my teeth.

✠   ✠   ✠

They came back at eleven. And I was waiting there, outside the house at the foot of that ladder, with Oliver's pistol in my hand.

He kept it on the crate of guns that Martha used for a nightstand next to their bed. I just crept past the bed, lifted it off, and went outside with it. Stood there in the moon-flooded night and listened to the frogs singing "Amazing Grace" with that cold, leaden, heavy, killing thing in my hand. It was an Allen & Thurbers revolver. Large sized. Probably the same one Oliver used to help kill those men in Kansas when he was sixteen.

I sat there on the ground thinking what a pitiful god-forsaken family we were, for all of Pa's Bible reading and Sabbath keeping. How we were all a little deranged from what Pa had done to us. Except maybe Sarah and Ellen at home. And their time would come, I was sure of it. Look at me. Fifteen and here I waited in the dark near midnight with a large-sized pistol in my hand, perfectly willing to shoot these two men in the feet if they didn't come home on time.

I could hear the sound of snoring men from the upstairs window. They'd kept Dauphin here tonight instead of sending him across the road. Kept him awake until ten. I patted Cuffee and waited. The night was silent except for the sound of snoring. And the frogs. Once I heard a hooty owl call. Another time I heard some creature of the night foraging in the brush. The rain had stopped. The moon came out from behind some clouds.

Then I heard them coming through the woods and across

the field. They had a lantern in their hands and it cast an unearthly glow on the ground before them.

"Hey," Hazlett nudged Leeman. "She's here."

"Told you she'd be. Crazier than a hooty owl. It runs in the family."

"Douse that lantern," I told them. "You're late."

Leeman drew out a pocket watch, peered at it and showed it to me. It was exactly eleven. He grinned, then doused the lantern.

"Get up the ladder," I said. "And be quiet. Dauphin's just gotten to sleep. He needs his rest. Pa will be home tomorrow and we can't let him know anything's amiss."

They started up the ladder. It wasn't so dark that I couldn't see the gleam of admiration in their eyes as I stood there with Oliver's pistol. It runs in the family, Leeman had said. What? Craziness? Or determination? "C'mon, Cuffee," I said. "Let's go to bed. I don't think it matters anymore, which."

Chapter Fifteen

Pa tried to get loans to save himself, but he couldn't. He'd wanted to be rich and done everything to try. Raised prize sheep, bred horses, invested in land. But always he failed. He lost Westlands, his farm in Ohio. A neighbor bought it at auction. When the neighbor came round to take possession, Pa, John, Jr., Jason, and Owen holed up in a barn on the property and held off the neighbor, the constable, and a posse. Pa was finally arrested. Later on they sold all his possessions at a public auction, but Pa was allowed to keep some things so the family could live. Things like dishes and wooden pails, blankets, bushels of potatoes, beans and soap, Bibles, inkstands, tools, and even two mares and two halters. And some clothing. Pa had to start over again. He had twelve children at that time. And Mama was expecting me.

WHEN PA CAME BACK FROM CHAMBERSBURG THE next day, I never saw his spirit so cast down. He went right upstairs to the garret to sleep. First, though, he asked Martha if she had any lemons.

"No, Father Brown, lemons are hard to come by. Unless a train comes in with a shipment of fresh seafood from the Chesapeake Bay. There could be lemons, if a ship from abroad put in at one of the ports down there."

"Send Watson to find out," he said.

"You want me to make a lemon cake, Pa?"

"No, I want a lemon to suck on, Martha."

She shuddered. "They're so sour."

"My spirit is sour. The Lord has sent me a bitter disappointment. And I need to mortify my flesh and discipline my soul so I am able to know what the Lord wants from me."

Martha and I stared at him. He was haggard and white in the face. He was wilted and there was a haunted look in his eyes. "You want some cool cider?" Martha asked.

"No. Give me water for now. Put some salt into it."

"Salt?"

"Until I get a lemon I'll drink salt water."

"It'll kill you, Father Brown."

"It'll make me strong. Now I'm going upstairs to pray. Have the men assembled in the dining room in an hour. Until then I want quiet."

Nobody knew what to expect. The men assembled in the dining room and waited. Owen, Oliver, Martha, and I stayed in the kitchen. We could hear the low murmurs of the men, their soft, whispered speculation burning low in the room, like a brush fire.

Was he giving up? Had Douglass backed out? Only Shields Green knew, and he'd right across the road to sleep.

"If Pa needs a lemon to suck on it's bad," Owen said. "Out in Kansas at a certain point we were starving. I thought that was sufficient mortification of the flesh. But no, he had to put small stones under his blanket roll when he slept. Said it made his spirit stronger."

It was bad. An hour later Pa stood before us in the dining room and told us that Frederick Douglass was not with him.

"He is a good man," he said, "but he thinks that if we attack federal property it will array the whole country against the abolitionist cause."

Douglass, Pa's darling, the slave who had escaped and made good. Douglass, the great Negro orator, Douglass the dark conscience of the North, Douglass the living instrument of God's will about slavery was not with him.

"We still have Harriet Tubman recruiting for us in Canada, don't we?" Tidd asked.

"No," Pa said. "Douglass brought a message. She's sick, up in Canada."

You couldn't read the men's faces when he told them this. Their faces were stone still. Steadfast. Determined.

"What does it matter?" Owen asked. "Douglass didn't come to our convention in Ontario when we drafted Pa's constitution, did he? Neither did Tubman. Stayed away from it like sheep stay away from slaughter."

"I pleaded for him to come with us. I promised to defend him with my life. I told him he would be the hive for the bees to come to us. But he said no. He will not draw forth his sword out of its sheath."

A movement of impatience from Owen. He was watching Pa. Thinking he was going to start preaching. He wouldn't tolerate that now, Owen wouldn't. And the other men would take their cue from him.

"So, my young Turks, we do not have Frederick Douglass on our side. Or Harriet Tubman. We have nobody but ourselves. And a few stragglers who may yet join us. If there is any man among you here and now who does not believe that, who wants to take the defection of Douglass as a signal to abandon me, let him stand now and tell me so to my face."

There was a general shifting of bodies in chairs. Those on the stairway got up and came down into the room. They just stood there. At first movement seemed absolutely necessary from all the men. And then stillness. Utter stillness and silence.

Then Owen spoke. "Where is Shields Green in all this?"

Pa took a long sip of salt water. "I gave him the chance to go back North. Douglass himself offered to take him."

"And?" Owen asked.

"He said, 'I believe I go wid de old man.'"

They came to life then. There was laughter. Foot stomping. Then yelling. Who needed Douglass? Who needed Tubman? Then hugging, backslapping, even applause.

Watson came in, stood there with bundles in his arms. They went and grabbed him. They drew him into the jubilation. The bundles fell to the floor. Coffee beans scattered. Lemons rolled all over the place. The men picked them up, started playing catch with them.

"Shields Green!" they started chanting. "Shields Green." And "We believe we'll go wid de old man." The more they said it, the funnier it became. Some of them had tears rolling down their faces at the absurdity, the simplicity, the beauty of it.

"And Douglass is the orator?" Kidd cried out. "Douglass? He couldn't put it into words like this. 'I believe I go wid de old man!' By God, it's better than 'I have not yet begun to fight!'"

Watson scooped up some lemons. He held one up. "You want one now, Pa?"

"Thank you, Watson, but no. I should like you to give them to Martha. Tonight we will have lemon cake," Pa said.

I woke up from a deep sleep as if somebody had put a hand on my shoulder.

"What was that noise?"

I strained my ears. Cuffee, too, heard it. He whimpered in his sleep. But all I could hear now was the steady breathing of Martha and Oliver on the other side of the room.

I pushed aside my calico bed curtain. The moon was so bright outside. An August full moon. I thought of home. Nights in North Elba a chill wind would rustle through the cornstalks. You'd need a blanket on the bed. Here it was still hot. As if time had stopped, or at least slowed down.

Is that what was wrong with the South, I wondered? Is that why they had slaves? Because time moved so slow down here they thought God would never catch up with them?

I always liked reaching for that first blanket in August, nights at home. There was such comfort in it. Suddenly I felt such a desire for Mama and home it was like a stabbing, piercing howl inside me.

Maybe that's what had woke me up. My own howling soul. But no. There it was again. Was somebody crying? Mumbling? "Stay here," I whispered to Cuffee, and I crept out of bed and into the hallway.

It was Pa. He was alone at the dining room table, the light of a single candle burning in front of him. He was leaning over his Bible, praying and crying softly. I hesitated, afraid to approach him. If he was sickly, I'd have to wake Owen. Maybe go for Mrs. Huffmaster.

"Pa?" I ventured into the room.

He looked up at me and smiled. "Kitty," he said. At least I think that's what he said.

"Pa? What's wrong?"

"Douglass wouldn't come with me, Kitty. Why wouldn't he come with me? I'm doing this for him and his race."

"It'll be all right, Pa. The men are with you," I said.

He nodded slowly. "He said we're going into a perfect steel trap. And once we're in there, we'll never get out alive. That's what he said. Only I can't tell the men that, can I?"

"No, Pa," I said.

"They believe in me, Kitty. He said that Virginia will blow me and my men sky-high rather than let us hold Harpers Ferry for one hour. That's what he said."

I wanted to run from the room. Go and wake Owen and tell him this. Wake all of them. But my bare feet stuck to the warm floorboards. And I couldn't run. I knew that a team of horses couldn't have dragged me away from that room.

Pa was talking to me. Pa was confiding in me. Pa was telling me things that he had told no one else here. Me. Annie Brown.

"So I'm sitting here praying. Should I go? Or should I retreat into the mountains and wait until a better time? What better time? The Bible tells us, 'there is a time to reap and a time to sow. A time for living and a time for dying.' But it doesn't say anything about a time to attack Harpers Ferry. That's what I told myself, sitting here. Then I thought, well, it doesn't say anything about it being the right time to fight in Kansas, either, does it?"

"No, Pa." I felt as if I were dreaming.

"I've been praying so hard, Kitty. And I think I've come up with an answer. I'm going to wait for a sign. The Lord will send me a sign. He always does. And I'll know it when I see it. I won't say anything to the men. No. But I'm going to wait for that sign. It'll come. Just like I know the pikes are coming soon. Don't you think that's a good idea?"

"Yes, Pa. I think that's a wonderful idea."

"The Lord is testing me. He always does. But I'll come through. You'll see, my girl. I will come through. You'll help me, won't you?"

"Of course, Pa. I'll do anything you want."

"Help me know the sign when it comes. That's all I ask."

"Yes, Pa."

"And don't tell the others what Douglass said to me. Promise me, Kitty."

"I promise, Pa."

He nodded and went back to his Bible reading. In the next moment he was not aware of me at all. It was like I was not even there. I went back to my room and crept into bed.

Had I dreamed it? Outside my window the moon-flooded night seemed alive with things. Eyes, beasts, creatures. The night here had a life all its own. You could almost feel it breathing out there. It was so hot! I lay awake a long time thinking about Pa.

He was taking this business about Douglass bad. And what about what Douglass had said?

A perfect steel trap, he'd said. Virginia would blow them all sky-high.

I ought to tell Owen that. Somebody should know. But how could I betray Pa the first time he'd ever confided in me?

Maybe he was testing me. Testing my loyalty. He did that sometimes with us. Yes, that was it, he was testing me. Tomorrow he'd act like it'd never happened. He'd wait to see if I ran and told anybody what he said.

He'd wait to see if the cock was going to crow for me three times. Like it had for Jason and Salmon. Well, he'd wait then, good and long. Because I wasn't going to let him trap me. He could test me all he wanted. I'd prove worthy.

Still, I was worried about him. And maybe I ought to say something to Owen about it. Just a little something. Oh, how I wished Mama were here. She'd know what to do.

"Owen, I'm worried about Pa," I said the next day. "He's all cast down because of Douglass."

"Pa never stays cast down for long, Annie." He was sitting at the edge of the garden under the arbor, stitching a shirt. It was pleasant and cool here. The vegetables were all at their peak, cabbages, squash, tomatoes. Martha had planted some flowers along the edges. Pink. They seemed so innocent.

I wondered how they could grow out here with all the turmoil and madness inside.

"The garden is pretty," I said.

"Yes." Owen looked around. "This is a right pretty place. I wouldn't mind owning it."

"How did Pa ever find it, Owen?"

He smiled. "He needed a hideaway. A safe house. Mr. Unseld told us about it."

"Safe house?"

"Yes. That's what they call a place where people who are in turmoil, or at war, can go and be in hiding. A refuge."

Safe house, I thought. This place is anything but safe. This place is a refuge for madness.

"I got up in the middle of the night last night, Owen," I said. "And Pa was praying and crying in the dining room. He's having misgivings, Owen. He counted so much on Douglass."

"Let me tell you about, Pa, Annie. He couldn't have misgivings if he tried. He has a fire burning in him, that's all. And that's why he sucks on lemons."

"You mean like a fever?"

"No. I mean like a prairie fire. It started in Kansas and it never went out. Sometimes it burns low, is all, and sometimes it takes a wind to whip it into a frenzy."

"Or a sign?"

"What do you mean by sign?"

"I don't know, but it scares me, Owen. He talked to me last night. But somehow I don't think he knew it was me. He looked at me and he called me Kitty. Who's Kitty, Owen?"

He threaded his needle, bit the thread off, and tied it.

He didn't look at me. "It's what he used to call Amelia. His kitty cat. You were too young to remember."

Amelia! Pa had spoken to me, and I'd felt so proud. Not

only had he spoken, but he'd confided his fears. With a voice so soft and a need so strong, I almost went and put my arms around him.

But he wasn't talking to me at all! He was talking to the dead Amelia!

"What did he say?" Owen asked.

"He said he was waiting for a sign. He looked right at me, Owen. And asked Kitty to help him know the sign when it comes."

"He mourns Kitty, Annie. I don't know how to explain it in the light of the fact that he lost so many young 'uns. But he was home when the others died. He held them in his arms. He was away from us for a year when Kitty died. In Springfield, Massachusetts, being a commission agent for wool growers. We were in Akron, Ohio. He'd write us letters from his little room in the Massasoit Inn, letters filled with fears. He was obsessed with the idea that the house would burn down, that we boys should be careful disposing of the fireplace ashes. Or that the snow would pile on the roof of the shed and it would break, killing the cows or one of us. Then something did happen."

I nodded. "I caused Amelia to be scalded."

"You didn't cause it, Annie. It just happened. But when Pa found out, he near went crazy. Blamed himself because he was more concerned with making money for the country's wool growers than being with his family. The separation from his family made him awful homesick, and he wrote to us often that his own plight should make him feel more for the slaves, ofttimes separated permanently from family. I think somehow Kitty is in the front of his mind now. She always seems to be when things get bad. He used to talk to her in Kansas, too. Right before we went on a raid. It's interesting. Maybe he's getting ready to act. Means all this sitting around will soon be over. Let's just hope he gets his sign, Annie, that's all."

Well then, I'd help him get it.

But how? I didn't know. What kind of a sign was Pa looking for? What kinds of signs were there? I wished brother John was here. He could tell me.

I remembered when I was little back in Ohio and Pa first went into the sheep business. I must have been about two, but I distinctly remember that one day he found a lost, near-frozen baby lamb, near dead, and brought it into the house in his arms. Pa had thousands of sheep, but this one was important to him, I suppose. He put the baby lamb into a pot of warm water and dipped it in and out until it became well again. It made a mess on the floor, and Ruth complained.

"If it lives, it's a sign," he told her, "that I'll make it in the sheep business."

It lived. Pa was a good man with sheep. The best. Which was why he was able to open a wool depot, and all the wool farmers in eastern Ohio, Virginia, and western Pennsylvania looked to him for advice and made him their agent.

Eventually he failed, of course. Like he failed in everything except quickening the country to the evils of slavery. But the failure wasn't his. As Pa explained it to us, it was because his wool went at a cheaper price in England. And because the British wool buyers ripped into his bales and pawed over the wool. "I was humiliated," he told us, "by some of the shameful, dishonest practices of some American wool farmers. They wrapped bad wool inside good wool at market, in England. And when the British buyers examined my fleece they injured it so that it was not able to be sold again."

I thought about all this as I walked the mile on the dusty road to Mrs. Huffmaster's.

She was setting out wash on the fence to dry. Her whites looked grayer than our men's shirts before they washed them. I wondered how she could see somebody's aura needed fixing and not that her own clothes needed whitening.

"Yer got trouble, ain't you?" she asked.

I shrugged. "What's a sign?"

She shook out an old pair of britches and threw them over a bush. "Depends."

"On what?"

"On who's doin' the lookin'. And how alert they be. And how much they believe in what they're lookin' fer. And at, when it comes."

Well, I thought, did you expect this to be easy, Annie Brown?

"I'm doing the looking," I lied. "My ma isn't going to be able to come down. She's feeling poorly this summer. And I was wondering if I should go back home or stay."

She was watching my face as I spoke. As if my words were live things. As if she could see them coming out of my mouth. Did they have horns? Or wings?

"'Pears to me, you should go home to yer mama."

"But she has my sisters Ruth and Sarah. And Pa needs me here. Martha's expecting and I can't leave the burden to her."

She nodded, satisfied. "Doan look too hard fer it."

"For what?"

"The sign. Just go 'bout yer bizness. Make like yer not lookin'. But take notice. Always. Be there a ring round the moon an' no rain follows? Is a certain body where they ain't supposed to be? Sayin' somethin' they couldn't know? Is the bread you burnt yesterday tastin' fresh and sweet? Do somebody say somethin' to you same as yer just thinkin' it? Or before? Could be anythin'. Doan look for grand, though. No burnin' bushes in the yard. Maybe a flower that got trampled yesterday is fresh and purty today. Look fer somethin' grand an' you'll never see it."

I nodded. "Thank you, Mrs. Huffmaster."

"Hope she be arright."

"Who?"

"Yer ma. I'll make a cornhusk doll. And soak it in cow's urine. Then I'll put it on the hearth. If it burns, your mother will get well."

"Thank you, Mrs. Huffmaster."

"I did it fer you when you had the concussion. Won't you come inside and set a spell? We could make the doll now if you want."

"No. I must get home. I have some mending to do." I accepted a cold cup of water from her well and started on the long, hot walk home.

I'd show Pa I was just as good as Kitty, any day.

Chapter Sixteen

I think Pa feared me as much as I feared him. Lord knows, he had reason to. The year I was born, four of his children died, Peter, Charles, Sarah, and Austin. Then there was baby Amelia's dying, and I know Pa holds me responsible for it, no matter what anybody says. Even though he's never said a word to me about it, I know he holds me accountable. And there I was at the Kennedy farm that summer instead of Ma. He was near beside himself when I first came, I know it. "Annie," he was probably thinking, "I know I invited her, but did she have to come? This is all I need for the whole thing to go wrong." I think that's why he kept me outside so much, and made me a lookout. He used to call me "strange Annie" in his letters home to Ma. "How is our strange Annie?" he'd write. I know I was always a hex to Pa. And things were strange enough at the farm to begin with.

HE LAST WEEK IN AUGUST DRAGGED LIKE A CROW WITH a broken wing. Everybody seemed to be tiptoeing around, waiting for something to happen.

"For what?" I asked Owen.

"For Pa to make his move," he told me.

"What'll decide him?"

"I suppose when he gets the sign."

He was teasing me. Owen believed in signs about as much as Pa believed in President Buchanan. But I was glad for the teasing. All the men seemed to have taken their cue from Pa, who was still cast down. There was no more singing at night.

And far less horseplay. They set about, instead, cleaning guns again, mending holsters, going over military manuals, and writing home. In that last week of August there was a regular spell of letter writing for some reason.

Watson wrote to Belle. "I dream of you at night. I would gladly come home and stay with you always, but for the Cause which brought me here. Kiss the baby for me. I scarce know him."

Stevens wrote love letters to someone named Jennie Dunbar in Ohio.

Jeremiah Anderson wrote to his brother. "We go to win at all hazards." Martha saw the letter.

Leeman wrote his mother. So did the Coppocs and Will and Dauphin.

Dangerfield wrote to his wife. "I love you, I miss you, I cannot come now, but will come in the future. This is why I am here." He showed me the letter.

Then Pa did something strange. For the first time ever, he read the letters. He walked into the dining room and picked them up, one after another. He put down Dangerfield's letter and spoke to the men. "After tonight all correspondence, except business of the company, will be dropped. If everyone must write some girl or friend telling or showing our location, and telling, as some of you have done, all about our matter, we might as well get the whole thing published at once in the *New York Herald*. Anybody who expects his friend to keep a secret for you is a stupid fool. Why should they? You can't keep it yourselves."

He insisted that all letters go out under the name of I.

Smith & Sons, Harpers Ferry. Then he enclosed them in one large envelope to John Kagi in Chambersburg, Pennsylvania. From here on, he said, all mail would come to us through Kagi.

Pa still brooded. He had days when he wouldn't speak to any of us. It seems that a man named Henry Carpenter of Medina County, Ohio, who had sworn allegiance to Pa, now wasn't coming.

Most certainly Pa didn't speak to me. And he never mentioned that night when he had confided in Kitty about his fears. I suppose he really thought he was talking to Kitty.

I was sitting on the porch reading Shakespeare the first week in September.

Sister, have comfort, all of us have cause to wail the dimming of our shining star. Richard the Third.

I looked across the yard at the leaves of the silver poplar tree, rustling in the September breeze. At that moment, two little birds came flying around my head, chirping and chirping. What were they? Oh, the wrens that had a nest under the porch. They flew around me, then perched on the porch railing, then went back to their nest, where their babies were setting up a grievous bad din. Then the wrens would appear on the porch railing again.

Something was wrong. I could see their distress. I dropped the book from my lap and ran into the house. Where was everyone?

No one but Pa was in the dining room, seated at the table pouring over his maps. "Yes, Annie?" he looked up.

"Pa, the birds. The ones who have a nest under the porch. They're fussing something terrible."

I expected to be chided for interrupting him. But he got up. "Let's go and see what the problem is."

We went down the porch steps and around the front of the house. The nest was between one of the supporting posts of the porch and the porch itself. Before we got to it, Pa put a hand on my arm. "Go no further, Annie. Fetch me that big stick over there."

I stared. A large, shiny snake was slithering up the post of the porch, making for the bird nest. I ran for the stick. "Be careful, Pa," I whispered.

How silly I sounded. Pa be careful of a snake? He was taking on the whole federal government! But a snake! It could coil itself to strike. If it touched him with its fangs, he would be poisoned!

Pa didn't stop to study on any of that. He just beat that old snake to the ground, then he picked up a large rock and smashed it. "Yea, though I walk through the valley of the shadow of death, I will fear no evil," he said, "for the Lord my God is with me."

He looked like some half-mad Moses, standing there praying. His arms were upraised. I should think he'd frighten the wrens more than the snake. But they were delighted with the whole spectacle. They flew right back to their babies in the nest. And by the time Pa got done praying, and we were back up on the porch, they were on the porch railing again, singing as if their hearts would burst.

Pa stopped, put his hand on my arm, and looked at them.

"They asked for my help, Annie," he said. "Don't you think it strange, the way they came and asked for my help?"

I said, "Yes, Pa."

"They were helpless and asked me for help. It's a sign, Annie."

I stopped dead in my tracks. A sign? The birds? The snake?

Then I heard Mrs. Huffmaster's voice. *Take notice. Always. But doan look for grand. No burnin' bushes in the yard. Maybe a flower that got trampled yesterday is fresh and purty today.*

Or maybe some birds about to have their babies eaten by snakes are now saved.

I felt the gooseflesh rise on me. A sign!

Pa was certain of it. He was jubilant. "It's an omen," he said, "an omen that I shall be successful." He went to the foot of the stairs to call the men to him. They came down reluctantly, cautiously, wondering what possessed him now.

"Annie called my attention to the birds," he told them, "and they were about to be eaten by a snake. A serpent, men. Ready to devour the innocent. I smashed him and he lies dead out there on the ground. Like all tyrants who oppress shall soon lie dead in Virginia. Annie? Annie, come in and tell them what happened."

So I went in and told them. And if I felt a little foolish, I also felt wonderful good. He had asked Kitty to help him find the sign. But Annie had found it. Hadn't she?

That night the pikes came. The long-awaited pikes, down from Chambersburg.

We were all asleep when the Pennsylvania Dutch farmer

leading his team came up the hill and into our yard. Cuffee heard them first and started barking. Oliver was out of bed like a shot, hitching his holster around his waist, pulling on his britches.

"Ho! Anybody to home?"

The house came alive. Lamps were lit. Boots clattered down the stairs. We all stood on the porch and held lanterns above the head of a rawboned young farmer in a black brimmed hat, next to a wagon and a team of four beautiful horses.

"Who's there?" Pa called out.

"Jacob Munster of Pennsylvania. I haf here a shipment for Isaac Smith and sons."

"Who sent you?" Pa asked.

"Mr. Kagi from Chambersburg. I haf boxes of goods. Some long. Some not so. Shipped down from Connecticut from a Mr. Blair."

A jubilant cry went up from the men. Pa hushed them. "He mustn't know what's he's brought," he whispered. "He's a Quaker. See the way he's dressed? We mustn't endanger him." Then aloud. "You are most welcome, Mr. Munster."

"I unload for thee?"

"No," Pa said, "no. My sons will unload. Come into the house, Mr. Munster. Annie, do you have any ham and bread? Coffee?"

I moved to go. Then Owen was beside me. "Keep him occupied and talking, Annie."

"About what?"

"Anything. Admire his team. Ask him about the ride down

here. Ask about his family. Just keep him talking, so he doesn't notice how heavy those boxes are and how many men it will take to lift them."

His hair was like yellow straw, and it hung below the collar of his fresh white shirt. His face was open and innocent. He wore black trousers and suspenders. He ate like a boy, requesting eggs with his ham and bread. "Thee haf chickens?"

"No. We buy eggs from a neighbor."

"Thee farms?"

"My pa and brothers are down here to buy cattle to take back to New York."

"Mr. Kagi told me I was carting farm tools."

I thought fast. "Yes. My pa is helping a lot of the farmers hereabouts to turn their fields into pastureland. Maybe raise sheep. My pa knows all about sheep. He raised them once."

I think he did not believe me. "The land here is good. Better even than Pennsylvania. I saw much of it on my journey. Here I would live if not for slavery."

"That's a handsome team you've got there, Mr. Munster."

"Why would farmers in Maryland want to raise sheep? They have slaves to tend their fields."

I shrugged. "Farmers are always looking for new ways to make money, aren't they?"

Now I saw something more in those innocent blue eyes. Knowledge. Anger, even. It made them bluer. Did he suspect he'd been carrying those deadly pikes? Had he pried open one of the long boxes? If he had, would he recognize them as weapons? He, a man of peace? And if he did, would he talk? We could be in a passel of trouble here.

"How big is your farm, Mr. Munster?"

"Five hundred acres. Corn and wheat. Potatoes, squash, beans. I haf only daughters. Five daughters. The oldest is fifteen. But they help good. Has thee seen slaves down here?"

"No," I lied. Thank heavens Shields Green and Dangerfield Newby were bedded down across the road.

"I have seen slaves in the fields as I drove along. It is an abomination to the Lord, slavery. A blot on our land. How does thy father feel about slavery?"

"He hasn't given it much thought," I said. "He hasn't had time, what with raising a family and all. Would you like me to pack you a napkin of food, to take back with you?"

His stare got bluer and graver. "Anyone can haf a good farm with all those slaves working in the fields. My girls work hard. But this summer the drought comes. And so now I must use my team to haul goods and make money. And then came the fire."

"Fire? Because of the drought?"

"No. Because of the Fugitive Slave Act. Because I harbor in my barn a runaway. They found out, the officials, and burned it down."

I felt a bolt of fear run through me. "Will you make anything for this trip?"

"Eighty-five dollars," he said. He stood up.

Eighty-five dollars? Pa will have kittens, I thought. Maybe I should have told him we're against slavery. He's madder than a wet raccoon about what he's seen here in Maryland.

And here I am acting like Pa doesn't give a tinker's damn about slavery. I wrapped some extra meat, bread, and cheese in a napkin for him. I cut some cake. I put some cider in a small jug. "This ought to hold you for a while, Mr. Munster," I said.

Were the men finished unloading the boxes of pikes yet? I prayed they were. He was going back outside. I followed.

Watson and Oliver had the last box and were bringing it into the storeroom. I watched Mr. Munster go over to Pa, who was patting the horses.

"I told Mr. Munster all about how you're going to use those tools he brought to help the farmers hereabouts turn some of their fields into pastureland for sheep, Pa," I said.

Pa was quick to take up on things. "Why don't you get some feed for those horses, Annie?"

I ran to do so.

"Nice team, Mr. Munster," I heard Pa saying. "I always admired those farms in Pennsylvania. God has smiled on you and your people."

"Perhaps because we go against slavery," Mr. Munster said.

Pa would never admit to coming down on slavery. I was sure of it. He'd lie at the gates of heaven to protect his plans. When I got back with the feed, I saw Pa was upset. All the men except Owen had gone back into the house. Owen helped me feed the horses.

"Eighty-five dollars!" Pa was saying. "That's dear."

"Took my team away from the farm for days. Left my wife and girls to tend to things alone. I haf no sons. My girls work the fields. Thee haf plenty of sons, sure 'nuf."

"It's nigh on to being outrageous," Pa said.

"My barn was burned because I sheltered a runaway slave."

I saw Pa's blue eyes darken, fill with something. What? Pity? Admiration? Distrust? The man could be lying, and Pa knew it. The man could be fishing for information. Or he may have found out who Pa was and was simply using a burned barn to raise the freight price.

If Mr. Munster knew what was good for him, he'd back off. Then I saw the man's eyes. Bluer than God's, defiant, righteous, angry at Pa. For having so many sons. For not standing up to slavery.

Pa reached into his pocket, drew out his beaten billfold, and withdrew the money. "Have a safe trip back, Mr. Munster," he said.

We watched him drive off, down the hill, with that beautiful team. I know Pa was thinking of the horses he'd once bred and trained back in Ohio, before he'd gone bankrupt.

"Let's get back to bed," Pa said. "It'll be a busy day tomorrow. The men have to fix the pikes. And I'll have to be up early, writing letters to my backers. This Quaker farmer took the last of my money. I'll have to beg for a little further aid, humiliating as it is to me."

Chapter Seventeen

In the summer of 1845 Pa told Salmon and Watson if they caught the flies that were badgering the sheep, he'd pay them ten cents a fly. Watson was ten then, Salmon nine. The flies caused the sheep to get worms in their heads. Well, Salmon and Watson worked so hard catching those flies. Then Salmon gave Pa a bill. But Pa never paid them. He used the money to buy The Rise and Progress of Religion in the Soul *and gave it to Salmon. He bought* The Saints Everlasting Rest *for Watson. The boys cried. So Pa bought Salmon a pocketknife he'd wanted, only he broke off the points. Salmon didn't want that pocketknife with the points broken off. I don't know what he bought Watson. Probably nothing.*

I NEVER DID UNDERSTAND THE FUSS OVER THOSE pikes. But now that I saw them, watched the men putting them together, I realized what dreadful things they were. Pa had paid Mr. Blair, a forge master, five hundred dollars for a thousand of them. Blair worked for Collins Company in Connecticut. They made the best edged tools.

These were edged tools, all right.

The poles were about six feet long. Then there were the ugly-looking, double-edged blades that came with them. And the job the men had now was to attach all those blades to the poles.

It kept them plenty busy. That was a lot of attaching to do.

Watching them, it all came together for me. The whole sanity of Pa's plan.

Or maybe the madness of it. I didn't know.

The reason for all those pikes was the slaves. Slaves had never been permitted to fire a gun, much less ever hold one. So Pa didn't contract for a thousand Sharps rifles. Slaves wouldn't know what to do with them. But shove a pike into their hands, Pa figured, and they would know. Anybody would know.

The men worked for a full week fixing those double-edged blades to those poles. Pa wrote his letters. I sat on the porch reading *Richard the Third*.

"Death and destruction dogs thee at thy heels; thy mother's name is ominous to children. If thou wilt outstrip death, go cross the seas, and live with Richmond, from the reach of hell. Go, hie thee, hie thee from this slaughterhouse, lest thou increase the number of the dead."

I could have been reading *Romeo and Juliet*, of course. But the mood of *Richard the Third* seemed to fit the nature of things at the farm better.

Besides, I didn't have to read *Romeo and Juliet*. They were doomed lovers, weren't they? I had the uneasy feeling that I was learning all about doomed lovers, watching Dauphin working on those pikes, sitting with the men, scarcely looking at me when I came in with cider or coffee.

I just knew that I'd already lost him. If not for good, then for now, at least. He wanted so much to be part of the men that he didn't look at me when I'd set the coffee down in front of him. Well, I'd done that myself, hadn't I? Hadn't I told him I didn't want to come between him and the men? Or was it just that he knew that death and destruction was dogging him at the heels? And the last thing he wanted was to look at me, to meet my eyes, to remember what we had between us.

I never saw anything as beautiful as Maryland in September. I always liked fall best. But up home it came and went like a redbird on the windowsill. One minute the leaves were yellow, next minute they'd be on the ground. Here the leaves stayed yellow longer. Some even turned red. And the sun was like filtered gold seen through them.

Yet, at the edges of the garden the Johnny-jump-ups, the sweet williams, the larkspur were still blooming. I thought I could stay here forever. There seemed to be a smoky haze over the hills, and the smell of wood smoke, mixed with that of a nippy morning, was the nearest idea to heaven I could think of. I wanted to live here with Dauphin. Maybe send for Mama and the younger girls. I thought with dread of the long, cold winters in North Elba.

We'd be going back there soon. That's what Martha said. Oliver told her likely we'd be leaving by the end of the month.

I was struck by some kind of dumb terror thinking on it, then wondered why. Had I thought this idyll would go on here without end? With me reading Shakespeare on the porch and learning new words like *idyll*? With Martha in the kitchen, always humming and making delicious bread? With the men joking and playing checkers and singing after supper?

I had fallen into the ways of it. I liked being one of only two girls here, being privy to the men's jokes, and feeling the warmth of loyalty amongst them.

Something was going on here of importance. And I was part of it. It came to me one night when Tidd was reading the *Baltimore News American.* "A man named Drake has found oil near Titusville, Pennsylvania," he said. "And the Constitutional Convention has opened in Kansas."

Tidd shook the paper out in his hands. "They'll be writing about us one of these days," he said.

He was right. And that's when it came to me. These men were going to make history.

"I just hope they spell my name right when they do," Edwin Coppoc said.

When their names did get into the papers Martha and I wouldn't be here, of course. We would be back home. And then I had another thought. But this one discomforted me. They would make history if they succeeded, yes. But they'd also make history if the state of Virginia blew them sky-high, like Frederick Douglass said it would.

And if that thought wasn't enough to afflict me, one day I wandered into the dining room and found a letter Pa was writing to Mama. I read it, and wished I hadn't.

". . . make sure Jason and Salmon put a new roof on the barn so the stock will make it through the winter. I shall be sending along four pairs of blankets. I have acquired them through Kagi in Chambersburg. They ought to help you get through the winter. Make sure Sarah and Ellen are warm enough. Also, I would like Oliver's Martha and Watson's

Belle to have a home with you, should they, and I, not return. For the present I can send no money, but shall try to send some home with Annie. For the present I give you my blessing and commend you always to the God of my fathers."

There were some lines written and scratched over. The letter was not finished. But it was as final for me as anything ever could be.

Pa didn't expect to live through the raid. And maybe Watson and Oliver wouldn't either.

The knowledge of it fell upon me like a blow. Like something final. Like a killing frost in North Elba. I hid the letter under some other papers on the dining room table so Martha wouldn't see it.

Two things happened the second week in September. Leeman and Hazlett, my invisibles, escaped again. And Johnny Cook and I mended our quarrel. I was glad for the chance of it. Things were coming to a head and I didn't want to leave off bad with any of the men.

Cook came to the farm one evening mad as a skunk in daylight at Pa. Nobody was expecting him. Supper was over. I was going out the door into the blue night that was gathering around the cabin to take my place of watch on the porch. Cook was coming up the steps.

"Where's your pa?"

I looked up into the face of this man who considered himself a crack shot, who wrote poetry and swore half the women in the Ferry were in love with him. I was about to make a smart retort, chide him for his rudeness. And then I saw the pain in his face.

"Inside. What's wrong?"

He was visibly trembling. "He's a devil, your pa. You realize that, don't you?"

"What's he done?"

"Made arrangements, without telling me, for my wife to be sent to Chambersburg."

"Sent your wife away?" I was confused.

"Made arrangements," he said again, as if I was simpleminded. "How does he know I want her in Chambersburg? She can stay right here with her mother, can't she? What's he doing in there?"

"Going over his maps. Writing letters."

"I'm going to have at it with him." But he didn't move. Just stood there, glaring at the blue dusk. "What kind of mood is he in?"

"Good. Martha made his favorite supper. Sunfish fried to a golden brown. Owen caught it in a nearby stream."

"Does he think he can just run everybody's life? Push us around like checkers on the board?"

I didn't answer. What did he expect me to say? He knew Pa as well as I did.

"I'm not afraid of him, Annie Brown," he said.

I understood, and smiled. "My brothers are. Watson's always saying that Pa wants his sons to be brave as tigers and still be afraid of him."

That took him by surprise. "Not Oliver and Owen."

"All of them. For all their bravado. So are the rest of the men, for all their drinking and cussing behind his back and mimicking him, like Edwin Coppoc does. One minute they're adoring him, next hating and fearing him."

He gave me a savage look. "And you?"

"One minute I love him, next I'm figuring ways to throw him off this porch. He's got me so confused, I don't know my own name half the time. Why should you be any different?"

That took the starch out of him. But he said nothing.

"Pa doesn't like being pushed, Mr. Cook. Makes him push back. And Pa's a hard pusher. My mama always told us, you get more out of Pa with honey than with vinegar."

He drew in his breath, shoved his hands in his pockets, and nodded. But I could see this was hard for him. He was descended from Puritan stock, Owen said. A hard-edged New Englander.

I felt sorry for him. He was all mooded up, twitching and pacing like a cat on a griddle. All the men were that way lately. The time must be coming close. "Likely Pa was trying to get her in a good safe house," I said. "With you part of the raid, you wouldn't want her anywhere near the Ferry, would you?"

"He still had no right to make arrangements without telling me. Shows you what he thinks of me. Nothing. After all I've done for him, too."

"I heard him say he was going to send you down the Charleston Pike, Mr. Cook. To get information on the slave population."

I knew that would bring him around. It did. It pleasured him. He'd always wanted to do this and Pa had managed to hold him back from it all summer. "You sure?"

"It's what I heard."

"Thank you, Annie. You saved me from making a fool of myself."

"It's all right, Mr. Cook."

"Maybe I can do something for you now. When I brought my horse around back a minute ago I saw Leeman and Hazlett in the woods. They were smoking and drinking. Said they'd lounge around there a while, then head for my house. Maybe we could do some drinking tonight at the Ferry. Aren't you supposed to keep them from wandering off?"

I started to move. "Oh, Pa will kill me."

He put a hand on my arm. "Look, maybe I can help. I'll go inside and talk to him. Keep him busy. You run around back and fetch them. Tell them I won't be home tonight. That I've decided to take my Mary Virginia to dinner at the Wager House."

"Oh, thank you, Mr. Cook!" I ran down the stairs and around back to find Leeman and Hazlett.

"Well, if it ain't Kitty," Leeman said.

I came upon them in the woods behind the kitchen garden. They were sprawled on the ground, smoking and playing cards. On the ground between them was a single lantern burning low and a silver flask. I think they were already well in their cups.

"Kitty?" I stopped short.

Leeman took a draw on his cheroot. "It's what the old man calls you when you ain't around. Didn't you know?"

"When did he call me that?"

"The business with the birds and the snake. After you told us about them and left the room, he says, 'That's my Kitty. Always knew she'd show me the sign.'"

There was no possible way Leeman could know about Kitty. There was no way, short of having uncommon powers, that he could know how what he had just said would undo me. And he did not have uncommon powers. His powers, if they could be called such, were of the variety found in the lowest species of man.

And right now the lowest species of man was looking up at me with a leer on his face.

But somehow, what he said did not diminish my spirit, but roused it. "Go back to the house! Now!" I said. "Go on back up that ladder and into the garret, or I'll tell Pa."

They thought that was a hoot, for sure. They looked at each other and laughed. And when they finished laughing, Leeman reached for the flask. I stooped down and took it up in my hands.

"Aw, c'mon, Kitty."

"Don't call me that!"

"Your pa does."

"It's what he used to call me when I was a little girl. I'm grown now. I can't help it if he still calls me that on occasion."

Hazlett nudged Leeman. "She's all growed now. You hear?"

"I hear. Like she had to tell us."

I blushed. In all my weeks at the farm none of the men had acted toward me with any bold intent. They had too much respect for Pa. And my brothers. But in their present state these two did not know the meaning of the word respect, if they ever had.

"Arright, Annie then," Leeman said. "Annie, is it?"

"Yes, it's Annie."

"Annie-all-growed. Gimme the flask. You're growed, then you know a man needs a little comfort now 'n' then. Only two ways to get it. A woman or drink. And not seein' any women a man can take a fancy to without gettin' himself in a heap of trouble around this godforsaken place, I need my flask. Bad. So give it on over, Annie-all-growed." Again the leer.

I held the flask away. "Get up and go back inside. And keep your filthy mouth to yourself!"

Leeman got to his feet. They both did. "We're goin' back to the Ferry with Cook," Leeman said.

"You're going back up to the garret."

"Says who?" from Hazlett. He was flinty eyed, though unsteady on his feet.

"Says I. Annie Brown. My pa has given me charge of you. And I say you go back upstairs." I didn't tell them Cook was going to take Mary Virginia to a late supper. I didn't want to use Cook. I wanted to do this myself. They must respect me. They must honor the position of authority Pa had given me. Just like I honored whatever authority he gave to everyone else.

"Thought we had an agreement," Hazlett said. "You let us go into town when we want and we'll take care of your little buttercup boy when we do the raid."

The raid. I didn't want to think about it. I hadn't, since I'd read Pa's letter home to Mama. I'd pushed it from my mind. But now I must think about it, it seemed. Now I must think about a lot of things.

How terrible that these two disreputable beings, the worst element in Pa's Provisional Army, should make me face those things.

But in those moments, with the blue Maryland night gathering around us, the first stars twinkling overhead, the lantern glowing at our feet, I looked at them as if through a cracked and smoky mirror. I saw fear in their faces. And it reflected my own.

You're all going to be blown sky-high when the state of Virginia catches up to you, I wanted to tell them. And you're not going to be able to protect Dauphin. Likely you won't even be able to take care of yourselves.

But they knew it. I saw that they knew it. And that was why they wanted to run away to the Ferry and drink the night away. To forget what they knew.

Why should they be allowed? When the other men were upstairs mending holsters, oiling revolvers, and studying military manuals. And likely they knew, too. And were going into it head on, without flasks or visits to Harpers Ferry to sustain them. Without their womenfolk.

Dauphin had even distanced himself from me so that he wouldn't weaken in his resolve. I saw that clear now. And I'd dishonored him by making deals with these two no accounts. Well, I would do it no longer.

"Dauphin doesn't need your protection," I said. "He can take care of himself. Now go back in the house. Or I'll tell Pa. I swear it."

They went. I picked up the lantern and blew it out. I followed them around to the side of the house and stood there while they climbed the ladder. I gave them back the flask. It was near empty anyways.

I didn't have Oliver's pistol this time. I didn't need it. I had Dauphin's honor. And if that wasn't enough, I had myself. Annie Brown. All growed.

Chapter Eighteen

All the while we were growing up, Pa was known for his honest and clean living. My brothers told me about the man who once worked in Pa's tanning yard in Pennsylvania, who stole some goods. Pa called him into the barn and made him confess, then told him to go back to work and be honest and no one would ever say a word about it again. Another time a man stole a cow and Pa helped send him to prison. Yet all that terrible winter he traveled through the snow to bring the man's family provisions, so they wouldn't starve.

I FELT CONSIDERABLE BETTER AFTER MY SET-TO WITH Leeman and Hazlett. It had decided me on a lot of things. For one, I wasn't about to take any guff from the men. For two, if they saw me as growed, to use their expression, I'd best start acting growed.

For three, it was too late now for any of us to do anything about the forthcoming raid. So I might as well face it with dignity and honor as with fear and whining.

Once you decide to do that, things change. You start to feel good and at peace with yourself.

Of course there were times when I backslid, when a terror would take hold of me right in the middle of the day, when I'd get a pain in my innards, contemplating what might happen. And I'd want to seek out Dauphin and beg him again to run off with me. Just leave.

And then it would come to me. I'm growed now, I'd tell myself. If I weren't, the men wouldn't have minded me. But there was the tricky part.

You can be growed and still be scared about things.

I felt cheated somehow. Like being growed wasn't worth all the effort that went into it.

September was going. I don't know where. It was sliding right past my eyes. Daily, I'd sit on that porch and see the leaves turning, feel the change in the air. It was like liquid gold pouring over the hillsides. And the sun had a different cast to it. The squirrels were busier than ever, too, scurrying about collecting nuts. I found a few woolly caterpillars. Owen said you could tell what kind of winter it was fixing to be by where the black stripe was on their brown fur. If it was right smack in the middle of their backs, the beginning and end of winter would be mild and the middle bad. If it was to one side or the other, either the beginning or the end would be bad and the middle good.

"Spring is one end of the caterpillar and fall the other," Owen said.

I asked him how he knew which end was which. Turned out he didn't. "It depends on how you want to look at it," he said.

I supposed that's how my life was right now. Good or bad. Depending on how I wanted to look at it.

✼   ✼   ✼

One evening the last week in September Pa came out to sit on the porch with me.

"Annie," he said, "come, let's take a walk."

This was not good. Pa never asked me to walk with him. Something was amiss. I searched my mind, went over my sins. Then I noticed he had a small box in his hand, but I couldn't see the real nature of it because he kept it in his left hand, and I was walking to his right.

We walked down the front slope. I waited.

"I've told Martha," he said. "Now I'm telling you. On the twenty-ninth, you two leave for home."

I caught my breath and calculated. Today was the twenty-second. So soon? I felt the world coming down on my head. I needed more time. For what I did not know. Thoughts jumbled in my head. How am I going to say good-bye to Dauphin? Suppose I never see him again? "Pa, do we have to?"

"There is no place for you here after the twenty-ninth," he said.

So then, the time was nigh.

"Oliver and Watson will accompany you to Chambersburg. Then Oliver will take you on as far as Troy, New York. From there you'll get the train for Whitehall. When you get home, Annie, I want you to care for your mother. And for Ellen and Sarah. Will you promise me to do that?"

I could not speak. I nodded yes.

"I also want you to remember our reasons for being here. People will be asking you how it was this summer at the Kennedy farm. Remember to tell them our reasons for being here. You know them. You've heard them all your life. A lot depends on you and Martha now. You were here with us. Speak kindly of us, Annie."

Oh daughter of troops, you have your marching orders. Don't question them. But I did.

"Pa, you talk like you're not coming back."

"We go to strike a blow for freedom. I have to talk like that. The tree of liberty has to be watered, every so often, with the blood of patriots. Thomas Jefferson said that."

I nodded numbly. There was no room for discussion here. When Pa started invoking Jefferson, I knew the time for debate was passed.

"The moral high ground hasn't much substance beneath it, Annie. It doesn't hold a man up too long. You have to take your place on it when you can. And draw attention to your cause."

"You're going soon then, Pa?"

"We have to. My money is run out. We can't afford to live here much longer. The men would have to take work. So we go, soon as we can in October."

So, it had nothing to do with Cook's full moon, then, or what might be festering in the souls of the local Negroes. It had to do with something as simple as running out of money.

But all I could do was nod, dumbly. My mouth was dry. Here I had my chance to talk to Pa, say things to him, and I couldn't get a sensible word off my tongue.

He had been speaking to me with his hands behind his back. Now he brought one hand around. It had the box in it. A small box, made of polished wood. "I want to give this to you, Annie," he said.

I just stared at it. Pa had never given me anything. Oh, he'd brought some raisins home for me once, when he came back from one of his many trips. But never anything you could hold in your hands after he was gone out of the room.

I didn't take it. I didn't feel right taking it. It was too beautiful. People only gave away things like this when they were fixing to die.

Maybe if I didn't take it Pa wouldn't die. Maybe none of them would.

"What is it, Pa?" I was stalling for time.

"My friend Dr. Samuel Gridley Howe gave it to me. You know who he is?"

I'd heard the name, but I looked at him, waiting for him to elaborate. He would love that, telling about his friends. And it would give me more time to figure out how not to take that old box.

"He's one of my backers. From Massachusetts. He's an agent of both the Massachusetts and the National Kansas Committee. He once fought in the Greek Revolution against Turkey. Another time he aided the Polish rebels in their insurrection against Russia. He and his wife, Julia Ward Howe, have fought many battles. For better ways to teach the blind. Better ways to help the insane and the feeble minded. He gave me this box. It had a fine Smith and Wesson revolver in it. I can't give you the revolver, Annie. But I want to give you this. Here, take it."

I accepted it. What else could I do? It was warm in my hands. I ran my fingers over the lovely wood. "Thank you, Pa."

"Another thing, Annie. I want you to continue your schooling. I've written to my friend Franklin Sanborn, accepting his offer to take you and Sarah into his school in Massachusetts. He offers to give you a plain but practical education. He says it will enable you to transact the common business of life, comfortably and respectably, together with a thorough training to good business habits that will prepare you to be useful and help you meet the stern realities of life."

What did he think I'd been learning here all summer? "Pa, I know the stern realities of life," I said.

"We all think we do, Annie. But they get sterner all the time. I would like you to take this opportunity, you and Sarah. I've written to your mother, advising her of this. Will you do this?"

I nodded yes.

"So then, all is settled between us," he said.

Settled? I looked up at him. Into his blue eyes. A prairie fire burning in him, Owen had said. A fire that had started in Kansas and never went out. That sometimes burned low or could be whipped into a frenzy. I thought, for a minute, I saw it smouldering there in those blue depths.

"Pa," I said.

"Yes, Annie."

"I'm sorry about Amelia, Pa. I know all these years you've held it against me."

"Amelia? Why speak of that now?"

"It was the red bird, Pa. I saw it on a fence. And I turned to chase it. Ruth was doing the washing and told me to watch her. And then Ruth turned away to bring a bundle of clothes to the line. And I went after the bird and Amelia went into the pot of water. Oh, Pa, I'm so sorry."

The blue eyes went opaque on me. I could see nothing in them now. "No need to speak of that now, Annie."

"But Pa, there is a need! My need! I need to know you forgive me!"

"Not now, Annie." He waved his hand in the air. He turned. He dismissed me. Our discussion was finished. Because he wanted it to be finished. He had that power. To summon you, to engage you in conversation, to build up your trust in him, make you care about pleasing him, make you think he cared about you. Then, when he got his own way with you, when he had what he wanted, your undying devotion and promises, he'd cut you down and leave you hanging.

"I've too much on my mind now, Annie. I've a lot to set straight. This is not the time."

"When, then? When is the time?" I yelled it after him as he walked back up the slope to the house. "When, if not now? You said you wanted things settled between us. So do I! Do only your things get settled?"

He was walking fast up that slope, away from me.

He had my promises, and I had nothing. Except the stern reality of knowing Pa could never forgive me. He left me there holding the empty box.

We had one week, Martha and I, to make our farewells.

Martha behaved the way she always did. The way the Martha in the New Testament did. She worked in the kitchen. That was our Martha's solution to everything.

When I could, I helped her. We made extra loaves of bread for the men, which we wrapped and put in the downstairs storeroom. Martha cured a ham and we picked and pickled the last of the tomatoes. She made a new shirt for Oliver. I made one for Dauphin.

But while she stepped lightly, even sang sometimes, my hands and feet were leaded. Every once in a while I would just stop what I was doing and stand there gazing out through a window, as if trying to fix in my head the line of silver poplar trees, or the oaks and maples behind the house. Or the corn-field next door. Or the sight of the half-blind horse standing patiently in the yard.

Martha would come past me and pat me on the shoulder. "Come on now, we've things to do."

"How can you be so cheerful? We could lose them all."

"We haven't lost them yet, have we?"

"Martha, you don't really think Pa will storm into the Ferry, take it and hold it and go on from there deeper into Virginia, do you?"

"I don't think on it, Annie. If I did I would go outside and jump off that porch in an instant. I just live one minute to the next. Keep putting one foot ahead of the other. It's the only way to be."

But at night when I couldn't sleep, I'd lie there and hear her and Oliver whispering, and I'd think, no wonder she can be cheerful, she's carrying Oliver's child. She takes part of him with her. They've become closer to each other here than ever before. What do I have?

Dauphin and I have grown apart here. This place has ruined things for us.

Every morning I got up and resolved to make it different.

Today I would seek out Dauphin. Or he would seek out me. And we'd have a coming together again. I could feel him looking at me across the room when I helped Martha serve at the table. I could feel his eyes on me. But he did not speak, he did not move outside the lamplight that enclosed him and the men.

Had he changed then, in his feelings for me? Didn't he remember how he'd told me that day at his father's place how we were betrothed, official-like? And we'd wed when this business at the Ferry was done with?

There was only one thing for it. Dauphin did not think he would survive this business at the Ferry. And he didn't want me building up my hopes. Either that or he was tired of being teased by Leeman and Hazlett.

I was wrong on all counts. Dauphin still did care for me, still did consider us betrothed, official-like. He was just waiting for the right moment to make his move, is all. Men! How silly they are! They need the right moment! They don't know that any moment is all right for the woman. They plan things like a military exercise. Feelings aren't enough. No. They have to have reasons!

Well, Dauphin finally got his reason. Cuffee.

Two days after Pa told me that Martha and I were to leave on the twenty-ninth, I decided that I was not leaving Cuffee. I could not leave Cuffee.

Who would take care of him? He was my dog now, my shadow. All I had to do was put my hand down and he would be there for me. There was no leaving Cuffee for me. I wasn't going to.

"Pa, I want to take Cuffee with me when I go." I stood there in the dining room one night. The men were outside, under cover of darkness, behind the house, smoking and talking. As usual Pa was at the table, going over his maps. Only one lamp. Oil was scarce. I stood outside the ring of light it afforded like a mushroom growing in the dark.

"Who's there?"

"Annie, Pa."

I wouldn't have been surprised if he'd said "Annie who?" He was finished with me. After all, in his mind he had settled things with me, hadn't he? I hadn't spoken directly to him since that conversation.

"What's the trouble?"

"No trouble, Pa. I want to take Cuffee with me when Martha and I leave."

"Cuffee?"

"The dog, Pa. He's become my dog. He depends on me. I want to take him home to North Elba."

"Impossible."

"Why?"

"You can't take a dog on a train."

"Are there rules?"

"Of course. There must be."

"I don't think so, Pa. When we were coming down here on the train I saw a lady and she had a cat in a little crate. She carried it all the way on the train."

He looked at me as if he'd never laid eyes on me before. Then I saw the blue eyes focus. Oh, it's only Strange Annie.

"I'm not leaving Cuffee, Pa. There's nobody to care for him. He needs a good home. And we could use him in North Elba. Our dog there is getting old."

He went back to his maps.

"Pa!"

"Annie, don't bother me with this now. Can't you see I'm busy? I've got more important things on my mind than a dog. And you should, too!"

"This is important to me, Pa. I can't lose Cuffee. I love him."

Well, I never should have said such. I should have known better. He started in then, preaching to me about the pet squirrel he'd lost as a child. And how he'd mourned it. "But I came out of it a stronger person," he said.

"I don't want to be a stronger person, Pa. And your squirrel died. Cuffee didn't. He'll just be separated from me and he won't know the reason why."

He didn't even hear me. Started right in on the slaves. And how they had husbands, wives, children sold away from them all the time. There was separation, he said. "What do you think I'm doing all this for, Annie Brown? To end this abomination of slavery. And the evils that go with it."

"Pa, please," I whispered. "Just let me take Cuffee."

He scowled at me. He looked so fierce that for a moment I thought he was going to get up and come across the room and hit me. But all he did was say, "Impossible. You need a crate. There's no wood to make one and nobody to make it anyway. The men are all busy."

"I can make a crate, Captain."

Both of us were startled at the voice. Dauphin. He came and stood beside me. "I'll be happy to make a crate for the dog, Captain," he said. "If that's all that's keeping Annie from taking him."

He took my hand. I wasn't sensible of the fact that I'd been shivering. But apparently I was. His hand was so warm over mine. It gave me strength. Dauphin standing beside me like that and facing Pa was all I needed. I felt strong as Mama. Built for times of trouble.

We must have put Pa on notice, standing together like that. He looked at us, nodded, and went back to his maps. "Go ahead, make the crate then," he said. "If you want to indulge in such foolishment. But Annie, you don't leave your post on the porch."

Chapter Nineteen

Dianthe Lusk, Pa's first wife, could trace her ancestry all the way back to John Adams. But I've heard whispers that there was insanity in the Lusk family. People say my brothers John and Frederick inherited it. I don't know. John was sane enough to stay away from the Ferry. Would Frederick have become involved in the raid if he wasn't killed in Kansas? He had some illness. Nobody could put a name to it. Was it insanity? Pa said Frederick was pretty wild when he was young. Did he take after Dianthe? Or Pa?

PA COULD NEVER GIVE HIS ALL. HE ALWAYS HELD out, keeping something back. I guess that's what Owen meant when he said don't ever make Pa look wrong, he won't stand for it.

Pa let Dauphin make the crate for Cuffee, but I wasn't to be with him while he did it. I was to stay on that porch. Still, I was happy.

Dauphin went right to the storeroom, pulled apart an old crate, and commenced to make one for Cuffee. I would have liked to be with him, to hand him the nails, watch him work. But hearing the hammer had to be enough. He was doing it for me. He'd stood up for me with Pa. And now he was building more than a crate for Cuffee down in that storeroom. He was putting back together, with each board, what we felt for each other. What had been broken apart in the last two months we'd been here. And he was making that crate good and firm, so it would never come apart again.

When I heard the hammering stop, finally, I crept down to the storeroom, Cuffee with me.

"How do you like it?" Dauphin stood there, beaming.

"It's the most beautiful crate I ever saw."

He showed me how the cover worked. It latched and un-latched. It went up and down. "You ought to put an old blanket in there so he'll be closed off and privatelike," Dauphin said. "Then you can poke it down a bit and give him some air. And I'll get a piece of leather and make you a leash. You'll have to walk him whenever you can on the trip. Maybe get him outside when the train stops."

We put Cuffee inside to see if he fit. He did. "Take a lit-tle bowl from the kitchen so's to give him some water. I'll find an old flask. I've been wanting to give you something to take back with you, Annie. But I never got to town. Wanted to buy you a book. Or a bolt of cloth."

"This is the best present I ever had, Dauphin," I told him.

He nodded and we stood there looking down at the crate. In back of us in the storeroom was that same drip, drip, dripping sound I'd heard the day I'd been here with Danger-field Newby when he'd been crying because he knew he couldn't rescue his wife and children. And that if he went on the raid, they'd likely sell her South. Newby had known then that he would never see his family again.

Did Dauphin know that now about me?

"I haven't treated you so right, Annie," he said. "Don't know if you took notice."

"I did, Dauphin Thompson."

He shrugged. "Don't know if I can tell why."

"I can."

He raised an eyebrow. "If you know, you know better'n me."

"You wanted to prove yourself worthy of the men. Be one of them. And so you had to push me aside."

"Didn't mean for that to happen, Annie."

"It's part my fault. I told you I didn't want to come between you and the men. But I think the real reason is because you know this raid may not work. And we may never see each other again. And so you had to put me from your mind, so as not to weaken your resolve."

There was a fair amount of wonderment in his eyes when he looked at me again. "How'd you come to know all that, Annie?"

"Because I love you."

He took me in his arms and held me then. Cuffee whimpered around our feet. "There's another reason. Don't know if I can tell it right."

"Just tell it any way you can, Dauphin."

"The other men. They don't have their women around. Watson doesn't have Belle and I know how it is with them. My brother Will doesn't have his Mary Ann. I just didn't think it right to make much of you in front of them, is all. Can you forgive me, Annie?"

This time I hugged him. "I love you all the more for thinking such, Dauphin."

"When the raid is over, we'll be married. Just like I said. Remember?"

"I remember."

"And we'll build our house. And have children. And Cuffee will be a father someday, maybe."

We laughed at that. The idea of Cuffee being a father! We laughed so hard we ended up crying. And I know it wasn't about Cuffee. I know that in the end it was because we both knew that we would never see each other again when the raid was over.

I asked myself, in the one little corner of my mind that was still open for asking, why we didn't just put Cuffee into that crate and walk off from the Kennedy farm, then and there. Just go out of that storeroom and down the hill with only the clothes on our backs. And make our way.

It would have been so simple, wouldn't it?

But life isn't simple. And we'd both come to a place in it where there was no walking out anymore. I loved Dauphin, my Dauphin, because of what he was. And what he was had to do with his not making much of me in front of the other men because they didn't have their womenfolk with them.

It had to do, too, with his being here in the first place, when he didn't have to be. He'd made some covenant with himself. And those men. And if he broke it, he wouldn't be my Dauphin anymore. So that if we walked out of that storeroom, it would be no good between us anymore.

And I guess that, too, is why we were both crying.

✳   ✳   ✳

Between my watch times on the porch, I helped Martha clean the whole house top to bottom. It was something to do. The labor was hard, but it kept me from thinking. Then we picked all the vegetables in the garden, washed and cooked and stored them. Seeing a garden die at the end of summer always curdles my spirit anyway. Seeing it die here, I knew I'd never be able to tend another garden again without thinking of this one.

After Martha went inside I said goodbye to the flowers, to the Johnny-jump-ups, the sweet williams, the larkspur. I hope you last well into the fall, I told them. But I won't be here to see you. The sun is good here and the house will protect you, so the killing frost won't get you for a long time.

Next we washed the sheets on all the mattresses for the men. That house was cleaner than it had ever been when we got finished.

I went back to my porch watch. Everything in the landscape was changing. At the foot of the trees the underbrush was turning red. Leaves were starting to fall. I knew the position of the shadows from the trees by now. I could tell the time of day from them. I finished reading *Richard the Third*.

"Go gentlemen, every man unto his charge. Let not our babbling dreams affright our souls. Conscience is but a word that cowards use, devised at first to keep the strong in awe. Our strong arms be our conscience, swords our law. March on, join bravely, let us to it pell-mell. If not to heaven, then hand in hand to hell."

The cadence of the words matched some drum in my

soul. And I read them over and over. Then I looked up. From the tree shadows I calculated it to be about four o'clock.

Then I saw the rider coming. I watched him turn his horse off the road and come through our gate at the bottom of the slope.

"Someone's coming!"

I ran in the house and told the men. They were lounging in the dining room. Pa was outside. Someone sent for him. He peered out the window. "Doesn't look like anybody I know. Everybody out of sight. Annie, go meet him."

"Yes, Pa." I went outside and down the porch steps. I started to walk down the slope.

First thing I noticed was he had one eye. The other had a black patch over it.

"Can I help you, sir?"

"Is this the Kennedy farm, where John Brown lives?"

"It's the Kennedy farm, but no one named Brown lives here. Isaac Smith and his sons are renting it for the summer."

He smiled down at me from his horse. "Who are you?"

I didn't like his smile. It was too knowing. "I'm Annie Smith. My pa rents this place."

"Well, Annie Smith, if that is what you must call yourself, you go and tell your pa that Francis Meriam of Framingham, Massachusetts, is here."

"Francis Meriam?"

"Grandson of the abolitionist leader Francis Jackson of Boston. Tell your pa, Annie Smith, that I have six hundred dollars in gold in my saddlebags for his treasury."

"Six hundred dollars?" I blinked. He was dressed like he was well-to-do. Good coat, silk cravat at his throat.

"Can't you do anything but repeat things, girl? I've been a long time looking for Mr. Brown. A Boston Negro told me to seek out Mr. Kagi in Chambersburg. Kagi directed me here. I have just come into an inheritance. After a trip to Haiti I am determined to give a large portion of it to the antislavery cause. That's what's going on here, isn't it? Well, are you dumb, girl? Is this where I may find Mr. John Brown or isn't it?"

"I'll go fetch Pa," I said.

So Pa had money now, money he needed. He was jubilant. He said the money and Meriam were signs that God wanted him to move soon. God was getting impatient. Get on with it, John Brown, God was saying.

He would make a trip to Philadelphia for more arms and supplies. That very afternoon he had Stevens read the provisional constitution to Meriam.

I didn't like the man, gold or no gold. He was slight. He coughed. He had one eye. He looked like the kind of man who had never done a thing of importance in his life, but dearly wanted to. He looked like a man who was not capable of doing a thing of importance. But he had money. And it was going to buy him what he wanted.

Pa administered the oath of fidelity and secrecy to him. And he took it. He was now part of Pa's Provisional Army. Then, that very day, a letter came from Kagi in Chambersburg telling Pa that Osborne Perry Anderson had arrived.

And could someone come and fetch him. Pa was ecstatic. Money, Meriam, and now Anderson all in one day. He left immediately to fetch Anderson. It was less than fifty miles to Chambersburg. He'd be back tomorrow, the twenty-sixth. On the twenty-seventh he would leave for Philadelphia.

Martha and I spent the next day doing more cooking. We even made cakes for the men, wrapped them in wet cloth, and put them in the storeroom.

Late the night of the twenty-sixth Pa arrived with Osborne Anderson, a free black, from Canada. He'd been at the Canada convention with Pa, when they'd made up their constitution. He was twenty-nine, quiet, soft-spoken, and being confined in a house wasn't going to bother him any, he told us. He was a printer by trade. He read books and kept to himself. We scarce saw him.

The next day when Pa left for Philadelphia, he left Owen in charge and instructions for the men. No one was to do anything to bring suspicion down on us now. Things were going too well. And no one was to go off the grounds for any reason.

"I was planning a supper," Martha said. "A special supper the night before Annie and I depart. I need some things from town."

Pa nodded. "Owen can fetch them this afternoon. But no one else is to leave here."

It was in that moment that I remembered that I meant to pay a goodbye visit to Mrs. Huffmaster. The garden had run its course, so she hadn't been around. She didn't know Martha and I were leaving in two days. But Pa looked so severe, I didn't dare ask permission.

He told Martha and me goodbye. He said that when we changed cars in the Harrisburg depot, he'd be returning from Philadelphia. We would meet there for final farewells, he said. Then he left.

That afternoon Owen went to the Ferry with a list of things from Martha. It was market day at the Ferry, and farmers and butchers filled the stalls with fresh produce, meat, fish.

"Buy a little from each stall," Martha told him, "so no one sees you buying too much. Remember there are only supposed to be four men here at the farm."

I ran outside to catch Owen before he left. "Could you get me some lavender water?" I asked.

He smiled. "Getting all gussied up for the trip home?"

"No. I want it for Cuffee. I'm going to bathe him before we leave. And I want him to smell nice."

"Lavender water for a dog?" He scowled. And for the moment I thought he looked like Pa.

"Please, Owen. Nobody wants to smell dog on the train."

"All right, Annie. You never ask for a thing. I suppose you deserve some lavender water. Even if it is for a mongrel dog."

All day, the twenty-eighth, Martha cooked. There was fresh sturgeon, which she stuffed. Buttered beans. Apple pie. There was Maryland duck. There were fresh fruit and good cheese. Buttermilk. Fresh-ground coffee. Owen had even brought home some local wine.

I helped some. But I still had to watch on the porch. Although, with Pa gone, I did my watching from down on the ground, where I bathed Cuffee. Owen filled up the big copper tub for me and I scrubbed him clean. Then Owen brought more water and I put some lavender water in it. Cuffee sneezed and fussed. But I told him he had to put up with the discomfort. It was the only way he'd get to go home with me.

Home.

I stopped what I was doing and gazed down the slope. Every bit of this place was branded on my mind, burned into it. The pioneer fence a little ways down that zigged and zagged. The trees, the bushes, the way you could smell the river in the distance. The wrens who had their nest under the porch. The way the sun sank behind the silver poplar trees in the west. The echo that bounced back at you from down the slope if you shouted or laughed.

I didn't want to go home. I wanted to stay here like this forever.

I looked behind me to the top of the roof of the log cabin. I thought of what Owen had said one day as he looked up at the house. "If we succeed, someday there will be a United States flag over this house. If we do not, it will be considered a den of pirates and thieves."

What would happen to the house when we were all gone? Would our voices bounce off the walls inside at night when the moon shone in the windows?

Martha's voice, singing? Mine, begging Pa to let me keep Cuffee? Cook's, telling Pa about Hettie Pease? Leeman's, calling Dauphin "Buttercup"?

Pa's, saying his prayers before meals?

Meriam's, taking the oath of fidelity?

Newby's, crying for his slave wife?

Green's, saying, "I believe I go wid de old man."

Oliver's criticism of Pa's plans for the raid: "You're dividing your forces."

Watson telling Pa how his baby boy, Frederick, was already turning over in his cradle?

Ed Coppoc's, begging Martha to let them have a little fun?

Dauphin's, saying "I haven't treated you so right, Annie. Don't know if you took notice."

Taylor's, telling us how he'd be the first one killed?

Tidd's, singing some ballad that would rip your heart out?

Stevens' voice, reading a military manual?

Will Thompson, mimicking Pa?

Kagi's, telling me how his kin near the Ferry wanted to lynch him?

What happened to a house when the people left it? Did the walls sag a little? The wind whistle through at night and sweep all traces of those who had lived in it out of the corners? Or did the house remember? When I was back home in North Elba, huddled under my quilts with four feet of snow outside, who would be here to witness the hooty owls calling to each other at night? Who would the little wrens sing to next summer?

I dried Cuffee off with an old piece of flannel, then brought him inside and set him on a piece of blanket in the storeroom. It would be time soon for our special supper. I hoped I could eat. I hoped it wouldn't last too long. Martha had promised that I could take a plate of leftovers and sneak out and say good-bye to Mrs. Huffmaster.

Chapter Twenty

When they passed the Kansas-Nebraska act in 1854, those who opposed slavery got scared to the quick. The slaveholders could fill up Kansas and Nebraska territories and multiply. My brothers John, Jason, Owen, and Frederick, went there a year later and became Free Soilers. They staked out claims in eastern Kansas. The slavers in Missouri thought the Free Soilers had come to free their slaves and sent Border Ruffians into Kansas to attack, to drive Free Soilers from the polls, to sack their towns and settlements. When my brothers wrote for Pa to come out, he said no at first. Sent Oliver, Salmon, and Ruth's husband, Henry. Then Pa went later on. If it wasn't war by then, it was when he got there. And after Kansas the country was quickened to the evils of slavery. Pa did that. Pa and my brothers.

UR SUPPER TABLE WAS DOWNRIGHT FESTIVE. ALL the men but Kagi and Cook were there, and when they gathered 'round the table, Owen said the prayer. But it wasn't one of Pa's prayers that had to do with serving the Lord or forgiving our sins.

Owen went right ahead and made up his prayer. "Lord," he said, "bless these vittles. And let them nourish our spirits as well as our bodies. And bless these here gathered together tonight in peace and harmony. Lord, these are all good men. And women. I know them personally, Lord, and I'll vouch for every one. And even though I just got to know Meriam, well, we feel You sent him to us, so he must be all right, too. That being the case, Lord, we ask that You let Your face to smile upon us. So that we may complete our assigned tasks and, someday soon, gather 'round a table together again, in peace and in harmony."

I never did hear such a prayer. It said nothing about the tree of liberty or the plight of the slaves or making the whole country bleed like Kansas had bled. If Pa was there he'd have had a regular hissy fit. But everybody nodded in approval. And it was fitting.

Owen had been thoughtful enough to bring candles back from the Ferry. Not plain tallow, like we always used, that smelled of the fat they were made from, but scented candles. Six of them were lighted in the middle of the table.

I picked some small twigs with colored leaves on them and brought them into the house. Martha, who knew how to do such things, arranged them in an old cracked pitcher in the middle of the table.

Martha had outdone herself with the cooking. With Pa not around, the men drank the wine, though Owen was careful to see that they didn't drink too much.

"I feel almost human," Will Thompson said.

"How does that feel?" Tidd wanted to know.

"Still, we've all come through something good here at the farm," Owen reminded them. But his eyes looked sad and I don't think he believed what he was saying. Not for one minute.

I watched him when he didn't think anybody was. And thought of the words from *Richard the Third*:

"March on, join bravely, let us to it pell-mell. If not to heaven, then hand in hand to hell."

Edwin Coppoc proposed a toast to Martha. For all the care she had given the men, the meals she had served, the dirt she had swept up, "the guff she had to listen to."

Martha blushed when they stood and toasted her. Her eyes sought Oliver's. "I was proud to be a part of it," she said simply.

"And to Annie, our watchdog," Edwin said.

Everybody's eyes were on me. When it came my time to speak, I was tongue-tied, though. I felt them all looking at me, waiting. "I'm proud to have known you all," I said.

"Hear, hear!" It was Leeman. "Let's cheer Annie, all growed."

They gave three huzzahs. I sipped my wine. I'd never had wine, but Owen said I could have a sip. I tasted it, while the men watched.

"Well?" Oliver asked.

"I don't see what all the fuss is about." It was tart and I made a face.

"You have to cultivate a taste for it," Oliver told me.

"I never had to," Edwin Coppoc said. And everybody laughed.

"We're corrupting your sister, Owen," Will Thompson said.

Owen smiled and said a funny thing, then. "If being here this summer hasn't corrupted her, the wine won't," he said. And the men laughed again, but a little more uneasily this time.

"You're brooding, Owen," Oliver teased.

"The correct word for it in the South is melancholy," Owen told us. "Aristocratic melancholy. I've been trying to get it right ever since I've been here. But it seems all I can ever manage to do is some good old-fashioned North Elba brooding."

"It always served us well at home, why not here?" Oliver asked lightly. And they all laughed again.

It would have been so easy for all of us to brood. And the men knew it. So they teased each other mercilessly, all through the meal. Martha, too, entered into the teasing, although I did hear a false note in her voice every so often.

I prayed the supper would soon be over. I didn't know if we'd all get through it. But we did, and then they sang for us.

Tidd insisted upon it. And led the singing. They sang "Home Again."

I saw tears on the surface of many of the men's eyes. But when I saw them roll down Dangerfield Newby's, I felt tears of my own.

I couldn't wait to get out of that dining room. When the singing was finished, an awkward hush fell on everyone. Then Owen suggested the men help clear. They fell to the task, eager to throw themselves into something. Then they went back into the dining room to linger with cigars and coffee.

I went into the kitchen to find Martha fixing furiously to wash dishes. The sink was full of sudsy hot water. She rolled up her sleeves. "Your covered dish for Mrs. Huffmaster is over there," she gestured to the table with her head. "But I shouldn't let you go."

I felt a jolt of alarm. "What's wrong, Martha?"

"You didn't speak up with your pa and ask his permission."

"Is that all that's vexing you?" I sighed with relief. So, we were to pull out that old bone again and pick it over between us.

"Not all," she said. "It's important. It's about time you stood up to him."

I picked up a rag to wipe the dishes. "There's no winning with Pa, Martha. Why try?"

"You keep letting him get away with it, he'll never learn, is why."

"He gets so stern looking," I said lamely.

She wouldn't leave off. Kept right at it, 'til I started to understand that it wasn't what was really plaguing her. What was plaguing her she wouldn't talk about. Or couldn't. She had to seize on something, so it might as well be this.

"You have to let him know you won't put up with his guff. You heard the men in there. You're all growed now and have to start standing up to him on your own."

I shrugged. "What's the use?"

"Now what kind of thing is that to say?"

Our eyes met. "It's all over now anyways," I told her.

"What's all over?"

I didn't answer. Everything, I wanted to tell her. Me and Pa. You and Oliver. Me and Dauphin. Watson and Belle. It's all over. What's the difference anymore if I don't stand up to Pa?

But I didn't say any of it. I couldn't. Not to Martha. I

think that if she let even one little corner of her mind think that anything was going to happen to Oliver, she'd just give out. I think that what kept her going all these weeks at the farm was that she and Oliver were going home to North Elba and she'd have her baby and they'd be a family.

"I'll try to speak up to Pa in the future," I said.

She slammed a dish down on the drying board. "Don't pacify me, Annie Brown!"

I didn't know what all to do then. It wasn't enough for her. Nothing I could say now would be enough for her. Because what was eating at her innards wasn't me and Pa. Good thing Oliver came into the kitchen just then. He took one look at Martha, smiled, kissed her cheek, then took the towel from my hand.

"I didn't do anything," I told him.

"I know," he said softly. "Run along on your errand. I'll dry. Me and Martha just need some time alone. I'll make it all right."

I looked into his placid face. He would make it all right, Oliver would. He knew how. I took the plate of food and started off for Mrs. Huffmaster's, wondering how anybody as uncaring and harsh as my pa could have begat such wonderful sons.

Lamplight spilled from her doorway. Though it was the end of September, katydids still chirped, frogs still croaked, and standing back from the little house I was taken with the weatherbeaten plainness of it, the chickens scratching in the yard, the line of sunflowers with bowed heads by the fence. It struck me as having a primitive kind of beauty. As if I'd never seen it before.

Maybe I never had. Maybe I'd never really looked.

"Sakes alive. Never expected to see you. Everythin' all right over to the farm?"

"Yes."

"How's yer ma?"

The children were running around behind the house. I saw that the baby was creeping now, in the grass. "Y'll mind that baby now!" she yelled. "Y'all don't let him near the barn!"

"My ma?" It was one of the things that I didn't like about seeing her. I had to remember my lies from our last meeting. "She's much improved."

"Thought so. The cornhusk doll soaked in cow's urine burned on the hearth."

"I'm beholden to you," I said. I hated lying to her. I wished we could have things out in the open between us. I wished I could speak plain with her.

"C'mon in and set a spell. I'll put up the kettle," she said.

"I don't have time. I promised Owen I'd be back in an hour. It's coming onto dark." I handed her the covered dish of food.

"What's this fer?"

"A present. For you. I wanted to give you something. I'm leaving tomorrow. We're leaving. Me and Martha."

She eyed me over the covered dish. "Goin' home?"

"Yes. It's time. Fall is here. My ma will need me."

She took my measure for a full minute there in the gathering September twilight. "Well, I'll miss you."

"I'll miss you, too, Mrs. Huffmaster." A lump rose in my throat. I would miss her. For all the terror her unannounced visits had brought. For all her peskiness. Right here in this very yard I'd bidden farewell to Amelia. I'd felt Amelia's presence. I'd known she'd forgiven me. And witnessed the lightness in me for letting her go. A lightness I'd never felt in any church. A knowledge no minister ever could inspire in me.

"Yer ain't wantin' to go though, are ye?" she asked.

"What?"

"Yer cain't fool old Mrs. Huffmaster. I got the power. I kin see yer ain't wantin' to go. Like it here in these parts, do ye?"

"It's nice," I allowed. My eyes misted with tears.

She walked over to put the covered dish down on a rickety wooden table that sat outside the door. "It'll work out just fine, Annie," she said. And her voice was all whispery, like the wind talking, the wind that seemed to have started a fuss, of a sudden, in the tree branches overhead.

Light from the whale oil lamp in the house spilled out behind her, and she was backlit for me in some kind of strange splendor.

"Yer carryin' a heavy burden, child. But yer up to it."

"Burden?" I looked at her dumbly. I wondered if she was really talking to me. Or if she was in some kind of trance.

"Come now. I all the while knowed. 'Tain't much I don't git a whiff of, if I sniff the air right. And I all the while knowed there wuz trouble brewin' over to that farm. Bad trouble, Annie child. Ain't it?"

I did not answer. I could not answer. Pa's training was in

me. I'd have died first, rather than tell what was going on "over to that farm," as she put it. But I felt a coldness come over me that had nothing to do with the night air.

She took my hand in her two bony ones, which were surprisingly warm and comforting. "Doan worry none 'bout yer pa," she said. "He's doin' what he wants to do. What he wuz born to do. Even if it ends bad, doan fret none 'bout yer pa."

I nodded wordlessly. And for just an instant it was as if my spirit were lifted out of my body and I was hovering over the two of us, up there by the swaying tree branches overhead, looking down on us as we spoke. A strange sense of calm came over me.

"The others," she croaked, "well, they's goin' into it with their eyes open. Nobody's put a halter on their necks an' leadin' 'em."

How did she know?

But she had known. All along. I felt that knowledge flowing through me, like my very blood in my veins. *But it doesn't matter. She won't tell. Her job isn't to tell. It's just to know.*

That, too, coursed through me. And I felt at peace.

"The 'portant thing," she said, still gripping my hand, "is that you done yer best. You done what you wuz brung here to do. Oh, I know. Yer frettin' cause yer pa ain't forgiven you for what happened to yer sister. Ain't that the truth?"

I nodded yes.

"It ain't in yer pa to forgive, Annie. If it wuz, he wouldn't be here, doin' what he's doin'. It's in yer pa to remember slights an' hurts, and grievances, and other people's sins. Always. And always to take it upon hisself to remind others. So doan you worry none 'cause he cain't forgive. But this, re-member this, Annie child." And she gripped my hand tighter.

"There be a time comin' years hence, when you'll be the only witness. An' everybody gonna be askin' you what went on here. You remember it plain, child. An' honest. 'Cause, long after they all dies, only you gonna be around to answer questions. An' that's gonna be yer job. To remember and tell what went on here."

She was making no sense now. But I put it down to the trance she was in. Then the mood broke. One of her children screamed from the back of the yard. She released my hand. "Go, Annie," she said, "an' the Lord be with you."

And in the next instant she was gone. As if she had never existed. Around the back of the house. I must hurry home, I thought. There's a storm coming. Oh, I hope it doesn't muddy the roads. We have to take the wagon all the way to Chambersburg tomorrow.

I ran out her gate. Wind whipped at my skirts. Then, out-side the gate on the path leading to the road, there was no more wind.

There was no storm coming. The tree branches were still. Not so much as a flutter in the broomsedge on the side of the road. No more whispering overhead. There were stars out already. And a lopsided moon overhead.

It had all been part of the spell she'd cast.

I felt unsettled, confused. *Years hence, you'll be the only witness.* I heard her scolding the children in the back of the house. Likely, I thought, she doesn't recollect what she says after one of her trances. Likely they just come on her, like a seizure. And after they're over, she's got no recollection at all.

I'll have to ask brother John, I thought. Maybe I'll write to him. Mama writes to him all the time and he keeps his counsel about things.

Oh God, I prayed, don't let Mrs. Huffmaster remember.

Chapter Twenty-one

Pa had himself an army in Kansas. Not only his sons, but James Holmes of New York, who was right out of college, August Bondi, a European engineer, Charley Kaiser, brother of Susan B. Anthony, the Partridge boys, John and Will Bowles, Augustus Wattles, and many others. Not land lookers or politicians making deals, either. Some were newspaper men who fought with him. Like Mr. Winchell from the New York Times, *Mr. Redpath of the* Missouri Democrat, *Mr. Hinton of the* Boston Traveller *and* Chicago Tribune, *and John Henri Kagi of the* New York Post. *Anybody who thinks the Civil War started with the firing on Fort Sumter should have been in Kansas is all I can say.*

'LL BE UP IN THE MORNING," DAUPHIN HAD SAID WHEN I got back from Mrs. Huffmaster's. "Early."

"Yes."

"We're having a meeting. In the house across the road. So's not to keep you and Martha up. You'd best get to bed now."

Then he'd kissed me quickly and I'd watched them all walk down the slope and into the darkness, jostling each other, teasing, throwing back and forth some kind of a ball. A meeting. Likely they were going to play cards well into the night. I felt their camaraderie as I watched them go. And my loneliness. But I knew better than to keep Dauphin from going with the men.

I was in the kitchen heating water for coffee the next morning when I looked out the window and saw him coming up the slope from the house across the road, out of the mist that lay across the lawns. Like an apparition, he appeared, with that easy gait of his, that special way he had of wearing his clothes, jaunty, almost careless, yet with enough style to draw the eye. And I thought, he is like something I have already committed to memory. I became afraid then and ran out of the house and down the porch steps and threw my arms around him. To make sure he was not a memory already, but that he was still here.

"Anybody up yet?"

"No."

He pulled me to the side of the house. And we just stood there, saying nothing, just holding each other close and hearing the morning sounds of the birds all around us. When it comes time to say goodbye there isn't any word that does it. And goodbye is the word you never use.

"When you get back to North Elba, you tell my ma I'm fine. She's not to worry. I'll be home soon."

"Yes," I said.

"You go see my folks first thing. Tell them what a grand time we had here."

I said yes to that, too.

"And if Pa wants to show you that piece of land he's giving us, you go with him to see it. We'll be building a house on it soon."

"Yes."

"And wait for me. When the raid is over I'll have done my part. I'm not going into the South with your pa. I'm coming right home."

I believed all his lies. And said yes to them. Because he believed them. When saying good-bye, no is a word you never use.

After a while I heard Martha stirring about in the kitchen and we went upstairs, my hand clutched in his. I warmed some cornbread while Martha made the coffee. Oliver and Watson came into the kitchen. We stumbled around bumping into each other, excusing ourselves, murmuring about what kind of day it would be and avoiding each other's eyes. Watson and Oliver ate quickly and went outside to get the horse and wagon. Last night Martha and I had packed all our things. They sat on the dining room floor.

We hoped to get away before the other men came down and avoid more goodbyes. But then I saw Shields Green, Dangerfield Newby, and Meriam coming across the road and up the slope in front. At the same time the other men started shuffling down, helping Oliver carry out our belongings.

Then somehow it was time. Too soon, I told myself, too soon. But time. Martha ran for my shawl and Dauphin tied Cuffee in the wagon and made sure the crate with the blanket was in there, too. The sun was just a rosy promise in the East behind the trees. From somewhere a rooster crowed.

"Martha, you've forgotten something," Owen called from the porch. "Annie, you, too."

We knew what it would be. And we were right. The men

were lined up in the dining room waiting to say goodbye. We had to go down the line and shake hands, one at a time. Martha went first. I followed.

They said things, then. Things I'd always remember. Things that were already part of me.

"Remember Annie, if you have to tell a lie, tell a whopper." Anderson.

"Try to remember the good things, Annie, and not how big the fleas were." Old Xcentricity himself. Owen.

"I believe I go wid de old man." Shields Green.

"Thank you for the vittles, Miss. And for all your listenin'." Dangerfield Newby.

"Thought anybody worth knowing we met in Kansas. 'Til I met you." Barclay the Younger.

"Always remember to put a cross on the bread before you put it in the oven." Stewart Taylor.

"Best jailer I ever had." Hazlett.

"Annie Brown, all growed." Leeman.

"My brother is no buttercup." Will Thompson. Everybody laughed.

"It is not the fight that troubles us, it is the leaving of our dear friends." Edwin Coppoc.

"Don't worry. We did it in Kansas, we can do it here." Aaron Stevens.

"Make a life for yourself, Annie Brown." Charles Plummer Tidd.

"Good-bye and good luck to you, Annie Smith." Meriam.

"Don't forget, we'll soon build our house." Dauphin.

I tore myself from Dauphin and stumbled outside. I

hugged Cuffee in the wagon. I looked back at that house, through my tears, as long as I could see it.

Before I was even born Pa moved his family so many times they lost count, Owen told me. I'd lived in enough houses to call none home. Except here. Here was the only place I'd felt was home. And now I was leaving for good.

Watson left us in Chambersburg. He would wait here for Pa and Kagi, who were now in Philadelphia. Oliver came as far as Troy, New York, with us, stayed over in the inn, and saw me and Martha onto the train for Whitehall. The trip is a blur to me. The wagon ride, the inns, saying good-bye to Watson, promising to kiss the baby for him, taking a letter from him for Belle. Then watching Martha and Oliver say farewell.

I was like someone in a trance all the way home. Like Mrs. Huffmaster when she told me about Amelia. I was no good to Martha. If not for having to see to Cuffee, safe and secure in his crate, I think I might not even have bestirred myself to eat.

In Harrisburg at the depot, we met Pa and Kagi. Oliver had told us they'd be along in Harrisburg, on their way back from Philadelphia. Pa had planned it that way. And I knew by now that when Pa planned things out they happened. We were waiting for our next train, standing there on the platform lost and bewildered, when Pa came rushing towards us as if he was on his way to a family wedding. That's how happy he was.

I suffered his embrace. Because he was beaming and I knew the only reason for his happiness was that they'd been successful in purchasing more arms in Philadelphia. And not because of us.

Martha assured him everything was fine at the farm. He and Kagi waited with us, then put us on the train.

Kagi took my hand. "Continue your education, Annie Brown," he said.

We got on the train. I waved out the window at them.

That was the last time in my life I saw my pa. The last time alive, anyways.

Cuffee behaved fine on the train. I didn't have a bit of trouble with him all the way home.

News of the raid came to us in pieces. Like broken things always do.

It was on Friday, the twenty-first of October. The Adirondack woods were already bare. Winter sat on the land, bleak and cold.

Mrs. Reed came up the hill, much as she had that morning so long ago now with the letter from Pa asking us to come to the Kennedy farm.

This time Mrs. Reed had a newspaper under her arm. The *New York Times.* It was dated October eighteenth.

"Nobody wanted to bring it, so I said I would." She came into the kitchen and held it out to us.

Nobody would take it. We'd heard just the day before from Dauphin's family that there had been a raid. And that everybody had died. We did not believe it. And nobody would touch the hateful paper for a while. It lay there on the table like some unclean thing.

We were all women, except for Salmon. Jason had gone back to Ellen and Ohio at summer's end. We were Mama, me, Sarah and Ellen, Martha. Belle, Watson's wife, was with the Thompsons, her family.

Salmon picked up the newspaper and read the account to us.

The raid had failed. Pa was prisoner. Watson and Oliver were dead. So were Dauphin and Will Thompson. Owen had escaped. So had some others. But no one knew to where.

Nobody said anything when Salmon finished reading. We thought first of Mama. Of Martha. "We must write to John," Salmon said, "and warn him. There may be bad feeling towards him now. And Jason. I think if Owen and the others who escaped are headed anywhere, it's to John in Jefferson County, Ohio."

Mama stood up then. "We must not wail," she said. "We must show a strong face to all. And we must send word to Ruth and Henry." They lived not far from us in North Elba.

Mama didn't have to worry herself about my wailing. I could not shed a tear at the news. Not for at least a week. They say I looked "wild-eyed" and heartbroken. They feared for my sanity, I think. About a week later my sister Ruth invited me to her house, which was not far from ours. She and Henry had a small supper for me. I didn't want to go, but I went. She had also invited Mr. Aphro, who had been our old music teacher in school. At one time he had taken part in an insurrection in Haiti and had fled to North Elba for his life.

He played the violin and sang for me. He sang "The Dying Warrior," and it was only then that I cried. I couldn't stop crying, it seemed. I cried for Pa, in jail, for the death of all the young men I'd known at the Kennedy farm, for Dauphin, for all I'd known and would never know again. I felt so old. I was within six weeks of being sixteen.

But I'd needed to cry. And to think, after all, that it was Ruth who saw it.

Somewhere in the first week after the news came to us, Martha's parents came to our door. They came in a buggy with pine knot torches. Martha's father held a rifle across his lap. When Salmon went outside to talk to them, Martha's father bellowed at Salmon.

"I told her if she wed that no-count brother of yours she'd come to grief! I told her your pa was a crazy man, didn't I? Where is she? Send her out here!"

"She's staying with us," Salmon said.

"Send her out here, or I'll come in and get her!"

Salmon never flinched. And then Henry Thompson, Ruth's husband, went out to stand with him. "You're not coming in this house," Henry told Martha's father. "We have grief here. We need no more."

"Who's gonna stop me?" the man demanded.

"I will," Henry said. And from somewhere he drew a revolver.

I was grateful to Henry. We all were. And I was glad in the end that he refused to go with Pa to the Ferry. Glad for us, for him, and for Ruth. I wish Dauphin had had the courage not to go. I wish I had the common sense Ruth had, not to let him go. Oh, I wish so many things!

We went on. Some of the neighbors got hostile. We had

to keep Sarah and Ellen home from school for a while for fear they would be harassed.

Nobody knew what to do. But wait. We didn't know the truths yet. And then on the thirty-first came a letter from Charlestown, Virginia, from Pa.

". . . Watson died of his wound on Wednesday. Dauphin was killed when I was taken, and Anderson I suppose also. I have since been tried and found guilty of treason, etc.; and of murder in the first degree. I have not yet received my sentence."

He went on to tell us that he was cheerful, that God reigned, and he had no guilt. He preached to us about God in the letter and told us to remember the poor, "though they be as black as Ebedmelch the Ethiopian eunuch who cared for Jeremiah in the pit of the dungeon."

He had a word for Ruth. "Copy this letter, Ruth, and send it to your stricken brothers. Write me a few words in regard to the welfare of all."

Then he ended with a postscript. It said: "Yesterday, Nov 2nd I was sentenced to be hanged on Dec. 2nd next. Do not grieve on my account. I am still quite cheerful. God bless you all."

Chapter Twenty-two

"We want men who fear God too much to fear anything human." That's what Pa said to the Massachusetts Legislature in February of 1857 after the second sacking of Lawrence, Kansas, by the Border Ruffians. "I believe in the Golden Rule, sir," he said to the gentlemen there assembled. "And the Declaration of Independence. I think they both mean the same thing; and it is better that a whole generation should pass off the face of the earth, men, women, and children, by violent death than that one jot of either should fail in this country. I mean that exactly so, sir."

OUT OF THE WHOLE CLOTH, HERE IS WHAT HAPpened at the Ferry. Here is what we learned. Most of it, in bits and pieces, in the months that followed.

Two more men arrived at the farm to join Pa's army after Martha and I left. John Copeland, a free black from Raleigh, North Carolina. And Lewis Leary, another free black from Fayetteville, North Carolina. He'd left a wife and child in Oberlin, Ohio. He was descended from an Irishman who fought in the Revolution.

At eight o'clock on the night of Sunday, October sixteenth, Pa and twenty-one men started off from the Kennedy farm. Pa left Owen, Barclay the Younger, and Meriam behind.

Owen said he had high words with Pa over it. But then Pa promised them that in the morning they, the rear guard, could bring the remainder of the weapons near to town and pass them out to all the slaves who would be joining them.

Tidd and Cook led the way. Their job was to cut the telegraph lines on both sides of the Potomac River, in Virginia and Maryland.

It took them two hours to get to the Ferry. Then they got the wagon with the weapons in it, the wagon pulled by the half-blind horse, onto the Baltimore and Ohio railroad bridge. Kagi and Stevens first took the bridge watchman, William Williams, prisoner. Then they all went through the covered bridge. And there, laid out before them, was the Ferry. Pa's dream. They went right to the armory, likely thinking how easy it all was.

But now there was another watchman. He came out of the fire engine house, the place he watched from. Pa and the men held rifles at him, ordered him to open the place up. The watchman, name of Daniel Whelan, did what watchmen do. He refused. But Pa's men had crowbars and the like, and so they went ahead and pried open the gates. Now they had two prisoners.

Pa told them he was come to free Virginia's slaves. Then he sent Oliver and Will Thompson to the bridge across the Shenandoah River to keep guard. Hazlett and Edwin Coppoc he sent to the arsenal. It was not guarded. Pa sent Stevens to the rifle factory on Lower Hall Island. Kagi and Copeland went with Stevens.

Everything was going according to plan. Pa must have been overjoyed.

They occupied the engine house. Then, about midnight,

Patrick Higgins, another guard, came on duty at the B & O railroad bridge to relieve Williams. Not seeing Williams, he yelled. That was all it took for Stewart Taylor and my brother Watson to do what revolutionaries do. Take Higgins prisoner.

But Higgins wasn't about to stand for it. He lashed out and struck Watson in the face and raced away. Taylor shot at him and grazed him in the head. But Higgins ran on to the Wager House. There is where the trouble began. Higgins told people in the Wager House what was going on.

Nothing happened for a while. Everything was quiet. Then Stevens, Tidd and Cook, Osborne Anderson, and Shields Green went on to Colonel Washington's house to bang on his door in the middle of the night and tell him they were freeing Virginia's slaves. And they were starting with him.

Washington, who was forty-six years old, came to the door in his nightshirt. But even in his nightshirt he had great dignity. He did not resist them, though I would imagine he told them what fools they all were. Because when you are the great-grandnephew of George Washington, you can stand there in your nightshirt in the middle of the night and tell men who have broken into your house with guns that they are fools.

They said they wanted his weapons. Cook lusted after those weapons. The pistol General Lafayette had given George Washington. And a sword sent by Frederick the Great at the end of the Revolution. The sword was inscribed. It said, "From the World's Oldest General to Its Greatest."

Cook must have felt like he had the crown jewels, taking

those weapons. Then they took five of Washington's slaves. The slaves were not at all happy to see their liberators, I am given to understand. They had been disturbed from their beds and were downright put out about it.

And they didn't want to be liberated. Especially if it meant going outside into the cold October night and down to the Ferry where a madman awaited them. Kept saying they were happy with Marse Washington. But they went, anyway.

On the journey to the Ferry they passed another slave owner's house. Owned by John Allstadt. More hammerings at the door. There they took Allstadt, his eighteen-year-old son, and six slaves. Back to the Ferry they rode and in front of the engine house Stevens gave the password.

"Number One, all's well."

Pa now had over a dozen hostages. And one with a very important name, who, besides being descended from the father of our country, was also an aide to the governor of Virginia. The hostages and slaves were herded into the engine house. The slaves were handed the precious pikes and told to guard the prisoners. They didn't want to do it, but they did. They must have taken one look at Pa, seen the gleam in his eyes, and thought that God Himself had taken it in His head to visit them this night. They were petrified.

Then something else happened. The Baltimore and Ohio eastbound passenger train was coming into the Ferry. Headed for Baltimore.

Had Pa counted on trains? I never heard him talk of trains, of timetables. The train was stopped just short of the Ferry by a clerk from the Wager House who told the engineer what was transpiring in that quiet little town of a Sunday evening. The conductor wouldn't allow his train to be brought into the Ferry. He sent his engineer and baggage master to investigate. Pa's men met them with guns and turned them back.

Then along comes Hayward Shepherd, station baggage man and free Negro. Everybody in the Ferry liked Shepherd. One of Pa's men saw him coming and told him to halt. Shepherd turned and commenced walking back to the depot.

One of Pa's men shot him in the back. Shepherd dragged himself back to the depot. He was hurt bad. Somebody sent for a doctor. John Starry, his name was. Everybody in town liked him, too. He attended to Shepherd. But Shepherd died the next day.

Pa was set on freeing the Negroes. The first man killed in his cause was a free Negro.

The night dragged on without much more happening and dawn came to the Ferry. A number of people began reporting for work at the arsenal. All of them were taken prisoner in the engine house.

At dawn Dr. John Starry took it upon himself to go around warning the townfolk. He ordered the bell in the Lutheran Church tower to be rung. He sent a messenger to Shepherdstown and to Charlestown to alert the militia. Pa had no worries about this. Remember, he called the militia dunderheads.

The people in Charlestown had faith in their militia, though. They called them the Jefferson Guards. The people of Charles Town also had a lot of fear. And it had to do with

Nat Turner's 1831 slave rebellion, in which fifty whites were murdered. They sent their militia right off.

At dawn Pa was gracious enough to allow that Baltimore and Ohio train to pass through the Ferry and continue on to Baltimore. But when the conductor got to Monocacy, Maryland, he telegraphed the news about the Ferry.

He telegraphed everybody he knew and some he didn't know. The president of the railroad got the message and sent one to President James Buchanan. And another to Governor Henry Wise of Virginia.

By seven o'clock some of the townsfolk at the Ferry started to make their move. Ordinary citizens they were. One was a grocer named Thomas Boerly. One of Pa's men fired and hit him and he soon died.

Meanwhile there were Pa and his men and the hostages in the engine house, waiting. Forty-five of them. No food, no water, nothing. They decided to release one hostage in return for food. But Pa wouldn't eat it when it came, and wouldn't let his men eat it. Said it was drugged.

And there was Kagi, secretary of war, still at the rifle factory, sending Pa messages, saying Pa and the men should leave the Ferry while the leaving was still good. Hie thee away from that slaughterhouse. But Pa wouldn't listen. He ignored the messages. He could have gotten away with all his men at that time. To the mountains. His holy mountains that he said God had put there for when the slaves made their run to freedom.

By noon the Charlestown militia came. The Jefferson Guards.

Oliver, Will Thompson, and Dangerfield Newby were guarding the Maryland end of the B & O railroad bridge. The Jefferson Guards attacked them. Thompson and Oliver made it back to the armory, but not Newby. They shot him, and he rolled into the gutter. They left him there.

Another part of the dunderhead militia sent some citizens to secure the Gault House Saloon at the rear of the arsenal and took command of the Shenandoah Bridge and armory entrance. They also had men at all the front doors of houses on Shenandoah Street. Anybody coming out the front of the arsenal grounds would now be a sitting duck.

Pa had no more chance of escape. The steel jaws of the trap that Frederick Douglass had told him about were closing.

Pa became sensible of this right off, of course. He sent one hostage and Will Thompson out under a white flag of truce. The townsfolk, who were just waiting to do something and show the militia how good they were, got ahold of Thompson and took him to the Wager House as prisoner.

Pa now sent Watson and Aaron Stevens out with another hostage. But they, too, got fired upon in the street. Watson fell. So did Stevens.

Then Leeman decided to hie thee from the slaughter-house by taking a back exit. He ran through the armory yard and jumped into the Potomac River. He swam out in the cold water to an islet. One of the townsfolk waded out there and shot him in the head.

The militia and townsfolk decided, for the rest of the day, to use his body as target practice.

There was a fearful lot of killing going on now. One of

Pa's men shot George Turner, a planter who came into town to take part in the fight. Next went Mayor Fontaine Beckham.

The people of Harpers Ferry were right fond of their mayor. But the way Edwin Coppoc saw it, what right did anybody have to come out into the street unarmed, even if he was mayor of the town? Coppoc, the Quaker, stood inside the engine house doors, got Beckham in his Sharps sight, and fired.

The mayor went down.

My brother Watson had dragged his shot-up self back to the engine house by this time. And I expect that's what made Edwin Coppoc do such a thing. Watson was in bad shape. Then my brother Oliver made ready to fire at another man in the street, but before he could aim his gun properlike, he was shot. And before long lay dying next to Watson.

The townsfolk didn't know what all to do now. Only thing they could think of was to drag Will Thompson out of the Wager House and onto the B & O trestle. Then they all fired guns at him and threw his body down into the Potomac River. And commenced to use it for target practice.

No slaves were coming, though. And this must have been a puzzlement to Pa, because by now the whole countryside at large knew what was going on at the Ferry. And the Negroes inside the engine house who had been handed pikes were shivering in their boots for this freedom Pa was giving them.

Kagi was still at the rifle works with Leary and Copeland. He had to make a real secretary of war decision then, because he and the two with him ran out the back of the building, across some railroad tracks, and right into the Shenandoah River. Townsfolk on the other side were just waiting for them, of course, and started firing. Kagi and the others ended up on a rock in the middle of the river.

Townsfolk kept firing, and Kagi was killed, Leary wounded, and Copeland dragged ashore, where the crowd decided he deserved lynching. The only thing that saved him was the sudden appearance of Dr. Starry, who said he belonged in jail. So he could be tried properlike and the lynching called a hanging.

Afternoon came. Another contingent of dunderheads arrived by train from Martinsburg, Virginia. They marched right on the engine house. Some smashed the windows and freed the prisoners. Pa and his men fired those Sharps rifles and wounded eight of the militia. But then more dunderheads arrived.

Across the Potomac were Cook, my brother Owen, Barclay the Younger, Meriam, Tidd, and some Negroes they managed to pick up along the way. They commandeered a little schoolhouse, sent the children and teacher away, and were stashing weapons into it. They heard firing in town, and Cook ventured forth just enough to see what was happening. He was shot but made it back to the schoolhouse.

He, Owen, Barclay, Meriam, and Tidd decided to start North.

Night came to the Ferry. How long since the men had eaten? And there were Oliver and Watson dying on the engine house floor.

Oliver begged Pa to shoot him. Martha's Oliver, who

would nevermore stir any softness into their bed. "Be quiet," Pa said. "If you must die, die like a man." So Oliver got quiet and died like a man.

Watson was begging for death, too, saying he couldn't abide the pain. Stewart Taylor lay dead already. No surprise to him. He'd known he was going to die. The five of the Provisional Army who were still on their feet in the Engine House were Pa, Edwin Coppoc, Dauphin, Jeremiah Anderson, and Shields Green.

Right about then, as I am given to understand it, Watson cried out again for Pa to shoot him. Pa said, "No, if you die, you will have died in a glorious cause." I doubt if Watson cared how glorious it was, just lying there in agony thinking of Belle and baby Frederick and how he'd never see them again.

Pa was too busy to care about any of that. He was trying to negotiate. He'd release the hostages, he said, if the militia would let him and his men go.

The answer was no, of course. It got dark and cold outside and inside. No slaves appeared to help. Outside the town was near crazed. Ordinary men with guns in their hands saw their chance to use them on something besides deer and rabbits. Many had been gathering all day and drinking and boasting. Somehow, in all the confusion with the militia dunderheads all around, Hazlett and Osborne Anderson managed to escape. If anybody could escape, Hazlett could. Hadn't he been one of my invisibles back at the farm, always running off? They crossed the Potomac and fled North.

Then came along more dunderheads. Ninety of them on

the midnight train. United States Marines under an army colonel. Name of Robert E. Lee. He took command of all the forces.

It was black as the inside of the devil's ear at Harpers Ferry. Militia were stationed all over town with rifles aimed at the armory. So were citizens. The mayor was dead, a grocer was dead, a free black Negro who worked at the depot was dead. Men who reported to work that morning were shivering and cold and scared in the engine house, with no food, no light, and men dying around them.

Bodies were lying on railroad trestles and in riverbeds, where they were being used for target practice. Townsfolk jumped on the body of Dangerfield Newby, fearful he was another Nat Turner.

Colonel Robert E. Lee, whose father, Lighthorse Harry Lee, was a hero of the Revolution, was in the street on his horse under the lamplight writing a paper. He was demanding surrender.

Inside the engine house Edwin Coppoc saw Lee out there in the street. He didn't know Lee was from a famous Virginia family, but he looked important, so Coppoc took aim. But a hostage, fearful for his life, told Coppoc who Lee was. And yelled that if Coppoc killed Lee it would be far worse than killing the mayor. And the militia would storm the engine house and kill everybody, white, black, revolutionary, and hostage.

Coppoc didn't care. Likely he had long since forgotten the teachings of his Quaker mother. He had Lee in his sight. The hostage threw himself against him, the gun went off, and missed Lee.

Pa answered Lee that he wasn't going to surrender. At this time Dauphin told Pa that he wanted to surrender. Pa paid no mind. Dauphin yelled it at the top of his voice as loud as he could. But he wasn't heard.

Well, Lee wasn't going to hold with no for an answer. Next thing you know Lee's Marines went crashing in. They fell on Pa and beat him with swords. Jeremiah Anderson they ran through with a bayonet.

Then they went for Dauphin, who all the while was yelling that he wanted to surrender.

They pinned Dauphin to a wall with a bayonet.

They took Pa and Coppoc and Shields Green prisoner.

When they questioned Pa, his hair was caked with blood, he was beaten around the head and face. He could not even sit up. But he preached to them. "You may dispose of me very easily, but this question is still to be settled, this Negro question, I mean." He went to jail, preaching.

In jail Shields Green tried to pass himself off as a captured slave made hostage. It didn't work. A young lieutenant of Lee's, by the name of Jeb Stuart, went to the Kennedy farmhouse and got Pa's carpetbag full of papers, maps, and letters from backers. And gave them to Lee.

Nobody was at the farmhouse to greet him. Except maybe the little wrens who were likely on the porch railing, singing their hearts out.

*   *   *

254

Owen, Barclay Coppoc, Meriam, Tidd, and Cook all escaped together. Owen took command. They would follow the mountains, travel to the Northwest. They must stay clear of the main roads and travel at night. He would not allow them to build fires. For the first couple of days they had no food except what they could steal from the late autumn fields. Sometimes they raided a barn.

They came to Chambersburg. Then Cook got brash and started into the town for food, something Owen begged him not to do. Cook was captured in Chambersburg, and the others ventured to the outskirts of the town. They wanted to try to rescue Cook, but couldn't. What Owen really wanted was to get near the railroad tracks, to get Meriam onto a train. Meriam was weak and helpless. But first, Owen decided, Meriam must be made presentable. He had his sewing things, dear Owen. His scissors and needles and thread. He mended Meriam's overcoat, clipped his beard, and put him on the track so he could walk to the first station north of Chambersburg.

Before saying farewell, Meriam divided his remaining money with the others. Then Owen, Coppoc, and Tidd headed for the North Mountains.

It was snowing badly. For weeks they traveled, through rough wooded hills and small mountains, into western Pennsylvania. They endured danger, they were hungry, the temperatures were freezing. They changed their names. Owen called himself Edward Clark, Tidd was Charles Plummer, and Barclay Coppoc was George Barclay.

They sought out and found Quakers who fed them and directed them to others who would help, good people who figured out who they were, but would not take a penny for helping. In late November they parted. Somehow, like Owen, Coppoc and Tidd found their way to safety. So did Meriam. Owen made his way to Jason's in Ohio. He dares not leave that state to this day.

Epilogue

Orchard House, Concord, Massachusetts,
May 1861

One of the ideas Mama held to was women's suffrage. I never will know why the women called what they were after suffrage, when they had suffered so up 'til now without it. But I do know that Mama counted Lucy Stone and Lucretia Mott friends, and they were suffragettes. Mama had gone to the Seneca Falls Convention in New York eleven years ago, where women adopted a Declaration of Independence. It caused a stir in our house, I can tell you. Pa said what did women want with rights? Mama said the same as Negroes wanted. But Pa just couldn't get a purchase on that idea, that women should be entitled to rights, same as Negroes. Mama took the water cure at a sanitarium in Massachusetts once, too. I guess she just never took The Book of Martyrs *to heart.*

I HAVE BEEN TWO WEEKS NOW TALKING TO THE AF-flicted part of myself. Talking the fire out.

To give everyone here credit, they have left me to myself. Oh, Louisa May knows I am writing and has smiled and nodded in approval on seeing me so set to the task, but she has not once asked to see my work. I do not know yet if I will show it to her or to anybody.

Concord has been in a regular frenzy over the start of the war. Thank heaven they have not made me part of the frenzy.

People have been in and out of this house like Mr. Lincoln presided here.

Speaking of Lincoln, he sent out a call for 75,000 men to serve for three months. A provisional army. What else would you call it? But such a number! Pa had twenty-one men.

Everyone is flying flags and men are rushing to join up. Women here in Concord are busy cooking and sewing, sending their men off with cakes and extra shirts, Bibles and blessings.

Today, the first week in May, the house has been very quiet, for which I am grateful. All, with the exception of Louisa's mother, Abba, have gone to see the Sixth Massachusetts Regiment off. Louisa took Sarah with her. Sarah is so excited about the war. "Isn't it wonderful?" she said to me.

I do not think it is wonderful. I think the men are going into a slaughterhouse. I think they all ought to be made to read *Richard the Third* before they rush off.

"Methought a legion of foul fiends environ'd me, and howled in mine ears. Such hideous cries, that with the very noise I trembling wak'd, and for a season after could not believe but that I was in hell."

That's how I feel. That's how I have felt since the October of the raid. As if I am in hell.

I think of Dauphin, of Johnny Cook, of John-secretary-of-war-Kagi. I think of Dangerfield Newby and Shields Green. I think of Martha, dear good Martha, who died in March of '60, not wishing to live anymore after Oliver was killed. Of her little daughter, Olive, who died in February, less than three days old.

We have still not seen Owen since he fled to Ohio. He writes to Mama on occasion under the name of Edward Clark. And if we write back we address the letter the same way. He seems fine, with Jason. But I hope no one captures him out there. We are comforted by the fact that there is a group in Ohio who call themselves the Ashtabula League of Freedom. They have pinned black stripes to their lapels to let people know they are in sympathy with what Pa and the others did. And they watch the roads out there lest any federal agents appear to arrest Owen or John.

Still I worry. And hope Mrs. Huffmaster was not right when she said someday I'd be the only one alive who could tell the story of those months before the raid.

Here is the rest of that story, which I wish I did not have to write:

Mama wanted to go right to the Ferry when Pa wrote that letter saying he was condemned to die. But he wrote another saying, "Don't come yet." He feared for her safety.

"What safety?" Mama asked me. "My safety is all fled. The worst has come about. I have lost two more sons. The others, all except Salmon, are afeared to show their faces in public. What have I to fear?"

So she sent for her friend Lucretia Mott, who feared nothing, either. And who came to North Elba to take Mama to Philadelphia to abolitionist friends. Mama wanted to be near a rail station to go to Harpers Ferry on a moment's notice.

Meanwhile, Pa was becoming something of a celebrity, which is a new word I have learned here at Mr. Sanborn's school, where I am getting the plain and practical education Pa wanted to help me meet the stern realities of life.

To get back to Pa. There he was in the Charlestown jail in Virginia, feeling like a caged animal, and all the newspapers were writing him up like he was an avenging angel. For the whole month after his trial was over and before he was executed, Pa was the man of the hour. And he wouldn't have had it any other way.

A famous judge and his wife from the North went to visit him. Russell was their name. She cleaned and repaired his clothing. They wrote to Ma that by the first week in November all his wounds were healed. They got him paper and pen and Pa wrote to everybody from jail. All his Northern friends, his sister, us.

Then a Mr. and Mrs. Spring from Perth Amboy, New Jersey, went down. She told her husband that all these years they'd been talking this abolitionist talk and now it was time to go and comfort that poor man, who had done more than talk about freeing the slaves. Mrs. Spring saw to Pa's comfort. And that of the other prisoners.

A sculptor from Boston visited Pa and did a bust of him. Many other old friends visited him, too.

Some wanted to launch an escape. Go right down there and get him out of jail. Thomas Wentworth Higginson, a reverend and one of Pa's backers, had a regular plan to get him out of jail. But Pa would not go for it. He said he would better serve the cause if he was hanged.

Most of Pa's other backers cut all ties with him. You never know about people. Mr. Sanborn, whose school we now attend, was part of the plot to get Pa out of jail. Then he was summoned to Washington by a Senate investigating committee and fled for a while to Canada. I think that's why he's being so good to me and Sarah now. Because of that flight to Canada. I don't blame him. He would have helped Pa escape. But, as he said, "What could any of us do for the cause lying in a jail in Washington?"

It's Frederick Douglass and some others I do blame. Douglass sailed for England. The authorities wanted to arrest him. And so many others who gave money for Pa's cause refused to be connected with it when the raid failed and fled, destroyed all correspondence with Pa, or denied that they knew anything about the raid at all.

I don't know if Pa ever discovered this. But I think they are all cowards, and that it is for them that the cock crowed three times. And not for Jason and Salmon.

But there were good things, too. Lucretia Mott went with Mama to the home of Mrs. Spring in Perth Amboy, where Ma wrote to Governor Wise of Virginia begging "for the mortal remains of my husband and his sons." The governor wrote back saying he'd do the best he could.

By the thirtieth of November Mama and her friends went to Harpers Ferry. They were met by a contingent of men from the Fauquier Cavalry and escorted to Charlestown on December first.

Mama stayed the afternoon with Pa in jail. He asked if she could stay the night, but they said no, so she went back to her friends in Harpers Ferry to wait for Pa's body to be delivered to her so she could take it home.

Pa spent the time after she left writing more letters. Next day they hanged him.

How do you spend a night alone in a cell when you know the next day you are going to be executed? How can you sleep? If you do, what happens when you awake? For a moment you don't comprehend things. We never do. For just an instant upon waking, the world is new, innocent as it was when we were babes.

Then we remember. Everything comes crashing down on our heads.

Oh yes, Pa must have thought, that's right. Today they hang me.

His jailers said he was cheerful and dignified. He shook hands with all of them and gave each guard a book. To the head jailer he gave a silver watch.

On the gallows platform he shook hands all around all over again.

They put his body in a pine box, and it was guarded by fifteen volunteer civilians on its way back to Mama in Harpers Ferry.

The officials were a little embarrassed about here. They wanted to find the bodies of Watson and Oliver to give Mama, too. But students from Winchester Medical College in Virginia, hearing about the raid, had rushed to the Ferry, stuffed Watson's body in a barrel, and took it back on a train to the college to use for medical experiments.

The officials couldn't find Oliver. He'd been thrown into a grave on the banks of the Shenandoah River. We found out later that they buried him with Dangerfield Newby.

Dangerfield Newby's wife, Harriet, was sold with her children to a Louisiana slave dealer.

Mama brought Pa home to North Elba. When their train arrived in Philadelphia the day after the execution a reception committee met it and led Mama away to make a fuss over her. And to take her to the Walnut Street Wharf where the coffin was to go by boat home. Ma and her friends went with it.

Every town the boat stopped in along the way, bells tolled, and the people came out to meet it and give Mama their sympathy. We didn't know it at the time, but soon as Pa was executed there were mass meetings all over the place. Cleveland; Baltimore; Philadelphia; New York; Rochester; Syracuse; Concord; Plymouth and New Bedford, Massachusetts; Concord and Manchester, New Hampshire. In Boston people went crazy with one of the most important meetings the antislavery people ever had.

On December eighth, Mama and the others arrived home with Pa's coffin. They laid Pa to rest by the great boulder outside our house.

It was a gray, dank day in North Elba. The long, freezing winter loomed all around us. I thought I was in a dream. I and Mama and Watson's wife had all been very sickly before Mama went to Charlestown. We could give no name to the illness, but dear Martha nursed us all through it. I had not yet sufficiently recovered. The biting cold of that terrible day we buried Pa ate into my bones. I thought I, too, was dead. Fog lay around the peak of White Face and the other mountains Pa had loved so well. You couldn't see their tops.

Salmon was the only one of Pa's sons present to greet the

funeral cortege. Salmon and Henry Thompson had dug the grave. Ruth, Martha, Belle, and Will Thompson's wife were there. Ellen, who was only five, clung to my skirts. If Pa was home, she reasoned, why hadn't he brought her any raisins? He always brought her raisins.

The Reverend Joshua Young from Burlington, Vermont, presided. Wendell Phillips, an orator of the abolitionist cause, gave a speech.

There were many Negroes there, too, from the surrounding farms. The family of Lyman Epps sang spirituals as the coffin was lowered into the frozen ground. The lilting songs, which had their origins in the cotton fields of the South, echoed off the hard earth and rang out over the bare countryside. Some crows picked up on the high notes and called them out over the barren fields and treetops.

I didn't cry at any of it. It was not that I couldn't. Ruth had already made sure that I'd done my share of crying. It's just that, oh daughter of troops, I knew Pa would not want it.

In Kansas, of all places, on December second, the day Pa was executed, a man named Abraham Lincoln gave a speech. He said Pa's effort to free the slaves was peculiarlike, being that it was a white man's attempt to get up a revolt among the slaves, in which the slaves refused to participate. He said the raid was so absurd that the slaves, for all their ignorance, saw it could not succeed. "We know slavery is wrong," this man called Lincoln said, "but that cannot excuse violence, bloodshed and treason."

That's all I have to write. Except that the war has started. If not for Pa it never would have.

I wonder if any of my brothers will enlist. I wonder, if Dauphin had lived, would he enlist.

I wonder how the men of Pa's Provisional Army, who were all so good and decent back at the Kennedy farm, could take aim and kill people the way they did at the Ferry. I wonder if any of us knows what we are truly capable of, if the occasion presents itself for us to find out.

I wonder if Pa ever really forgave me for Amelia. Or if I can ever stop loving him and hating him all at the same time. I wonder what Mrs. Huffmaster thought when she found out about the raid. I wonder sometimes if my meeting with her, when she told me about Amelia forgiving me, ever really happened, or did I dream it? I wonder if my aura is healed now that I have written this.

I wonder what ever happened to Hettie Pease. And if Dangerfield Newby's wife and children will survive until the war is over and they are freed.

I wonder if the war will ever be over. And if the slaves will ever be free.

I wonder what this man called Lincoln thinks about Pa now.

I wonder if I have talked all the fire out.

Author's Note

Everyone is familiar with John Brown and his raid on Harpers Ferry, it seems. By now he is part of American folklore. But like most of our history that is relegated to the "folklore" category, the three months John Brown and his Provisional Army spent at the Kennedy farm in Maryland that summer of 1859 are not widely known. So most people don't know about Annie Brown, John Brown's daughter.

Indeed, in all the factual books on Brown and his famous raid, Annie appears as a walk-on, a bit player. But she leapt out at me like a star begging to be born. Fifteen years old in 1859, Annie came down from the Brown place in North Elba, New York, with her seventeen-year-old sister-in-law, Martha, to help keep house for the Provisional Army and to make life at the Kennedy farm appear normal.

She was assigned the task of "watchdog" — keeping watch on the porch for approaching strangers. The farmhouse was soon full of men, eighteen in all (one arrived right before Annie and Martha left, two after). It was Annie's job to keep the men from running off, warn the inhabitants of the house when a stranger was approaching, and generally keep curious eyes at bay. John Brown could not have it known that so many men were living at the farmhouse, that he was receiving and storing arms there, and that some of the men were Negro. So Annie had her work cut out for her.

Indeed, in some of the books on John Brown there are

excerpts of Annie's account of life on the farm that summer. From these accounts, written by Annie in her later years when she was Mrs. Annie Brown Adams, I learned the nucleus of facts about that summer in Maryland, her descriptions of some of the men, her chores, the newspapers her father subscribed to, the dog Cuffee, the description of the house, and, of course, Mrs. Huffmaster.

In my research I pursued other sources to round out the picture that Annie gave me in those written accounts. My California sources proved very fruitful.

Still, there were gaps, as there always are in doing research. At best history gives us a fragmented picture. We know what people did and when, but not why. We are not privy to their private emotions, their fears, hopes, or wishes. So historical writers must create and fill in the gaps.

Annie, therefore, is an historically accurate character. But her personality, feelings, and interaction with those around her are of my making. Mrs. Huffmaster was a real character. She haunted the Kennedy farm that summer, she saw Shields Green, as I have her doing, she poked around and asked questions, and plagued Annie and Martha.

But, again, her relationship with Annie is of my creation. As is Annie's conversation with Mr. Munster, the Quaker farmer who delivers the pikes (although Owen did tell Annie to distract the wagon driver who delivered the pikes, so he would not discover what he'd been carrying).

While I had brief, thumbnail sketches of all the men in John Brown's Provisional Army, there is, again, no record of their conversations with Annie. I created them, tailoring scenes out of information I learned about the men. Leeman and Hazlett, for instance, did constantly run off, and it was Annie's job to keep them in tow. She called them her "invisibles." Dangerfield Newby's wife was a slave in captivity who did write, begging him to come fetch her, and who was sold South after the raid. Shields Green was a favorite of Frederick Douglass, who did go with John Brown to meet with Douglass at the quarry when Douglass refused to throw his lot in with Brown. And Green did opt to stay with Brown, saying, "I believe I go wid de old man."

The men almost did mutiny when they found out about the proposed raid. Some had been kept in the dark about it, and when they found out, thought the plan sheer madness. Owen Brown conferred with them and gave his father the exact words I have him saying when they decided to stand behind Brown and go through with the raid after all.

Owen had a withered arm and sewed his own clothing. And he did walk to Antietam and back to buy corn so the men wouldn't steal it from the field next door. Everything about Owen and all Annie's brothers in the book is true. Everything about the Brown children in childhood is true, as is everything about John Brown and his sons in Kansas.

Salmon and Jason refused to be part of the raid, because they had seen so much violence in Kansas. Kagi was an ex-schoolteacher, and Tidd left the farm in anger after the argument about the raid to go to the Ferry with Cook and "cool off." Annie was betrothed to Dauphin Thompson.

Everything about the raid, as related by Annie, is true. She and her sister Sarah did stay at the home of Bronson Alcott, father of Louisa May Alcott, in Concord, Massachusetts, at the time I have Annie there in the prologue and epilogue. They were attending Mr. Sanborn's school; Sanborn was one of many abolitionist friends of John Brown.

What eventually happened to Annie Brown and some of the others in the book?

Shortly after the Battle of Gettysburg in 1863, Annie and her mother, Salmon, his wife Abbie, Sarah, and Ellen crossed the continent to settle in California. They stopped in the Midwest to visit John Brown, Jr., who lived there with his family. Jason and his family lived nearby. So did Owen. Ruth Brown and Henry Thompson also had migrated there.

After visiting with family, Mary Brown, Salmon and Abbie, Ellen, Annie, and Sarah joined a wagon train on the Overland Trail to California. They joined up with about eighty wagons. The trip was fraught with the usual dangers posed by unfriendly Indians. But the Browns had other concerns. Southerners in the wagon train learned of their presence and decided to give the Brown family the kind of treatment John Brown had given slave owners in Kansas. The Browns and their party had to leave the wagon train in the middle of the night, take an alternate route through Idaho, and flee to the safety of a Union fort. They did arrive safely in California, however.

There, in Red Bluff, Sarah and Annie found positions teaching. Annie taught in an African-American school. Eventually they all moved to Humboldt County. Salmon started a sheep ranch. Annie married Samuel Adams, carriage maker and blacksmith, reared his children from an earlier marriage, and bore eleven children of her own.

Eventually Owen Brown, Ruth Brown Thompson and her husband Henry, and Jason and his family emigrated to California, too. Mary Brown, Annie's mother, was constantly being contacted by important people because of what her husband had done. And Mary Brown was in constant contact with abolitionists in the East.

As for Annie, she lived until 1926 and was frequently sought out by historians to tell about that summer at the Kennedy farm. Owen, the only other living Brown child who was there, died in 1889. So, as I have Mrs. Huffmaster predicting, Annie became the only one who could tell the truth about that summer before the Harpers Ferry raid. She took the role seriously, though it haunted her for the rest of her life.

A final accounting of the men who took part in the raid on Harpers Ferry:

Jeremiah Goldsmith Anderson: killed in the raid.

Osborne Anderson: escaped. Served as a non-commissioned officer in the Civil War. Died of consumption in Washington, D.C., 1872.

Oliver Brown: killed in the raid.

Owen Brown: escaped. Died in California, January 1889.

Watson Brown: died of wounds incurred during the raid.

John Cook: escaped with Owen and others. Captured near Chambersburg, Pennsylvania, on October 25 and was hanged on December 16, 1859.

John Copeland: captured in the raid, executed December 1859.

Barclay Coppoc: escaped. Enlisted in the Third Kansas Infantry and was killed when a train he was riding on fell forty feet from a trestle into a river. Died from injuries September 1861.

Edwin Coppoc: captured in the raid and hanged in December 1859.

Shields Green: captured in raid. Hanged, December 1859.

Albert Hazlett: escaped. Later arrested in Carlisle, sent to Virginia, and hanged in March 1860.

John Henry Kagi: killed in the raid.

Lewis Leary: killed in the raid.

William Leeman: killed in the raid.

Francis Meriam: escaped. Enlisted as a captain in the Third South Carolina Colored Infantry. Served under General Grant. Died November 1865.

Dangerfield Newby: killed in the raid.

Aaron Dwight Stevens: captured, wounded, sent to prison with four musket balls in his body. Executed March 1860.

Stewart Taylor: killed in the raid.

Dauphin Thompson: killed in the raid.

William Thompson: killed in the raid.

Charles Plummer Tidd: escaped. Enlisted in the Twenty-first Massachusetts Volunteers in the Civil War and died of fever on the transport *Northerner* as first sergeant, February 1862.

John Brown's Children

CHILDREN FROM HIS FIRST WIFE, DIANTHE LUSK BROWN:

John Brown, Jr. Born July 1821 in Hudson, Ohio. Married Wealthy Hotchkiss in 1847. Went to Kansas in 1854 and became a political leader in the Free State movement. Captured, beaten, and put in chains in Kansas. Became mentally unhinged afterward but helped forward arms into Chambersburg, Pennsylvania, for the Harpers Ferry raid. Died May 1895 in Ohio.

Jason Brown. Born January 1823 in Hudson, Ohio. Married Ellen Sherbondy in 1847. Went to Kansas with John and Ellen in 1847 to fight in the Free State movement. Lost taste for violence after Kansas and refused to be part of the raid. Died December 1912 in Okron, California.

Owen Brown. Born November 1824 in Hudson, Ohio. Went to Kansas in 1847. Fought bravely. Never married. Took part in raid. Died January 1889 in Pasadena, California.

Frederick Brown (first). Born January 1827 in Richmond, Pennsylvania. Died 1831 of unknown causes.

Ruth Brown. Born February 1829 in Richmond, Pennsylvania. Married Henry Thompson in September 1850. Died January 1904 in Pasadena, California.

Frederick Brown (second). Born December 1830 in Richmond, Pennsylvania. Went to fight in Kansas, where he was shot and killed in August 1856. Buried in Kansas.

Infant son, unnamed. Born August 1832; died at three days. Dianthe Lusk Brown died in the next few days.

CHILDREN FROM HIS SECOND WIFE, MARY DAY BROWN:

Sarah Brown (first). Born May 1834 in Richmond, Pennsylvania. Died of dysentery in September 1843 in Richfield, Ohio.

Watson Brown. Born October 1835 in Franklin, Ohio. Did not go to Kansas. Married Isabella Thompson in 1858. Shot at Harpers Ferry; skeleton preserved at the Winchester Medical College, Winchester, Virginia. Later buried in North Elba, New York.

Salmon Brown. Born October 1836 in Hudson, Ohio. Took part in fighting in Kansas. Married Abbie Hinckley. Refused to go to Harpers Ferry. Died by his own hand in May 1919 in Portland, Oregon.

Charles Brown. Born November 1837 in Hudson, Ohio. Died of dysentery in September 1843 in Richfield, Ohio.

Oliver Brown. Born March 1839 in Franklin, Ohio. Fought in Kansas in 1855. Married Martha Brewster in April 1858. Killed at Harpers Ferry in October 1859. Buried along Shenandoah River. Remains later returned to family.

Peter Brown. Born December 1840 in Hudson, Ohio. Died of dysentery in September 1843.

Austin Brown. Born 1842 in Richfield, Ohio. Died of dysentery in September 1843.

Annie Brown. Born December 1843 in Richfield, Ohio. Joined her father at the Kennedy farm in Maryland at age fifteen. Married Samuel Adams. Died in October 1926 in Shively, California.

Amelia Brown. Born June 1845. Died from accidental scalding in October 1846. Buried in Akron, Ohio.

Sarah Brown (second). Born in September 1846 in Akron, Ohio. Never married. Died 1916 in Saratoga, California.

Ellen Brown (first). Born April 1848 in Springfield, Massachusetts. Died April 1849. Buried in Springfield, Massachusetts.

Infant son, unnamed. Born April 1852 in Akron, Ohio. Died three weeks later of whooping cough. Buried in Akron, Ohio.

Ellen Brown (second). Born September 1854 in Akron, Ohio. Married James Fablinger in 1876. Died July 1916. Buried in Saratoga, California.

Bibliography

Boyer, Richard O. *The Legend of John Brown: A Biography and a History*. New York: Alfred A. Knopf, 1973.

Greene, Laurence. *The Raid: A Biography of Harpers Ferry*. New York: Henry Holt and Company, 1953.

Hinton, Richard J. *John Brown and His Men*. New York: Arno Press and *The New York Times*, 1968.

Libby, Jean. "John Brown's Family and Their California Refuge." *The Magazine of California History* 7, no. 1 (January/February 1988).

National Park Service. *John Brown's Raid*. Based on reports by William C. Everhart and Arthur L. Sullivan. Washington, D.C.: U.S. Government Printing Office, 1974.

————. *The Wives and Children of John Brown*. Harpers Ferry, West Virginia: National Park Service.

Oates, Stephen B. *To Purge This Land with Blood: A Biography of John Brown*. New York: Harper & Row Publishers, 1970.

Sanborn, F. B., ed. *The Life and Letters of John Brown: Liberator of Kansas and Martyr of Virginia*. Boston: Roberts Brothers, 1885.

————. *Recollections of Seventy Years*. Vol. 1. Boston: Richard G. Badger, The Gorham Press, 1909.

Saxon, Martha. *Louisa May Alcott: A Modern Biography*. New York: The Noonday Press, Farrar, Straus, and Giroux, 1995.

Stavis, Barrie. *John Brown: The Sword and the Word*. South Brunswick and New York: A. S. Barnes and Company, 1970.

Villard, Oswald Garrison. *John Brown 1800–1859: A Biography Fifty Years After*. New York: Alfred A. Knopf, 1943.

Warren, Robert Penn. *John Brown: The Making of a Martyr*. New York: Payson and Clarke Ltd., 1929.